Staging Wars

The Laura Bishop Mystery Series
by Grace Topping

STAGING IS MURDER (#1)
STAGING WARS (#2)

Staging Wars

A Laura Bishop
MYSTERY

Grace TOPPING

HENERY PRESS

Copyright

STAGING WARS
A Laura Bishop Mystery
Part of the Henery Press Mystery Collection

First Edition | April 2020

Henery Press, LLC
www.henerypress.com

Trade Paperback ISBN-13: 978-1-63511-591-8
Digital epub ISBN-13: 978-1-63511-592-5
Kindle ISBN-13: 978-1-63511-593-2
Hardcover ISBN-13: 978-1-63511-594-9

Printed in the United States of America

*To Terryl Paiste, Martha Huston, Antoinette Pavone,
Susan McNally, and Sandra Pierce.
Friends, mentors, and book club members.*

ACKNOWLEDGMENTS

Writing a second book can be more daunting than writing the first one. I appreciate more than I can say the encouragement, advice, and help I received from Connie Berry, Ellen Byron, Kait Carson, Annette Dashofy, Ellen Dubin, Lin Fischer, Kaye George, Lynn Heverly, Rhea Killinger, Libby Klein, Joan Long, Shari Randall, Kathy Reardon, and Barbara Sicola.

Thank you to the members of the Sisters in Crime Chesapeake and Guppies Chapters; my agent, Dawn Dowdle of the Blue Ridge Literary Agency; my editor, Maria Edwards; and everyone at Henery Press.

And a special thank you to my husband, John, and daughters, Lesley McArthur and Laura Goulet, for their loving support.

Chapter 1

A certified home stager will help you sell your home quickly and
for more money.

"There's a body in Hendricks Funeral Home!"

I looked up to see my friend, Nita Martino, racing toward me. Her face was flushed and her voice raspy and breathless. Minutes before she had been handing out pamphlets about our business, Staging for You, and laughing as she talked to people gathering in the town square for the Louiston Small Business Fair. Now her smile was gone and her eyes looked wild and confused.

Grasping the table for support, she gulped for air and sputtered, "In the home—a body."

"Well, it is a funeral home." I tried not to laugh, knowing how Nita avoided them ever since two of her brothers had locked her in a viewing room during a family funeral.

Our position in front of the old Victorian building wouldn't have been my first choice to place our table at the fair, but it had the advantage of shade from large trees fronting the funeral home and a restroom inside, where Nita had slipped away to visit.

"This one has a knife in its back."

I stared at Nita, wondering if my friend, who possessed a wicked sense of humor, was trying to pull me into another one of her zany escapades. Seeing the look of shock and disbelief on her face convinced me otherwise.

Shaking myself, I turned to Mrs. Webster, who helped occasionally with my home staging business. "Can you stay with Nita while I check on this?"

"Not on your life, girl. I'm coming too." The spry older woman jumped from her chair with more vim and vigor than would be expected of an elderly grandmother. Nita followed right behind her.

We dashed up the steps to the large Victorian home that had been a funeral home for more years than anyone could remember. Once inside, I paused in the foyer long enough for my eyes to adjust to the dim light and then scanned the large rooms on either side of the hall, looking for a body. The fragrance of carnations permeated the building, even with no flowers present. Every time I smelled carnations I thought of funerals.

Seeing nothing, I continued down the center hallway, stopped, and stood rigid—Mrs. Webster plowing into me at my sudden stop.

At the end of the hall lay a man prostrate on the floor with a long-handled knife encased in the middle of his back. Nita hadn't been playing a joke on us.

When we reached him, Mrs. Webster, a retired nurse, leaned over and placed her fingertips along the man's neck, while I dug in my pocket for my cell phone. After a few seconds, she shook her head—a sure sign the man was dead. I didn't know how anyone with what looked like a large kitchen knife in his back could survive, but people have survived worse. Unfortunately, in this case he hadn't.

I felt numb. Nita came up behind me. "Is he dead?" Her voice wavered. It wasn't every day you stumbled on a body, much less one with a knife in its back.

I nodded and punched 911 on my cell phone and waited for someone to answer. Remembering how I had fallen apart when faced with a recent death, I forced myself to speak calmly.

"This is Laura Bishop. I'm at Hendricks Funeral Home. We've found a man on the floor. He's been stabbed in the back."

"Are you okay, Laura? Is there anyone with you?" I easily

recognized the voice of Patty Charles, Louiston's senior dispatcher, and put her on speakerphone so the others could hear her.

"Nita Martino and Mariah Webster are here with me."

"Good. Is the man breathing?"

"No. Mrs. Webster checked his pulse, examined him, and said he's dead."

"Can she start chest compressions until the EMTs get there?" Patty asked.

Mrs. Webster leaned closer to my phone. "Patty Charles, I said he's dead. No EMT is going to revive him. He's got a large knife dead center of his back." We all grimaced at her unintended pun.

Mrs. Webster had cared for dying patients in their homes over a number of years and could recognize when a person was dead. Though probably not many of them had been murdered. I gave Patty the address of the funeral home and my callback number, thankful I'd recharged my cell phone that morning.

"Police and an ambulance are on their way. Stay on the line with me until the team gets there." Her use of old phone terminology made me smile, in a situation that didn't warrant any smiles.

"Thanks, Patty."

"You said the man was stabbed. Do you feel safe?" Patty asked.

We had been focused on the victim and hadn't given any thought to his attacker. Could that person still be in the funeral home? Unlikely, but I didn't plan to look around to be sure. How long would it take for the police to arrive?

"We haven't seen anyone else," I said.

I heard footsteps behind me, and my heart leapt into my throat. "Hold on, Patty, someone's coming."

"Well, hello, everyone. Come in from the heat to cool down?"

We all turned in unison to see Warren Hendricks, director of the funeral home, ambling down the long hall from a side entrance, looking as though he didn't have a care in the world.

When none of us answered, he raised his eyebrows. "Anything wrong?"

Mrs. Webster, the calmest one of us, pointed behind her. "You have an unexpected guest."

Warren peered behind us, gawked at the man on the floor, and dropped the white paper bag he'd been carrying. "Have you called for an ambulance?"

"Hold on, Patty, we're okay." I waved my cell phone at Warren. "I'm on the phone with Patty at the dispatch center. She's sending police and an ambulance." Seconds later, the front doors to the home flew open and two EMTs rushed in, quickly followed by a uniformed policeman.

"They're here, Patty. Thanks for your help."

Experience gained from reading mystery novels made me realize we should move away from the area. We'd probably already messed up the crime scene just by being there. I motioned to Nita and Mrs. Webster for us to go into one of the empty viewing rooms to stay out of the way. We took seats in the ornately carved wooden chairs lining the walls.

Thinking of the body made me wonder. "Did either of you recognize the man?" From the little I could see of his longish blond hair and the side of his deeply suntanned face that wasn't pressed into an Aubusson carpet, he didn't look like anyone I knew.

Nita took a Kleenex from her pocket and wiped her sweaty face. "It was hard to get a good look at him, but he didn't look familiar." Her eyes were still wide from shock.

"How old would you say he was?" I asked.

Nita shrugged. "Somewhere in his late thirties or older. It was hard to tell with that deep suntan."

Mrs. Webster shook her head. "Dang, it's a sad thing when someone can't even go into a funeral home without getting murdered."

Warren came into the room, perspiration running down his forehead and into his graying beard. He removed a folded white handkerchief from his back pocket and wiped his face. A ceiling fan high above us did little to cool the room, which was becoming warmer by the minute. It was surprising since funeral homes were usually cold.

Over the years, I'd seen Warren under a number of trying situations, but this one seemed to unnerve him.

"Did you recognize the man, Warren?" I fanned my face with a pamphlet outlining the history of the funeral home.

"Unfortunately, I did. At least I think so. I haven't seen him in nearly twenty years."

"Can you tell us who he was?" The voice of Detective Alex Spangler made me look up in surprise. I had dealt with him before, and seeing his tall figure looming in the tall archway didn't give me warm fuzzy feelings.

Before Warren could answer, Detective Spangler scanned the room and stopped when he got to me. "You again." Obviously, he didn't have warm fuzzy feelings about me either.

That morning all I'd wanted to do was promote my home staging business—so I could make a living and save enough money to someday travel to places I yearned to visit. Instead, I was going to be questioned by police about a murder victim I didn't know. And by a detective I didn't want to be interrogated by again.

Chapter 2

To successfully stage your home, detach yourself emotionally from it and think more like a home seller and less like a homeowner.

"You're next, Laura."

I looked up from the ornate carpet I had been studying to see Neil Stanelli, a Louiston uniformed policeman and one of Nita's numerous cousins. Nita, Mrs. Webster, Warren Hendricks, and I had been waiting in separate areas of the home before being interviewed one at a time by Detective Spangler. Most likely we were separated so we couldn't confer on our stories before he could question us.

I'd been glad for the time alone in a separate room—time to collect myself. It was one thing reading about a murder victim in a novel and another thing actually seeing a victim. Thinking of the man's sudden death at the hands of someone vile enough to stab him left me chilled to my very core.

Now it was my turn to be questioned. I rose from the ornate Victorian chair that had been designed for torture and not comfort, and stretched, trying to work the kinks from my body. I'd been sitting there for what seemed like hours, although I knew it hadn't been that long. But it had been long enough for me to study the mishmash of old-fashioned wallpaper patterns on the walls in garish hues of peach and green; the heavy, ornate draperies; and the variety of chairs and sofas from different eras, none of them comfortable. I knew because I had tried them all. I regretted not having ear buds with me so I could have listened to an audiobook on my iPhone to fill the time. A Nero Wolfe mystery by Rex Stout, where I didn't see the body firsthand, might have helped take my mind off this sad business.

Neil led me into a viewing room across the hall from where I'd waited, slid open tall oak pocket doors, and ushered me in. It was fortunate Warren hadn't had any viewings scheduled that day. We were running out of rooms, and the police activity would have been disturbing to the family and friends of any deceased there.

"Laura Bishop's here." With that, Neil slid the doors closed behind us.

Detective Spangler studied a notebook in his hands, ignoring us. When he finally looked up and saw me, he grimaced. His dark eyes and handsome features didn't appeal to me—much. I have this thing about handsome men. They always seemed to be at the root of any unhappiness I'd experienced in my life, and I tended to steer clear of them.

Detective Spangler pointed to the chair in front of him. "Take a seat." *Said the spider to the fly.* This was worse than being called to the principal's office.

"Please tell us what happened." His eyes held my gaze, which unnerved me somewhat. His intense gaze looked powerful enough to make suspects confess.

I told him succinctly everything that had occurred from the time Nita left the square to use the restroom until the police showed up. No emotion, no embellishments, no theories. I was sad for the man, whoever he was, and felt emotionally drained. My throat was parched, but I was determined not to ask for anything to drink. I couldn't wait to get out of there and return to our table at the fair and a world without bodies.

"Did you recognize the man?" Detective Spangler tapped his pen on his notebook.

"No. I don't believe I ever saw him before. If I did, I don't remember him. Didn't he have any identification on him?"

"We didn't find a wallet." He looked at his notebook as though to confirm that. "Do you know if any of the others knew him?"

I'd seen each of the others going in to be interviewed, so I knew he was interviewing me last. Was he thinking I knew something they weren't willing to say? Perhaps rat on them in some way?

"Nita and Mrs. Webster said they didn't recognize him. Warren said he thought it was someone he knew but hadn't seen in nearly twenty years. You arrived just as he was about to name him." *So there, Detective. If you hadn't arrived when you did, I might be able to give you a name.*

I sat up straighter and reminded myself not to be so grumpy. But something about Detective Spangler always put my teeth on edge. Besides, I had nothing more I could contribute.

"Warren Hendricks said the victim's name was Ian Becker. Does that name mean anything to you?" Detective Spangler again tapped his pen on his notebook.

I shook my head.

"What was Nita doing in the funeral home to begin with?"

Uh, oh. Was he keying in on Nita as a possible suspect in the murder? "She went inside to use the restroom. Warren had told us that it would be okay. She'd been gone only a short time before she returned to tell us what she found."

I stopped and thought about the sequence of events. "The man was lying in front of the door leading to the restrooms, so she hadn't made it that far. When I ran into the building, Nita and Mrs. Webster followed me."

Then it struck me. Nita might have missed the killer by only minutes. I shuddered to think what would have happened if she had witnessed the attack. Detective Spangler could now be investigating her murder as well.

Detective Spangler scribbled something in his notebook and stood. I took it as a signal I could leave.

"That's all for now. I don't need to tell you not to discuss this with anyone else."

"I need to explain to my assistant outside what happened. He was scheduled to arrive to help us about the time the ambulance and police cars pulled up. With all the people in the square, what happened won't be a secret for long."

"Okay, but don't go wild spreading Ian Becker's name."

I rolled my eyes, something I frequently reminded my young assistant *and myself* not to do. Childish I knew, but Detective Spangler always brought out the worst in me.

I left the room wondering who had wanted Ian Becker dead.

Chapter 3

Staging your home with touches of luxury will help buyers view your house as special.

Outside the funeral home, I took several deep breaths to relieve the stress I'd felt building. The warm summer day was glorious, and I took a moment to enjoy the view of the Allegheny Mountains in the distance. Seeing the green, rolling mountains always calmed me. It was a beautiful time of year in Pennsylvania—but Pennsylvania was beautiful any time of the year.

I went back to our table in the town square, glad that only our team was there at the moment. The thought of how close Nita had come to danger had shaken me, and I hugged her. Close friends since second grade, and without sisters, we had become more like siblings and worried about each other.

Tyrone Webster had arrived to help and was sitting with the others. His dark good looks and outgoing personality would help attract people to our table. Tyrone was Mrs. Webster's grandson, and I'd known him since he was young. Now a design student at nearby Fischer College, he assisted me part-time in my staging business.

"Hey, Tyrone. I'm guessing Nita and your grandmother filled you in on what happened this morning." I reached for one of the unopened bottles of water on the table and gulped down half of it before I came up for air.

"Man, that was terrible. When I saw the emergency vehicles and then didn't see any of you here, I freaked out."

Since his grandmother was his only family, I knew how alarmed he must have been. "I'm sorry. One of us should have come out to tell you what was going on, but everything was happening so fast."

"Not to worry. A policeman outside the funeral home told me you all were inside and okay. So I came back here. The crowd came down to this end of the square to see what was going on, so I got to talk to a lot of people about the business."

Nita fanned herself with a handful of the pamphlets we'd been handing out. "Emergency vehicles outside a funeral home were bound to attract attention."

"It sure attracted the ghouls," Tyrone said. "I overheard some guy say that maybe one of the bodies brought in hadn't been quite dead."

"Ridiculous. We're not living in the dark ages." Mrs. Webster took off her hat and swatted the bees buzzing around the drinks we'd left on the table.

It was getting hotter as the day went by. Tyrone reached for a fresh bottle of water, opened it, and tossed the lid into a nearby bag of trash. "Thanks to the big crowd at this end of the square, I handed out lots of pamphlets. Nita, your before and after photos in the pamphlet impressed people."

During the past few months, Tyrone and I had staged a nineteenth-century mansion, making it more attractive to buyers. It sold for far more than expected. The new owners had bought the mansion and all the furniture and turned it into a fantastic bed and breakfast. It was our first staging job and helped establish our reputation in Louiston. Since then, we'd completed a few more places. Nita joined us, first taking photos of our progress, and now completing online classes to become a certified home stager.

Mrs. Webster helped when we needed her skillful needlework or on occasions like the fair today. She enjoyed being able to spend more time with Tyrone—and to keep an eye on him. Having raised him since he was orphaned at five years old, she was quite protective of him.

Nita didn't respond to Tyrone's comments about her photos. It was most unusual, since she was thrilled to be using her photography skills. Could she be thinking the same thing I thought earlier—that she might have missed the killer by minutes or even seconds?

"How did your interview with Detective Spangler go?" I asked her. Having been questioned by him before and how uncomfortable it could be, I worried he might have intimidated her. I always found him intimidating.

Nita expelled a long breath. "He asked me several questions, often the same ones over and over but worded differently."

"The police do that. It must be an interrogation technique to see if your story stays consistent. How about you, Mrs. Webster?" I asked.

"Don't you worry about me, girl. I didn't let him intimidate me. I stared him right in the eye and told him everything I knew." She sniffed. "I nursed his grandmother in his family's home when he was a youngster. He knows I'm not going to let him scare me into saying something I shouldn't."

Nita fanned herself faster now. Her face was flushed and her shoulders slumped. With the sun directly overhead, the heat had become intense, and the nearby trees no longer shaded us. Mrs. Webster handed Nita a bottle of water and a tube of sunblock. "Put some of this on, and tomorrow, bring a hat. You young people need to be more careful. In my career, I've seen some terrible cases of skin cancer. Tyrone's already lathered up."

Tyrone and Mrs. Webster, with their dark brown skin, showed no effects from the sun, but Nita's face was reddening, either from the sun or from the earlier stress of finding a body. The hat Mrs. Webster was never without helped protect her skin. I planned to bring one of my straw hats tomorrow when we would again be at the square. The two-day fair was enabling us to educate homeowners about what a home stager could do to prepare their homes for sale. And it was helping to promote our fledgling business.

Tyrone reached into a box on the ground and placed more pamphlets on the table. "What I can't understand is why someone would want to kill somebody at a funeral home? But if you are going to get killed, a funeral home sure would be a convenient place for it to happen."

"Young man." Mrs. Webster swatted him with a pamphlet.

"Sorry, Gran."

It was sometimes easy to forget how young Tyrone was. Even at nineteen, the boy in him still came out.

I studied Nita again. Earlier in the day she had been cracking jokes and now she was subdued. Not surprising after the terrible experience of finding a body. It had affected all of us but especially her.

"Nita, why don't you go home? We can handle this. And if you don't feel better, stay home tomorrow."

"I'll be okay. Tyrone is picking up lunch for us soon. Once I've eaten something, I should feel better."

To Italian-American families, good food helps in any situation. It's like the British and a soothing cup of tea. I wasn't convinced food would help Nita right now, but I decided to let it go for the moment. I felt quite shaken by the experience myself and longed to call it a day, but I had to hold it together for my business. The fair was held only once a year, and it was too good an opportunity to miss.

Tyrone walked away from the table, talking into his cell phone. When he returned, the uncharacteristic frown on his face was a dead giveaway I wouldn't like whatever news he had.

"Laura, did you cancel the rental truck we reserved for Monday? I just called to confirm the rental, and they said someone canceled it. I told them they must have mixed us up with someone else, but they said the caller specifically said to cancel the reservation for Staging for You. Worse than that, they don't have another truck available for Monday."

"What? I didn't. Nita, did you cancel it?" I couldn't imagine why she would have. We needed that truck. We'd reserved it to transfer furnishings to stage an unoccupied house that was soon going on the market. Nita shook her head and looked as puzzled as I felt.

That was strange—this happening right after someone had anonymously left us a bad review online and some other things that I was beginning to wonder about. It was starting to unnerve me. "It's too late now to wonder how it happened. Let's work at getting another truck—that is if we can find one at this late date. Tyrone, can you work on that?"

Nita sat up in her chair. "If you can't locate one, let me know and I'll check with the family about borrowing a vehicle." Nita's father and five brothers owned a construction company, and they had often come to my aid.

"Thanks for checking on the truck, Tyrone. If you hadn't, we would have been in a real fix on Monday." I'd known Tyrone since he was a youngster, and he had proven himself time and again to be an asset to our small team. Not only did he provide the brawn we needed to move furniture, but he also had an excellent eye for good décor and design. He designed stage sets for the Louiston Players, the local community theater group, and could do a lot with very little.

I pondered who else could have a truck we could rent or borrow. "We could call Ernie Phillips. If he doesn't have any window cleaning scheduled for Monday, perhaps we could rent his truck. In fact, I'll check with the homeowner to see if they can work window cleaning into their home staging budget. That will help make it worth his while." Houses for sale with sparkling clean windows help them stand out from other houses on the market.

As the number of people attending the fair dwindled, we began packing our promotional materials to place in my car overnight. After church in the morning, we would start again. Closing the back door of my car, I let out a big sigh.

"Was that a sigh of relief, or are you tired? Nita asked.

"Neither. I was thinking about Aunt Kit's arrival this evening. She's coming to town to attend the Louiston Arts Festival and is staying with me for a few days." Aunt Kit was my mother's older sister who had moved away from Louiston several years ago to take a job. She had never married, and was, to my knowledge, my only living relative. Her outlook on life was about as grim as my mother's had been.

Nita laughed, a sound I was glad to hear coming from her. "You mean Aunt Kit with the glass-half-empty-smudged-and-cracked outlook? That will sure help lift your spirits after the depressing events today."

"It must be genetic. She's as dour as my mom used to be. I hope I didn't inherit the same genes." With the bearing of a stern mother superior, Aunt Kit had missed her calling.

"Give her a small glass of the Harvey's Bristol Cream Sherry she likes. Then she'll be halfway pleasant."

"She doesn't drink often." Maybe that was just as well. Cream sherry sounded innocuous, but the potent sweet drink could provide a real punch to an unsuspecting imbiber.

"Then serve her some sherry trifle—with an extra dose of sherry."

"That reminds me, I need to pick up a bottle of it. If Aunt Kit becomes too much to deal with, I'll have it to drink."

"Glad you mentioned that Aunt Kit was coming into town for the arts festival. Don't forget you're helping with the art intake on Tuesday. Come prepared for an interesting session. If we don't hang the artists' works where they want them, they can get pretty upset."

Chapter 4

Most homebuyers form an opinion fifteen seconds after entering a home. Stage your home to ensure their first impression is a good one.

After a draining day, I happily returned to my craftsman bungalow and was greeted by my tiny black cat, Inky. Unlike many cats who only tolerated their owners, Inky was affectionate and curled around my ankles, displaying how happy he was to see me. He was even more so when I put clean water in his bowl, with two ice cubes, which he loved, and fed him his favorite salmon dinner. It smelled awful to me, but he loved it—it pays to have a happy pet. I'd heard too many horror stories from pet owners about how their pets had taken revenge on them for minor infractions.

After tending to Inky, I stepped in the shower, wishing the hot water pouring over me could wash away memories from earlier that day. I hadn't realized how stressed I had become. The water helped relax my stiff muscles and reminded me again how wonderful it was to have a shower. My father frequently talked about how much he appreciated a shower. As a Marine, who had served in both the jungle and the desert and frequently had only cold water to bathe with; he viewed a hot shower as pure luxury. Memories of him caused a sharp pain to hit. Even after so many years, I still missed him. After my parents' divorce when I was young, he gradually disappeared from my life, and I didn't know whether he was alive or dead.

I dressed quickly and went about preparing dinner so Aunt Kit could have something to eat following her long ride. It didn't matter what I fixed. She would pick at whatever it was and say she wasn't hungry. But she always had room for dessert.

The doorbell sounded just as I slid a frozen pizza into the oven. I had doctored it with red peppers, onions, mushrooms, and olives to make it healthier.

Aunt Kit stood at the door, a tall, erect figure, holding two large cases that would have weighed down anyone far stronger. She hadn't even bothered to rest them on the porch floor while waiting for me to come to the door. It always amazed me that someone who ate so little could be so strong.

"Well, you took your time," she said, every bit as imperious as Maggie Smith in *Downton Abby*.

Lovely greeting. "Hello, Aunt Kit." She was so much like my late mother it was like having her there—just when I thought I had exorcized her disgruntled spirit from the house I had grown up in. My mother resisted any bit of happiness that tried to fight its way into our lives. Fortunately, I'd had Nita's family to show me how good life could be. As a result, I had a much better outlook on life than I would have had without them.

"Here, let me give you a hand with your cases." I made the mistake of reaching for one of them.

She pulled back. "I can still manage on my own, thank you very much."

I shrugged and led the way to the guest room.

Inky scooted around us and launched himself onto the bed. I held my breath, wondering how Aunt Kit would react, but I needn't have worried. She was fond of me in her gruff way, but she loved Inky. And for some inexplicable reason, he loved her too. He would be her constant companion while she was there.

I was ravenous, but as I expected, Aunt Kit toyed with the pizza I placed in front of her. As I cleared our plates away, I told her about Nita finding the body in the funeral home. I knew if I didn't, someone would tell her about our involvement. She had grown up in Louiston and still knew lots of people in town who were bound to tell her.

"How do you get yourself involved in things like that?" She stated it as though I went looking for trouble.

There was no explanation for it, so I ignored her question.

Aunt Kit continued. "How is that little business of yours going?"

Hearing people use the term *little* in that way had the same effect on me as hearing fingernails scrape across a blackboard. It was as though they were dismissing the subject as having *little* value.

"It's growing. Nita is working with me now. Also Tyrone, when he isn't at school or one of his other part-time jobs. We have enough work that I'll occasionally call in Will Parker to help. Do you remember Will? He's the retired rodeo star who was hit by a car this past spring, but he's doing a lot better now."

"I remember you telling me about that, but I don't think I've ever met him."

"He's a real character, but I like him a lot. He lives with his daughter and her big family up near the B&B."

"I'm glad he helps you out, but how you could give up a well-paying job in IT to go into a business moving furniture about is beyond me. I can't imagine what your mother would think if she were alive."

I knew how my mother would think—exactly like Aunt Kit. As young women, neither of them had any sense of adventure. It made me wonder what their parents had been like with both their daughters viewing the world so glumly. Maybe it was just as well I didn't know.

"Working in IT bored me. Home staging allows me to use my talents for decorating. And there's a lot to be said about being my own boss. But best of all, I'm doing work that makes me happy. And I'm doing it while still young enough to try it.

"What does being happy have to do with making a living? You'll never be able to make the money you made in IT. I wasn't happy in my work, but it's given me a good retirement that I can depend on. Derrick wouldn't have approved of you chucking your job."

Uh, oh. She'd used the D-word. My late husband, Derrick, had never had time for anything I wanted. Everything had always been about him. I was elated that I no longer had to worry about what *Derrick thought*.

"Frankly, Aunt Kit, I've reached the stage in my life where I'm doing what I want to do—even if I go broke doing it." Entering a new field, that was always a possibility, but I wasn't going to let a fear of failing stop me from trying. "You don't have to worry about my finances. The home staging field is growing, and the more people recognize its value, the more they'll be turning to businesses like mine."

And then she softened. "Just take care, dear. I worry about you."

That statement deserved a reward. I opened the freezer and surveyed the two containers of ice cream stored there. Should I give her butter pecan to butter her up, or rocky road, which seemed to hold a warning? Decision made, I placed a bowl of butter pecan ice cream in front of her. Her face broke out in a wide smile. Dessert always put a smile on her face.

I scooped up a bowl for myself. Maybe after the day I'd had it would put a smile on my face—and help me prepare for whatever tomorrow held.

Chapter 5

A home stager knows what helps to get a house sold fast.

The next morning after church, I waited for Nita at Vocaro's Coffee Bar, where we met most mornings and she read our horoscopes. None of the horoscopes came true, but since she enjoyed reading them, I listened and attempted to sound interested. She was running late that morning. I'd asked Aunt Kit if she wanted to join us, but she said she planned to relax in my hammock and read a new release by Cindy Brown, whose humorous mysteries featured a different Broadway play.

As I sipped my cappuccino and waited for Nita, I spotted Warren Hendricks coming in and waved at him to join me. I hadn't talked to him since the tragedy at his place, and I was curious about what he knew of the man we'd found there.

As Warren approached, I noticed how unlike himself he looked. His usually neat hair was standing up from his head in spikes. And instead of the immaculate somber suit he wore during the day, he had thrown on jeans and a sweatshirt with a logo that had long since faded beyond recognition. At one time it might have said Penn State.

"Hey, Warren, take a seat. I'm sorry about what happened at the funeral home."

Warren pulled out a chair, turned it, and straddled it, facing me. "I'm surprised you want to be seen talking to me."

"Why ever not?"

"Since I'm being considered for the role of villain in Ian Becker's murder."

In addition to operating the funeral home, Warren directed the Louiston Players, our local community theater group. He could be every bit as dramatic as any of the characters he directed.

"I don't think Detective Spangler is going to consider you involved in the murder just because it occurred at your place. Besides, what motive could you've had? Did you even know Ian Becker? Was that his name?

"Yeah, Ian. He used to spend summers here in Louiston with his aunt, and we hung around together. I was two years older, but we got along okay. The last summer he came was about twenty years ago. I remember it because it was the summer before my last year of college."

"And you haven't seen him since?"

"No. After that summer, his folks moved the family to New Zealand, and that was the last I heard of him—until he called me on Friday. Quite frankly, I was really surprised to hear from him, especially after so many years. He said his aunt had died, and he was in town to help settle her affairs."

"Who was his aunt?"

"Doris Becker. We handled her burial. I thought he might be calling about that and told him his aunt had made all the arrangements and set money aside for it years ago, so her estate didn't owe us anything. But he said he wanted to come by and say hello for old times' sake. With his parents traveling so much when he was a kid, he'd spent a lot of summers here. Louiston probably felt more like home to him than any place."

"That's so sad." I thought about him lying on the floor at the home and shuddered.

"And weird. He comes back here after twenty years, and as soon as he walks into my place, he gets murdered. And with his wallet gone and no other ID on him, if I hadn't recognized him, the police might have been unable to identify who he was."

"Did anyone else know he was meeting you at your place?" I was starting to sound like Detective Spangler.

"That I couldn't tell you. We made arrangements to meet at the home at noon. I told him to come for lunch—that I'd get us hoagies. He used to love them, and we ate a lot of them that summer. I figured he probably hadn't had a good one since moving to New Zealand and thought it would be a treat for him. I went to get them just before noon."

So that's what Warren had in the bag he dropped when he saw the body—hoagies? "Where did you get them?"

"Johnny and Kathleen's. Their salad on the hoagies is the best."

"It is." Just the thought of the foot-long bread roll filled with Italian meats and cheeses and heaped with lettuce coated in the best salad dressing in the state made me hungry. "Could someone there say they saw you and when?"

"I doubt it. The place gets busy, and I don't go there very often these days. Someone might remember I'd been there but not what day or time."

"Detective Spangler and his team will check it out. How long were you gone?"

"About twenty minutes. I hadn't planned to be away long, so I didn't lock up, especially since I'd told your group they could use the restrooms. I didn't want you to find the doors locked and think I had forgotten. Also, I'd told Ian that if I wasn't back by the time he got there to go to my apartment upstairs. He knew the way. We planned to eat lunch there."

I took a sip of my now-cold coffee. "Do you have any security cameras near the entrances to the home?"

Warren shook his head and laughed. "People aren't usually dying to get into the funeral home. Sorry. That wasn't the best way of expressing that. People breaking in hasn't been a problem."

"Too bad. A camera would have shown who entered and left," I said. "Since Ian's wallet was gone, robbery was probably the motive. But why stab him in the back?"

"Maybe to keep Ian from identifying him. It's all so strange. I'm not convinced the police are thinking it was simply a robbery. That's why I'm worried they're looking at me as a suspect."

"But what motive could they think you had for killing him? Especially since you haven't seen him for so long. Could he have been involved with someone's wife or girlfriend that last summer he was here and that person wanted revenge?"

Warren shook his head. "That doesn't sound like Ian. And who would want revenge after so many years?"

"Don't they say revenge is a dish best served cold? Or could he have been here long enough this time to cross someone? It doesn't take some people long to get into trouble."

"He said he'd only just arrived in town." The corners of Warren's mouth tightened. "Why are you so interested? You aren't planning to get involved are you?"

"Definitely not. You know me, Warren. I'm intrigued by a mystery. That's why I read mysteries over other novels. I love trying to solve a puzzle. Someone in this town murdered Ian. Doesn't it drive you crazy thinking it could be someone we know?"

Since Warren seemed to relish being in the police spotlight, I didn't say what I was really worried about. With Nita being the one to find Ian's body, Detective Spangler might also consider her a suspect. Worse, Nita walked in just minutes after the stabbing. Could that person have seen and recognized Nita and wondered if she saw him commit murder?

Chapter 6

The cost of staging a home is always less than your first price reduction.

Warren left Vocaro's, taking his paper coffee cup with him. He was probably a nervous wreck since he hadn't taken a sip the whole time he sat there. I hoped Detective Spangler wasn't considering Warren a suspect, or Nita, for that matter. As I'd learned in the past, once he strongly suspected someone of a crime, it was difficult to have him look elsewhere.

A few minutes later, Nita took the seat Warren had vacated and put her coffee and croissant on the table. "Sorry I'm late." She took a sip of her coffee and sighed. "I needed that. After tossing and turning all night, I overslept and nearly missed church. Now I can hardly keep my eyes open."

"I was just about to call to see if you were okay. Warren was here, so I filled the time talking to him."

"I saw him as I came in. Poor Warren. He looks about as bad as I feel." Nita's normal healthy color was gone, and she had dark circles around her eyes. She definitely hadn't gotten much sleep the night before. Finding a dead body is more traumatic than mystery books portray.

"He's afraid the police suspect him of killing Ian Becker. That's the name of the man killed at the funeral home." I eyed my now-empty cup and contemplated getting another one.

"Not a name I know. One of my brothers may have known him. I'll have to ask the guys. Why does Warren think the police suspect him?"

"Warren's always been a bit dramatic and a worrier. And with things slow at the funeral home, he has time on his hands to worry. Frankly, I think he secretly enjoys the thrill of being a suspect." I finished the last of my muffin and crumpled the wrapper.

"Not if they put him in jail. Thankfully, tryouts for the Louiston Players will be starting soon. That'll help keep his mind off murder."

I was a fan of the local community theater group Warren directed and rarely missed a production. "What show are they doing this season?" I hoped it wasn't a production featuring murder. Last season Warren had directed a production of *Arsenic and Old Lace,* which had numerous murders.

"*Music Man,*" Nita said.

Oh, good. No murders in it. "That'll be a fun production."

I studied Nita's solemn face. She needed some fun. Both of her college-aged kids had taken summer jobs at the shore, and Nita missed them. Now with the shock of the murder at Warren's place, she'd need more things to keep her occupied. Working with me and taking the online home staging classes weren't enough of a distraction for someone as energetic as Nita. Her husband Guido would probably appreciate having her involved with more things that could channel her excess energy.

"Why don't you try out for a part? I don't have any acting or singing talent, but you'd be a natural. I could see you playing Marian, madam librarian."

Nita took a bite of croissant, chocolate oozing from the ends, and shrugged. "I don't know. They'd probably want someone tall and thin, and that's not me."

"There's always the role of the mayor's wife."

Nita laughed. "Much more my speed."

When we finished eating, we left Vocaro's, retrieved the

promotional items from my car, and headed to the town square for the second day of the fair. Tyrone and Mrs. Webster were already there, Mrs. Webster looking like a thundercloud. Her eyes were narrowed and she had a frown plastered on her face.

When we greeted them, the response we received was less than enthusiastic. I looked at Tyrone and arched an eyebrow as if to say, "What's up?"

Tyrone nodded and took the box from me and began spreading the pamphlets and other items on the table. "Don't mind Gran. She got another one of those telephone calls this morning."

"What calls?" Who could be calling that would make her look like she could spit fire?

Mrs. Webster looked up from the needlework in her lap. "Those dang calls from people identifying themselves as representatives from the IRS, social security, or from collection companies. Calls preying on the elderly, saying that if I don't respond they could come after me."

"You know those calls are fake, right?" I worried that she might be taken advantage of like so many other people had been. "Don't even answer them."

"Don't you worry about me. I know the sweet voices of the callers disguise corrupt souls. I get riled thinking about the people they've fooled. When I can control my anger, I play along and ask them questions—like whom are they calling. Most times they don't even have a name—so how can they be calling me?"

"I told Gran to record the number and report them to the organization they are supposed to be from. One time she told a caller that she'd sold her soul to the devil doing what she was doing."

"Dang right she had. I'm not letting some crook scare me into doing something stupid."

I should have known better than to be worried about Mrs. Webster. I could see her wringing a confession from the caller and making him promise to go into a more legitimate line of work. People foolish enough to try something illegal with her deserved what happened to them.

I looked around the town square at the colorful umbrellas and tables that were beginning to draw a crowd. A good number of small businesses in town had taken advantage of the opportunity to promote their businesses, and people were starting to spread out and head to our end of the square. Soon we were handing out pamphlets and answering questions about Staging for You. Staging a home for sale was a new concept for many people, and we found ourselves explaining how our services could help people prepare their homes for sale. We were able to describe how staging had resulted in quicker sales and better offers for those homes. Not everyone who stopped to talk to us was ready to sell their homes, but I hoped they would tuck a pamphlet away for the future or give it to someone who might be.

The people milling about our table—the candy we were giving away attracting many—prevented us from discussing the murder yesterday, which was just as well.

Nita was deep in conversation with a woman nearby. Her usually bubbly personality made her perfect for sales and promotion. Even with her more subdued demeanor today, she would be excellent at promoting our business. However, as she walked back toward the table, I wondered what had caused the sudden frown on her face.

"How's it going?" I added another stack of pamphlets to the table.

"Great until the conversation I just had. I talked to that woman last week about possibly doing a staging consultation with her. At the time she wasn't certain when she and her husband were going to put their home up for sale. They've finally picked a time frame, but she said she was having someone else work with them on the staging."

"Someone else?" I couldn't hide my surprise. "I don't know of another staging group in town—unless her real estate agent is giving her advice. That's always a possibility."

"No, she definitely said a home stager." Nita sat down heavily in her chair.

"I haven't seen anyone advertising about home staging. Did you ask her who it was?"

"No. I could tell she was uncomfortable, since the last time I talked to her she'd seemed interested in working with us. I didn't think it would do any good pushing her on it."

"Disappointing, but it doesn't matter. This is a big enough community for more than one staging business." I laughed. "Now whether they can do as good a job as we can is another matter."

Tyrone who had been standing nearby leaned closer. "Glad you brought that up. I meant to tell you what I heard at Vocaro's." Tyrone, working as a barista, picked up a lot of gossip at the coffee shop. "Monica Heller is jumping into the staging business with both feet."

My stomach clenched. *Anyone but her.* Monica, a local interior decorator, had made my life in school miserable with all her taunting. She'd been the thorn in my side that had festered and oozed all through our school years. If that wasn't enough, I strongly suspected she'd been involved with my late husband, Derrick. But then, he had been such a womanizer there probably weren't many women in town he hadn't been involved with—except Nita, of course.

Why would Monica be moving into home staging? She had a successful interior design business, helping homeowners put personality into their homes. Home stagers take a lot of the personality out so prospective homebuyers can see themselves living there. Maybe the rumor was wrong.

Could anything more go wrong this weekend? A dead body, having to deal with Detective Spangler again, Aunt Kit arriving, a canceled truck, a bad review, and now possible competition from Monica.

"Hey, Laura."

I turned to see two tall and very lean men behind me. I immediately recognized Geoff Clarke and Ron Zigler, the men who'd bought the Denton's nineteenth-century mansion Tyrone and I had staged in the spring. They had turned it into a fabulous bed and breakfast. It was early days for the venture, but the B&B was fast developing a reputation as *the* place in town to stay.

"Well, hello." I was pleased to see them again, especially since they had liked the work Tyrone and I had done on the mansion and hadn't changed too much—yet. I quickly introduced Geoff and Ron to everyone.

Geoff, who frequently served as the spokesman for the duo, pulled off his baseball cap and shook hands with everyone. I saw Mrs. Webster nod in approval. Geoff's good manners had just earned him high points with her.

"Meeting the small businessmen and women in town?" Mrs. Webster asked.

"We have some work we'd like to do at the B&B, including eventually finishing the basement. We thought meeting some of the business owners would give us a head start with that."

Nita went into promotion mode and pointed to the square. "You've come to the right place. If you don't find the people you need to talk to here, let me know. My family is in construction, and they know all the tradesmen in town."

"Thanks, we'll keep that in mind. Next, we'll be looking for some furnishings. Any places you can recommend, Laura?"

"Start with Josh Sheridan at Antiques and Other Things. He has more *other things* than antiques, but you never know what you might stumble on there. I'm going there this week to talk to Josh about renting some storage space. If you'd like to meet me there, I'd be happy to show you around."

Geoff and Ron liked that idea and we agreed on a time to meet. "Thanks. Sounds like a plan," Ron said.

Seeing Geoff and Ron reminded me of Will Parker. "Have you met Will Parker yet? He's the man you'll see along Battlement Drive near your place. He voluntarily maintains that road, picking up trash that accumulates along the roadside. Be sure to make friends with him. He'll keep an eye on things for you."

"First person we met," Ron said. "He told us about some of the adventures you all had there this spring."

"Will is a real character, but a good guy." I quickly gave them the names of some other antique stores in the area, not wanting to discuss our experiences at the Denton house, where the homeowner had been murdered. "How's the B&B business?"

"Great so far—although something strange just happened. We had a guest check in and spend the night. The next day he went out, and we haven't seen him since."

"Did you get a deadbeat who skipped out without paying?" Mrs. Webster asked.

Ron took a seat next to Mrs. Webster. "He'd paid for several nights, so we didn't suspect he skipped out. He said he was in town to settle his aunt's estate and planned to stay with us only until he could find out if her house was in reasonable condition for him to stay there. We thought perhaps he'd decided to stay at his aunt's place and would be back later for his luggage. Now we're not so sure."

A shiver ran down my body. A missing guest. A man found dead in the funeral home. This didn't sound good. I looked at Geoff's and Ron's open, unsuspecting faces.

"Guys, I think you need to contact the Louiston police."

Chapter 7

Key rooms to stage include entryways, living rooms, kitchens, and master bedrooms.

The next morning, Ernie Phillips parked his truck in my driveway ready for us to load the furniture stored in my garage. The truck was hard to miss. On the side of it Ernie had painted *Window Wizard* in bright neon green, using a wide paintbrush. Not the most professional job, but no one would miss it.

I had a list of items we would be taking to the staging site and started to check off the carefully wrapped items as Tyrone, Ernie, and Will Parker loaded them. My current inventory wasn't large enough to fill a house, but between what we had stored in my garage and at Nita's place, we had enough to make a house look cozy and attractive. Getting a large storage area would enable us to expand our inventory.

The owners of the home we were staging thought my idea of having the windows cleaned was a good one, so I hired Ernie for his window cleaning capability, the use of his truck, and his loading skills. We would have to make more than one trip, but it would work out.

When Nita arrived, I knew something was up. Her sparkling eyes and wide grin usually meant she had news to share. "I saw Neil. Guess what I learned?"

Poor Neil. Even as a grown policeman, he could never stand up to his older cousin, Nita, especially when she was seeking information. He frequently ended up spilling police news he shouldn't be sharing.

"What were you able to wheedle out of him this time?" I asked.

"They found Ian Becker's phone at the funeral home—under a chair. Maybe it flew out of his hands when he was struck down. His phone records showed he'd made calls to his aunt's attorney, Warren Hendricks, Anne Williamson—one of his aunt's friends from the arts group—and Emily Thompson. He dated her during his last summer here."

"Interesting."

"So what are we going to do about it?" Nita asked with sudden interest. "If the police arrest Warren for the murder, we need to help him."

"What do you mean what are we going to do? Nothing. We aren't getting involved in this. We didn't even know Ian Becker. And I don't think the police are seriously linking Warren to the murder."

"But it's all so intriguing."

"As intriguing as it sounds, we have a house to stage today. Let Detective Spangler handle it."

We made quick work of the staging. Ernie, standing on a ladder to the upper floor, yelled down, "Laura, I hate to say it, but I think these are the dirtiest windows I've ever cleaned. I don't know how the homeowners could distinguish morning from night."

"Do your wizardry, Ernie, and make them sparkle. We need to brighten the inside of this house, which is really dark. Clean windows will help, especially as dirty as these are."

We opened all the shades and blinds, and removed window dressings that overpowered some of the windows. It did a lot to brighten the rooms.

"Where do you want these, Laura?" Will Parker stood in the doorway holding rolls of area rugs. It was good seeing him well recovered from a hit-and-run accident that had almost killed him months ago. I directed him where to put them. After everything was in the appropriate rooms, we arranged the furnishings and added some artwork, making sure not to make holes in the freshly painted walls.

This was a much simpler job than some since our contract with the homeowners had us bringing in minimal furnishings. After setting up some furniture in the living room and kitchen, Nita and I made up the bed in the master bedroom, added a bedside table and lamp, and some accessories. Fresh white towels in the bathrooms gave them a spa look. A few accessories completed the job.

I stood back and looked at the results—simple but elegant.

Now that the feverish pitch of activity to get the staging work done was over, I thought more about the phone calls on Ian Becker's phone. Who was Emily Thompson?

Asking around out of curiosity wasn't the same thing as getting involved, right?

Chapter 8

Turn a small condo balcony into a charming area by adding a small café table and chairs.

The following day, I arrived at Antiques and Other Things to find Geoff and Ron waiting outside for me. It was a beautiful but unusually cool morning—one requiring a light jacket. But the cool day didn't prevent Geoff and Ron from enjoying the small seating area outside the main entrance. Josh Sheridan, the owner, had put out small café tables and chairs, surrounded by planters and hanging baskets filled with blue and yellow petunias. Ron entertained himself by throwing small pieces of donuts from a Hibbard's Bakery bag to three tiny birds that pecked at the crumbs.

Both men gave me a warm hug in greeting. "Before we go in," I said, "let me tell you a little something about Josh. He loves old movies and frequently dresses as a character from a film he watched. If you can guess who he's dressed like or what movie it's from, you'll have a friend for life."

The old-fashioned bell over the door jangled as we entered, alerting Josh he had a potential customer. Today he sported a long Madras print shirt hanging outside his trousers and khakis.

"Hey, Josh. I've brought in some new Louiston residents. This is Geoff Clarke and Ron Zigler. They own the new B&B in town."

After the introductions were over, I pondered what movie

character Josh was dressed like. He enjoyed this aspect of my visits so much I didn't want to disappoint him. The Madras shirt was reminiscent of the fifties or sixties, so I made a wild guess. "The main character from *State Fair*?"

"Wrong." It didn't help much that he only gave me one guess.

Ron stood back, studied Josh, and rubbed his chin as though deep in thought. "I'm going to guess *American Graffiti*."

Josh gaped at him in astonishment. "Right!" Just that fast they became movie-loving kindred, and Geoff found himself a friend forever.

"Josh, I'm going to show Geoff and Ron around, but after that, I need to talk to you."

"Y'all go on ahead. I'll be here when you're ready." Josh's Georgia origins were still recognizable in his accent. "Give a holler if you need me."

After giving Geoff and Ron a quick tour, I left them to browse, and I returned to the front entrance where I found Josh stacking wooden crates.

"Take a look at these, Laura. I refinished them. They were crates used to ship matches and gun cartridges. They sure look pretty, don't they?

"Oh, they are nice." I took a closer look.

"I was able to preserve the labels on the sides." Josh stacked up two more of the crates. "There's lots of demand for them, and they nearly fly out the door as soon as I put them on display."

I liked the look of them and could think of a dozen ways I could use them, but I didn't want to look too interested until we could negotiate a price. After a few minutes, Josh and I came to a price we were both happy with.

Josh dumped some matchbooks and small matchboxes into a large bowl he placed on the counter. "Someone spent years collecting these, but most of them don't have much value." He reached into the bowl and pulled out two. "Here, take a couple. You never know when you might need a match."

"Thanks, Josh." I slipped the matches into my jacket pocket."

They'll come in handy. I keep candles in case the power goes out, but I can rarely find a match to light them with."

"Now you'll be prepared."

Time to get down to business. "Josh, a while ago we talked about me renting some storage space. Now that I've accumulated a fair amount of furnishings we use when staging empty houses and plan to obtain more, I'm running out of space at my house and at Nita's place. Since you've taken over those two new mill buildings, do you think you could find space for us to rent?"

"I just might be able to. Let me check the buildings and see what kind of space I can find for you. You'll need an area you can secure and get things in and out easily. How about I look around and call you this week?"

"That would be great. Thanks." I picked up my new acquisition.

"What do you have there?" Ron asked, coming up from behind me. He pointed to the crate. "That's a nice piece."

"It's a crate Josh refinished. I think it'll make a good end table or maybe an occasional table. Nice isn't it? He has more."

Josh pointed to the crates he had stacked behind the counter. "Interested? I'll give you a good price on 'em."

Ron ended up purchasing two of them, and Josh was a happy businessman.

"By the way, Laura," Josh said, "your old friend Monica Heller came in here the other day—along with that artist who's teaching at Fischer College."

My old friend? I would definitely not describe Monica as such. Just the thought of her raised my hackles. "Oh, yes?" I feigned interest.

"Yeah. She introduced Damian Reynolds—one of those artistic types—wearing a black silk shirt. Not many guys in Louiston wearing silk shirts. I could've bought a tank of gas with what he probably paid for his haircut. The interesting thing was he came back a couple of days later on his own and asked if he could consign some artwork." *So much for keeping his customers' business confidential.*

"Was that unusual?" The curiosity bug bit me again.

"Sort of. Him being so big in the art world, you'd think he'd take his stuff to an auction house. He'd get better prices than I could get for him here."

"Don't sell yourself short, Josh. He obviously felt comfortable bringing you the pieces."

I studied a collection of colorful vases on a shelf nearby. Why would someone well-known in the art world consign pieces to a small-town business like Josh's? It was great for Josh, and a good idea if Damian didn't want word getting out that he was selling his stuff. Had he fallen on hard times?

Geoff had been standing nearby. "Did you say Damian Reynolds came in here? He and his agent stayed at our B&B recently while he looked for a house in town. It was exciting having someone so famous as one of our first guests."

"Yeah, but his stay wasn't without drama," Ron said, putting a bust of Jefferson on the counter.

Josh, who loved a good gossip, was all ears.

"One night, he and his agent got into a big row," Ron said. "We thought we were going to have to break it up. Fortunately, it didn't come to more than words. We didn't want our B&B to become known as the place a famous artist was murdered."

Chapter 9

A good design guideline is to hang artwork sixty-two inches from the floor to the center of the piece.

That afternoon, Nita pulled up in her lime green VW bug for our ride to the Fischer College Arts Center. She was involved with the Louiston Arts Festival and had convinced me to help with the art intake. Aunt Kit had volunteered to come along.

When we approached the car, Aunt Kit insisted on squeezing her tall frame into the small backseat—too stubborn to let me sit back there. I'd hoped to get in first because I knew I'd later hear how the backseat caused her sciatica to flare up. There was no winning with Aunt Kit.

Nita looked perkier today. "How'd your meeting go with Josh? Is he going to rent us storage space?"

"He's going to look around his buildings for a spot large enough to meet our needs. Also space we can lock to keep his customers from picking through our things looking for a bargain."

Aunt Kit squirmed in her seat, trying to get comfortable. "Why do you need all that furniture?"

"We use it to stage houses that are unoccupied," I said. "For an occupied home, we work with things the homeowner has—many times removing some furniture to make a place look bigger. But if the home is unoccupied, we furnish it to make it look lived in.

Furnished homes sell faster than empty ones."

As Nita and Aunt Kit chatted, my thoughts strayed back to Warren and his worries about being a suspect in the murder. I wondered how he was doing. Warren and I had been friends for years, and I couldn't imagine him striking out at anybody in anger much less stab a man in cold blood. It just wasn't consistent with his gentle nature, which was perfect for comforting the bereaved at his funeral home.

"You sound quite knowledgeable, Nita." Aunt Kit's words brought me back to the present. I could tell she was impressed and relieved I'd finally begun to build a team of helpers.

"Nita's been taking online courses to obtain her staging certification. Having two certified home stagers will give us more creditability," I said.

Aunt Kit grunted. She was still convinced I'd made a mistake leaving my well-paying job in IT to start a home staging business. She was also upset about our discovering a body at the funeral home. So was I, but it was hardly my fault. Nothing I'd said so far relieved her worries. As her only living relative, she worried about me far too much.

Nita pulled into the Arts Center parking lot, and after much back and forth maneuvering, she managed to park. Nita's driving and parking abilities, or lack of, were her biggest challenges. I helped Aunt Kit pull herself from the backseat where she had been curled up like a pretzel. Once we alighted, we helped Nita unload her bags of gear and the framed photographs she was submitting to the festival and carried them into the center.

Nita had joined the arts group after she'd become serious about her photography. I was happy to see her more active and involved in things for herself and suffering less from empty nest syndrome. Being a part of the arts group inspired her to do more with her photography than just take photos of the houses we staged.

When we walked into the Arts Center, the place was bustling with activity. Aunt Kit wandered away and hopefully would stay out of trouble. She tended to direct people how to do their jobs. Once she'd told the bishop which priests he should assign to the various parishes in the diocese. The funny thing was the assignments nearly matched her recommendations. Pure coincidence?

Volunteers had already started to erect the wooden display boards the artwork would hang on. The boards created a maze throughout the large room. When the volunteers saw us, they bombarded Nita with questions about the body she'd found.

She assured everyone she didn't have anything more to say other than she'd found the body, and that was it. Again it made me wonder who could have wanted to kill someone who hadn't been in town in over twenty years.

"I remember Ian Becker," a voice called from the back. "He was a nice kid. Occasionally got into trouble, but nothing serious—just enough to keep his aunt chasing after him."

I glared at him and he must have gotten the message we didn't want to hear anymore because he faded into the crowd.

When everyone returned to work, Nita assigned Mrs. Webster, another volunteer Nita had recruited, and me to direct the artists where to take their artwork and check off their names. It was an assignment we could handle that didn't require any experience in dealing with the artwork. My only involvement with artwork was recognizing pieces I liked and selecting ones to use in homes we staged. As the pieces came in, I kept my eye out for any that would be a good addition to our inventory. Some of them were brilliant.

The pieces would be displayed in various categories and labeled with the name of the artist, the name of the piece, and a price for each.

Mrs. Webster's eyebrows shot up. "Heaven sakes. Do you think anyone is going to pay these prices?"

"The artists set their own prices. From what Nita said, they have to be willing to sell the piece to enter. If they don't want to sell it, they set the price high to discourage buyers. But that doesn't always work. I understand one artist priced her piece for what she thought was an outrageous amount so it wouldn't sell and was shocked when it sold."

Later, Nita stopped at our table to see how we were doing. "Have they all checked in?"

Mrs. Webster nodded and handed her the check-off sheet. "Who is the juror for the show?" The juror would select first, second, and third places in each category as well as honorable mentions.

"Damian Reynolds," Nita said. "He's famous for his wild abstracts, and you see his artwork everywhere. He recently joined the faculty of Fischer College, either as an instructor or guest lecturer—I don't know which. Great for the college, but people wondered why someone so famous would come to a small town like Louiston."

"That is a bit surprising," Mrs. Webster said.

"Anne Williamson still can't believe she was able to convince him to serve as the juror." Nita pointed to a short, stout woman with a head of tight gray curls, hanging paintings. "That's Anne over there."

Nita grimaced. "I tried to convince her to hang the art so the center of each piece is sixty-two inches from the floor, a decorating standard. But she insists the top of each piece is to be seventy inches from the floor, regardless of size. It makes the smaller pieces look funny. But she heads the organization and holds it together— almost singlehandedly—so I don't make an issue of it."

"Anne always likes doing things her way." Mrs. Webster knew most of the people in town and their idiosyncrasies.

"She usually refuses help. And everyone is happy to let her do it so they don't have to. Except for this festival." Nita pointed to the gallery. "She couldn't do all this on her own."

Mrs. Webster sniffed. "You know what they say. People often don't want anyone involved to cover up their mishandling of the funds."

Nita laughed. "Believe me, Mrs. Webster, there isn't much money to mishandle. And from what I understand, there never has been. Besides, Anne is a very talented artist and her work sells for *lots* of money. Come on. I'll introduce you."

As we approached, Anne Williamson hoisted a large framed piece and started to hang it on a display board. Aunt Kit came over to join us.

I rushed over to the older woman. "Here, let me help you with that."

"Don't you worry, dear, I've got it." With that, she dropped the frame into place and slapped her hands together to remove any dust that dared cling to the frame. "I'm stronger than I look."

When the others approached, Nita made the introductions. Anne beamed at our compliments about the artwork that was beginning to surround us. Her pride in the work of her members was obvious.

"We're very fortunate to have talented artists here in Louiston. We're especially happy that Nita joined us. Nita, you'll have to take your friends over and show them your photographs. They've all been hung. Now if you'll please excuse me, we have an artist who is unhappy with where his work was hung, and I have to go deal with it."

We said our farewells to Anne and followed Nita to the photography area. The variety of images was amazing, but it was Nita's two photos of Inky that immediately drew my attention.

"Nita, they're wonderful." My friend didn't realize how talented she was. The photos she had taken of my cat were truly imaginative. How she was able to get him to pose with such interesting expressions, I'd never know. He wouldn't have done that for me.

Not comfortable with the attention she was receiving, Nita blushed and pointed to another area. "Come on, let me show you around. Most of the works are up now, so you'll get to see the exhibit before anyone else does."

"Maybe I'll find some pieces we can add to our staging inventory." I thought the original works were fabulous, but seeing the prices made me realize that for now, I would have to stick to shopping at resale shops or garage sales for artwork.

When we walked into the room containing the two-dimensional pieces, a large painting of a woman dressed in shades of black, purple, and lavender immediately caught our attention. It was dramatic and breathtaking.

"That's Anne's submission," Nita said. "Stunning isn't it?" That was an understatement.

Mrs. Webster whistled at the price. "Did she set it that high to discourage buyers?"

"No. That's what her artwork sells for. You see why we don't have to worry about her mishandling our little treasury."

"You could buy a small car with that kind of money," Mrs. Webster said.

Aunt Kit, who was really into art, stood looking at the piece. "I wouldn't be surprised if it doesn't sell for even more than that if two or more people start bidding on it. I need to get to know Anne Williamson better." With that, she left us in search of her.

I looked up to see Tyrone weaving his way around the art boards. Mrs. Webster had said he'd be arriving soon to give her a ride home.

"Laura. Glad you're still here. I just came from Vocaro's. Word is out the police are questioning Warren again." Uh, oh. Would Nita be next?

Chapter 10

Attractive artwork can breathe new life into a room. Framed photos will make a room look more contemporary.

Two days later, the art show opened, and a reception was being held that evening to honor the award winners. Damian Reynolds, the juror, had judged the artwork the day before and Anne Williamson had notified the winners. We were thrilled to learn that Nita had won an honorable mention for her photographs.

"I can't believe my simple photos of Inky got an honorable mention." Nita accepted the flute of champagne her husband Guido handed her. He leaned over and kissed her gently. "Your photos are great."

"Don't sell yourself short, Nita. It took skill in getting such terrific photos. Of course, using my gorgeous Inky as your subject might have helped."

Nita laughed. "Possibly. It's hard to find a cat more beautiful than Inky."

The room was jammed, but the crowd parted when Monica Heller entered. She radiated superiority. A tall swarthy man with long dark hair tied at the back of his neck accompanied her. As they walked by, Monica paused in front of us, like Queen Elizabeth stopping to talk to well-wishers in the crowd.

"Congratulations, Nita, on your little award," Monica said.

Little award. I forced myself not to shake my head in disgust. Or curtsy. Would Monica ever change? "We didn't see you at the Small Business Fair over the weekend, Monica," I said.

She wrinkled her nose as though she smelled something bad. "Oh, my dear, no. I have more business than I can handle as it is. No need to drum up more." She whisked a flute of champagne from a tray held by a passing waiter and walked away, never bothering to introduce the man with her.

I turned to Nita. "Did Monica enter anything in the festival? She knew about your award."

Tyrone stopped chewing on the ice from his glass and pointed to the retreating figures. "She probably knows because of him."

At my puzzled look, Nita added, "That's Damian Reynolds, the artist—and Monica's latest client. He bought a mid-century modern house near the campus, and Monica is helping him decorate it."

"Is that what they call it now?" Mrs. Webster bit on an olive that was probably as sour as her feelings about Monica. "They looked a lot chummier than homeowner and decorator."

"According to word at Vocaro's, they're *together*." Tyrone took another mouthful of ice.

Between Tyrone and Nita's hairdresser, we had the best sources of information in town.

A short while later, Anne Williamson thanked everyone for coming and introduced Damian Reynolds. After the applause died down, she thanked him for serving as the juror and handed him a gift-wrapped box. "A small token of our appreciation." He placed it on the table behind them and took his place next to Anne for the awards ceremony.

Anne announced the winners in each category, and Damian presented envelopes containing cash awards to the recipients. With lots of Nita's family present for the ceremony, the applause when she accepted her envelope was thunderous. I was thrilled for my friend, who deserved all the recognition she could get.

Nita's joy of winning the award was obvious from her broad smile. "Can you believe it? I get money as part of the award."

Later as everyone mingled, I bumped into Anne Williamson who was standing near her piece.

"Congratulations on your best-in-show award. Your piece is fabulous." I sounded like a gushing fan, but I admired anyone who could paint such a beautiful and dramatic piece.

"Thank you. It's one of my favorite pieces. It will be hard to part with it."

"Does that mean you've sold it?"

"Let's just say I'm entertaining offers."

Damian Reynolds, holding a champagne flute in his hand, walked up to the piece. He studied it for a long time and then moved closer as though memorizing every brushstroke. When he walked away, I turned to Anne. "I wonder what they look for in a piece when they judge the different categories? He certainly admired your piece, giving it best in show. High praise coming from a famous artist."

"Yes, it was quite an honor," Anne said with a huge smile. "I think this deserves another glass of champagne." With that, she went in search of a waiter.

Mrs. Webster, who had been standing nearby, stared at the painting. "All that money for a painting." She continued studying it.

"You are so entranced by it, perhaps you should put in an offer for it." I leaned over to take a close look.

"If I had that much money, I could pay for Tyrone's next year of college." She shook her head. "There's something about that painting."

"It's definitely mesmerizing."

Nita came up from behind us and pointed toward Damian who was talking to Guido. "Quite a handsome guy. I predict every young woman at the college will become infatuated with him before the end of the summer semester."

"Too handsome for my taste." I finished the remainder of my drink and looked around for a place to put my empty glass.

"I know—you and your belief that handsome men are trouble. In this case, you may be right."

Chapter 11

Ensure artwork and furniture are in scale and in proportion to the room size and other items around them.

I searched the crowded reception room for Warren but didn't see him. It was unusual for him to miss a function like this since he was a big supporter of anything related to the arts in Louiston. Could the police have detained him?

Tyrone, biting into a cookie, approached and handed me a serving plate of cookies. It looked like he had eaten most of them already. "Laura, I need to leave. Got a date. Could you give Gran a ride home?"

"I'm riding with Nita and Guido, but I'm sure they'd be happy to drive her home." I looked around. "By the way, have you seen Warren? I thought he'd be here. Since the police wanted to question him again, I'm worried that he's not here."

"He came into Vocaro's this afternoon. Said the police had wanted to ask him about who else Ian Becker hung around with when he lived here. They didn't detain him."

"That's a relief."

Behind us, we heard raised voices and turned to see Monica and Damian. Her face was reddening and her hands curled into fists. Damian kept trying to quiet her, but as Monica became more agitated, her voice grew louder.

"I can't let you do that!" Monica screeched.

Damian, noticing the crowd had turned toward them, took Monica by the arm and ushered her out a side door. The room remained silent for several seconds before the buzz of conversation started again. Monica always knew how to make an entrance—and now a dramatic exit.

"Well, that was interesting." I started picking up paper cups and plates from a nearby table and disposing of them in a trash bag. Nita had used her strong arm to find volunteers to help clean up after the reception—me among them. "That was one scene I could have done without."

Tyrone took the bag from me and held it open as I cleared another table. "I gather their decorating collaboration, or whatever they call their relationship, isn't going well."

"Doesn't sound like it. But Monica never has a smooth relationship with anyone. If nothing else, it makes life interesting for the rest of us."

At the end of the evening after Nita and I finished cleaning up, I noticed a box sitting on a side table. I held it up and motioned to Nita. "This got left behind."

"Agatha Christie!"

"What?" I stared at Nita, wondering what had gotten into her.

Guido laughed. "Since finding that body and being stressed, she's started using a few expletives and wants to cut them out before the kids come home. Now when she's upset, she uses the name of somebody famous. What's wrong, Nita?

Nita pointed to the box. "That's the thank you gift Anne gave Damian for serving as the juror. In his haste to get Monica out of here, he probably forgot it."

I handed her the box. "He might come back for it."

"Yes, but we're ready to close up, and if he doesn't come back soon and we leave it, someone might take it. It's too valuable to leave."

Nita turned to Guido. "It's not too late. Do you mind if we drop this at his place when we take Mrs. Webster home? He doesn't live far from her."

During the short drive to Damian's house, I found my eyelids becoming heavy and noticed Mrs. Webster's head bobbing and occasionally jerking upright. We'd all had a tiring day, and I was anxious to get home and curl up in bed with Inky, if he wasn't deserting me again for Aunt Kit's bed. Aunt Kit had joined old friends for dinner that evening, so I wasn't sure what time she would be getting in.

Damian's mid-century modern house was set back from the road in a grove of pine trees. The large front windows typical of that style of home were dark and the place looked rather foreboding. Guido pulled into the long driveway and stopped the motor. We could see a dim light from a side window, which could mean Damian was still up.

Nita hopped from the car with the box. "I'll knock quickly, and if he doesn't answer, I'll leave it near the front door and send him a text letting him know it's there."

The cool night air and the lovely fragrance of pine coming in from an open car window helped relax me. I rested my head on the seatback, planning to sleep the rest of the way home.

A piercing scream jolted us fully awake.

Looking toward the sound of the scream, we saw Nita by the front door frantically beckoning to us. We scrambled from the car, nearly stumbling over ourselves, and ran toward the house. Our relief at seeing she was okay was overwhelming.

When we reached the front door, Guido entered first, with Mrs. Webster and me following. Not knowing what we'd find, I tried to push in front of her, but she wouldn't have it.

We gaped at the scene in front of us. There, wide-eyed and covered in blood, stood Monica Heller—a knife in her hands. At her feet lay Damian Reynolds.

Chapter 12

Arrange furniture to provide balance to a room.

Guido grasped Nita to his chest, trying to soothe her and to assure himself that she was okay. Monica looked dazed and was keening like a sick animal.

"Monica, drop the knife." I attempted to keep my voice calm, feeling more like running away than trying to talk a crazed killer into giving up her weapon. If we didn't get it away from her, would she come at one of us with it? Me in particular, given our history.

Monica didn't appear to absorb what I'd said. Finally, she focused on me with a questioning look, as though wondering why I was there.

"Drop the knife," I repeated. Monica looked down at the knife in her hands and abruptly thrust it away from her. It landed on the terrazzo floor with a clatter, splattering spots of blood as it skittered across the shiny stone surface.

Mrs. Webster knelt on the floor next to Damian Reynolds and checked his pulse. She pushed aside his long ponytail, matted in blood, and exposed an expanding dark circle in the middle of his back. *Not again.*

Assured that Nita was okay, Guido pulled his phone from his pocket and punched in 911. Behind me, I could hear him giving details to the dispatcher. *Would it be Patty again?*

Monica stood as though rooted next to Damian's body. Now that she was unarmed, I took her by the arm, gently led her to the sofa, and eased her into it. She rubbed her sticky hands together as though to rub away the blood on them. My instinct was to get some wet paper towels in the kitchen so I could wipe her hands clean, but on reflection, thought better of it. The police would need to see things the way they were before we entered.

Monica's eyes came back into focus and with a jerky voice asked, "Is he...going to be okay? I tried to save him."

Save him? "How, Monica? How did you try to save him?"

"I found him...on the floor. He wasn't moving...the knife." She started to sob. "I pulled it out...trying to save him."

If Monica pulled the knife out, had she thrust it into his back to begin with? Regretted what she had done and then pulled it out? But if she hadn't stabbed him, who had?

If she hadn't stabbed him, it was natural her first instinct had been to remove the knife. If she read mysteries, she'd have known not to do that. Now she was covered in blood, been seen holding the knife, and looked every bit as guilty of stabbing him. *Oh, Monica, what have you done?*

Given all the evidence of what four people had seen, would the police be willing to believe her story about finding him and removing the knife to save him? Especially after they had argued so publicly?

We could hear the wail of sirens in the distance and knew it would only be a matter of minutes before the emergency response team arrived. At this point, I didn't know if Damian was alive or dead, but it didn't look good for his chances of survival.

When we heard the sound of vehicles screech to a halt nearby, Guido left Nita's side and went outside. From the window, I saw him talking to the policemen who had arrived with the EMTs. I was grateful to have Guido running interference for us. The EMTs nodded their heads, and I assumed that Guido had apprised them it was a crime scene. That way they could take steps to attend to the victim and try their best to preserve any evidence.

With the EMTs there to take over, Mrs. Webster stepped back from Damian's body and came over to where Monica and I sat. The grim look on her face confirmed my fears that Damian was dead.

Leaving us, Mrs. Webster poked her head into several doorways, and when I heard running water, I realized she had gone to wash her hands. I looked over and saw Monica rubbing her hands on her skirt, looking unaware of what she was doing. She stared anxiously at the EMTs as they went into action.

Guido had taken Nita outside. I looked through the large front window and could see them sitting on a bench near the front door. I desperately wanted to join them and not be here, witnessing what was happening in front of me. But I didn't want to leave Monica alone in the state she was in. Would there be any effect on the investigation if we removed her from the immediate scene of the crime? If we left through the front door or even a rear door, we could end up harming the crime scene. What a mess.

It was times like this that I wished I'd read more true crime and police procedural novels instead of traditional mysteries. Perhaps then I would know how to handle the situation better.

I looked up to see Detective Spangler coming through the doorway. He caught sight of me and shook his head. After conferring with the uniformed police officers and the EMTs, he came over to where Monica and I sat.

"Am I going to find you near every body that's found in town?" He flipped open the small notebook he was never without.

What could I say? Given my ill luck, that was about what was happening. And with each instance, it wasn't getting any easier.

Chapter 13

Each room should have a focal point. To provide a focal point for a bedroom, use a headboard that is about sixty inches high.

In the morning after a late night, I dragged myself from bed, fed Inky, left a note for Aunt Kit, and made my way to Vocaro's to meet Nita and Tyrone. We were scheduled to stage another unoccupied home that morning and couldn't put it off. Fortunately, the truck we had reserved hadn't mysteriously been canceled, so we were set to go. Nita, just as bleary-eyed as I felt, arrived soon after I got there.

It had been quite late by the time we had given our statements to Detective Spangler and were allowed to leave. Fortunately, he'd felt compassion for Mrs. Webster and directed a police officer to take her home, saying he would get her statement in the morning. With four of us to attest to what we had witnessed when we arrived at the house, he could get most of what he needed from Nita, Guido, and me—and later get Mrs. Webster's story.

When Detective Spangler had broken it to Monica that Damian was dead, it was as though she had gone into shock. Her vacant stare unnerved me. When she parted her lips to speak, words didn't come out.

Later when Detective Spangler questioned her, she mumbled her responses. It surprised me that he'd allowed me to stay at her side during the questioning. The last thing we saw that night was Monica being driven away in a police car for further questioning. It hadn't been her finest hour.

Now with little sleep, Nita and I stared up at the menu board hanging above the counter, trying to decide on something we could stomach. The shock of finding a second body within days of each other was taking a toll on us, and neither of us felt very hungry.

Tyrone stood behind the counter, ready to serve people as they came in. Soon he would be getting off work and we could leave to pick up Will Parker and then the furniture we were taking with us. Tyrone still amazed me at his ability to hold several part-time jobs and manage to get passing grades—in fact, more than just passing.

Today, however, after hearing about the events of last evening from his grandmother, he didn't seem as buoyant. Monica wasn't among his favorite people either, but with his experience of being accused of a crime and then proven innocent, he could well sympathize with her plight.

We finally decided on muffins and coffee and claimed our favorite table in Vocaro's rear seating area and sank into our seats. We'd both ordered large coffees in an attempt to become more alert.

Vocaro's served as a crossroads for the community, and a large segment of the population came through it during the day. So it was no surprise when Nita's cousin Neil came in. His wrinkled police uniform and mussed hair a sure sign he'd pulled an all-nighter.

When he saw us, he put up both hands, palms out as though stopping traffic. "Don't bother to ask, I'm not saying *anything* about Damian Reynolds's murder or about Monica Heller."

"Relax, Neil. Have a seat." Nita patted the chair next to her. "We know you wouldn't have information about what's going on." Knowing Nita so well, I knew her words, innocent on the surface, were meant to goad her younger cousin into saying things he shouldn't. He could never resist trying to show her how much in the know he was.

She turned away from him as though ignoring him. "What do

you think, Laura? Did Monica stab Damian? Or was it as she said—she found him on the floor when she got there and pulled the knife out to save him?"

I pondered the question, glad I wasn't in a courtroom being asked that—it was a tough one. "I don't know. We didn't see her stab him, but what we witnessed was pretty incriminating. I heard her tell Detective Spangler that after she and Damian argued at the Arts Center, he dropped her at her place. Later, she got in her car and drove to his house. The door was ajar, and getting no answer when she called his name, she stepped inside. That's when she saw him on the floor. Without thinking, she pulled the knife from his back, hoping it would help him. We arrived to find her holding the knife."

"If what Monica says is true, and she didn't stab him, who did? We didn't pass anyone on the road near Damian's house. But who knows how long Damian could have been lying there before Monica arrived." Nita shuddered, probably reacting to the memory of finding them there.

"It couldn't have been too long, because they left the Arts Center only about an hour before we did," I said. "Perhaps a little longer since we helped clean up."

"Two stabbings within a week. Could we have a serial killer on the loose in Louiston?" Nita looked at Neil out of the corner of her eye, hoping he wouldn't be able to resist adding something.

Neil didn't resist for long. "Did you know that Damian fellow is a famous artist? Or was." The color rose in Neil's cheeks at his blunder. "You should've seen the reporters coming into the station. They were shouting questions at the Chief about the murder—and about the murder of that man from New Zealand. The Chief wasn't happy, especially after he received a call from the New Zealand Embassy. The whole squad later heard him yell at Detective Spangler to get those cases closed—and fast."

Suddenly, Louiston was becoming an international hotbed of criminal activity, and we'd been caught up in it.

Chapter 14

Buyers will be in and out of a vacant house within minutes but will linger in a furnished home an average of forty minutes. The longer they stay, the greater the opportunity for them to picture themselves living there.

When we reached the site of the unoccupied home staging, I grabbed my check-off list and went to work directing Tyrone and Will Parker in unloading the truck and telling them where to take the furniture and rugs we'd brought. Nita carried in the large canvas bag we brought with us to each work site. We didn't always need everything from the bag, but being able to pull out things like furniture sliders, two-sided tape, or removable picture hangers when we needed them was helpful.

The hundred-year-old house, built in a Victorian style with a wide front porch, was typical of the homes in that section of Louiston. Tyrone, who was studying design, found the old homes interesting. Standing in front of the house, I pointed out some of the characteristics of the house style. "Real craftsman built these old homes. Look at the decorative trim in the gables." I pointed to the house across the street. "That one has fish scale shingles on the sides."

"I never paid much attention to them before." Tyrone looked up and down the street at the homes with various decorative trim.

I pointed to a little door in the porch foundation. "See that? It opens to a coal chute. Workmen used to deliver coal to a bin in the cellar by dumping it into the chute. When people switched to gas, most of the chutes got covered up. I imagine most people living in these homes don't even know there is a coal chute."

"Probably lots of things in these old places people don't know about," Tyrone said.

On the porch, I then took a can of brass cleaner from our tool bag and wiped some on the house numbers. With a little buffing, they looked brand new. People could either be attracted to or turned off by a house based on a first impression—and that started at the front entrance.

After a busy morning, we stopped for lunch at noon and pulled out the sandwiches and drinks we'd brought with us, gathering around the kitchen table we'd set up. It gave us the break we needed from all the physical work we had been doing.

Will took off his cowboy hat and fanned himself. "I can't believe you ladies stumbled on another body."

Nita's phone rang. She got up and walked away to answer it.

"This has been a bad week, Will." I unwrapped my sandwich and took a bite, savoring the taste of the tuna and dill pickle on pumpernickel bread I'd packed.

"That's for sure. I didn't know either of those two gentlemen, but I sure was sorry for 'em. Doesn't it make you wonder about two murders so close together and both of 'em stabbings?"

Tyrone sat down and pulled the tab from a can of Pepsi. "Sure sounds strange to me. I had an art class with Damian Reynolds last semester. Man, he was a tough instructor but a talented guy."

Will had a rapt audience in Tyrone. "What could connect a man who lived outta the country for more'n twenty years and an artist who just moved to this area and probably never met him?"

"Right now—nothing but pure coincidence." I finished my sandwich, wadded the wrapper into a ball, and placed it in my bag. "There's been talk about a serial killer, but with Monica being found as she was, that possibly rules out the serial killer theory."

"Lessen you consider Monica could be the serial killer—killing both that Reynolds fellow and the man in the funeral home. Did you ever think that?" Will looked smug as though he had solved both crimes.

He was another reader, who enjoyed stories of intrigue—the more outlandish the better. To my mind, Monica was the Wicked Witch of the West and could have stabbed Damian. But a serial killer? Not even I could swallow that. *Serial bully maybe.*

Nita returned and slumped into a chair. "That was my niece Jaime. She found the home of her dreams."

"That's great. Why are you looking so grim about it?" Tyrone asked.

"Because her place isn't ready. If she doesn't sell it right away, she'll lose the house she wants." Nita unwrapped her sandwich. "To top it all off, she just learned about Damian's murder and is really upset."

"Upset? Did she know him?" I stopped gathering our trash and stared at her.

"That I don't know." Nita took a long swallow of water. "She works at the college, so maybe she knew him. But getting back to Jaime's house, before her husband went on active duty with the Army Reserves, they did all the major things that needed to be done, like making repairs and painting. But it still needs to be staged."

"We can help her with that." I wiped some crumbs from the table with my hands and brushed them into the trash bag.

"In their situation, she wouldn't be able to pay you much."

"Nita, are you crazy? She's family. I wouldn't charge her anything." Nita's family had been good to me over the years, and I was willing to help any of them. "As soon as we leave here, let's go see what her place needs. We can come up with cost-effective ways for her to make the place appealing to buyers. And while there, we can find out why she's so upset about Damian Reynolds."

I called Aunt Kit to let her know I wouldn't be home until late that evening and asked her to feed Inky. She said she and Anne were going to see a movie and she would see me in the morning.

With our break over, we returned to work. I referred to our master list to see what remained to be done. Nita and I had developed a routine. We all did certain things, which prevented us from duplicating effort. I always did accessories with recommendations from Tyrone, who always had good ideas. Sometimes a single pop of color could make all the difference in a room.

Once the rooms were set up to our satisfaction, Will and Tyrone removed all the wrappings we used to protect the items we'd brought with us and took them back to the truck.

Tyrone shouted goodbye and left to return the rental truck.

Will waved his hat in farewell. "See ya'll next time. I'm headin' home to walk Pinto and do a cleanup along Battlement Drive."

Nita and I waved goodbye to Will and then began our final check of the place. We looked for any stray bits of dust or lint, vacuumed the room to fluff up the rugs or carpets, plumped pillows, and checked that the accessories weren't overdone. Before we left, Nita photographed each room, and we checked the list of items we left there so we could update our inventory. Another job completed. I sent a text to the real estate agent listing the house to let her know the staging had been completed.

Now, what were we going to do about the emergency facing Nita's niece?

Chapter 15

Home stagers offer various levels of home staging—from giving homeowners a list of things they can accomplish themselves; to staging a vacant home by bringing in furniture; to arranging for work to be done by painters, plumbers, landscapers, etc.

"Thank goodness you're here." Jaime was pacing on the front sidewalk as we drove up. Her red eyes showed she had been crying. When she saw us, she patted her hands together like a small child anticipating a surprise. "I couldn't believe it when Aunt Nita said you were willing to help me." Her eyes welled up with tears. "Sorry. This has been a terrible day."

I felt sorry for the young woman. To have such highs and lows in one day would be almost too much for anyone to handle, much less someone left handling the sale and purchase of a home while her young husband was away. The timing couldn't have been worse for her. And learning about Damian Reynolds hadn't helped.

I used my most soothing voice—the one I used with clients who are desperate to sell their homes and have become stressed. "Let's sit down and talk about what needs to be done."

"Everything," she wailed. "The house Frankie and I have been watching finally came on the market. I have his power of attorney, so our agent put in a bid for us. The homeowners accepted our contract, but it's contingent on our selling this place first. And they've only given us a few days to sell it. To make it look good enough to sell quickly, I have so much to do. And with Frankie away, it's all on me. And now, hearing about Mr. Reynolds, I'm so upset I can't function."

I was surprised the homeowners were willing to give Jaime and Frankie time to sell their house and wasn't sure they could sell it within the short time allowed. But Nita and I would do everything we could to make it happen.

Jaime went to get a Kleenex to wipe her eyes.

"What do you think, Nita?" I surveyed the living room while Jaime was gone.

"I recommend we remove some of the oversized pieces. Right now the rooms look too crowded, making the place look smaller than it is."

"Good idea, but what I meant was why do you think she is so upset about Damian?" It felt strange calling him by name since I had never had any dealings with him. But I didn't want to keep referring to him as *that famous artist*. "Is she just super emotional and cries easily at someone's death?"

Nita shrugged. "Sometimes. It's hard for young people to deal with death."

"It's hard for any of us, especially when the person was murdered."

When Jaime returned, Nita didn't hesitate to question her. "Jaime, why are you so upset about Mr. Reynolds? You weren't involved with him were you?"

Jaime's head jerked back. "Aunt Nita. Of course, I wasn't."

"Your aunt is only teasing you." I frowned at Nita. Would she ever learn to be subtle? If she wanted to know something, she'd ask direct questions without any subtlety. Like the time she'd asked Sister Madeleine, our second-grade teacher, what kind of underwear she wore beneath her habit. She hadn't improved with age.

"Did you know Damian Reynolds well?" I wondered how broadly she'd interpret my question.

"I provided admin assistance to him at the college. He'd only been there a short while, but I found him to be very nice. Except for the last time I saw him. He was preoccupied with something, and I had to keep calling his name to get his attention. That seemed to annoy him. It's just so sad that he was murdered. And no, Aunt Nita, I wasn't involved with him. He was seeing a lot of that interior decorator he hired. She used to wait for him outside in that red convertible of hers."

Apparently, Jaime hadn't heard about Monica's involvement in his death.

"I once saw him get in the car and kiss her," Jaime said.

So as we suspected, Monica and Damian had more going on than business dealings. I wondered if I should tell Detective Spangler or let him figure it out for himself. But he probably already suspected Monica had killed Damian during a lovers' quarrel.

It was a relief to know that Jaime hadn't been involved with Damian. Now it was down to business getting her house ready for sale.

"Who's your agent?" In the short time I'd been in the home staging business, I had met many of the agents in town and received referrals from them.

"Doug Hamilton at Hamilton Real Estate."

Doug Hamilton and his movie star good looks. A stunning lookalike for a young Robert Redford, Doug had been involved in the sale of the Denton mansion Tyrone and I had staged. He was a nice enough person, but I still had a deep-seated aversion to handsome men, or perhaps more a wariness. Let's just say that based on my experience with good-looking men, I steered clear of them. Doug had retired from the Navy and had come home to help his ailing father with his real estate agency. Since then he'd obtained his real estate license.

"Doug is a nice guy. I think you are in good hands." I pulled out my tablet and checklist to make notes. "Okay, let Nita and me tour the house on our own, and we'll work out a plan." It was better to look at the house without being escorted by the homeowner, who often would talk throughout the tour and be distracting—especially when the homeowner was extremely upset and worried about the sale, causing us to miss things.

Jaime's house was typical of one owned by a young couple. A bit bland, too cluttered, and lacked cohesiveness. Fortunately, following Nita's advice, Jaime and Frankie had recently painted the walls a neutral dove gray and made needed repairs.

In each room, we noted what we could do immediately, what things we recommended Jaime purchase, and what we recommended she remove. Some of the things we would help her with and others we would make recommendations, and it would be up to her to decide how she wanted to proceed. Nita took before photos.

After that, we got busy rearranging furniture, boxing up items Jaime didn't need until after they moved, rehanging prints on the wall that had been hung too high, switched a rug from one room to another, and did myriad things. At the end of the night, we were exhausted but pleased with the result. It was a cute cottage and would appeal to a young couple or a single person. I was hopeful someone would fall in love with it in the next few days.

As we drove home, I thought again about what Jaime had said about Damian. What had he been so preoccupied with the day he was murdered?

Chapter 16

Show off the amount of storage space your home has by clearing out unnecessary items from closets and shelves.

The next morning, I received a call from Josh, saying he had identified a place in one of his warehouses that might work for us. I made arrangements with him to check it out.

On my laptop, I pulled up my inventory of furniture and home furnishings. Since we had just furnished two unoccupied houses, we didn't have as much inventory on hand, but we'd soon be adding to it.

I'd just disconnected from Josh when another call came in, this one a result of the Small Business Fair, asking if we could meet with the homeowner about staging her place. It was a relief to know the fair and the expense of printing the brochures hadn't been a waste and that new staging work had come from it. Hopefully, we'd get even more business from the fair.

The third call I received wasn't as welcomed. Not the message anyway.

"Laura, this is Nita. Neil just called to say Monica has been formally charged with Damian Reynolds's murder."

I went through the rest of the day in a fog. If we hadn't arrived at Damian's house when we had, would Monica have gotten away from there? Would it be our testimony that convicted her of murder? The thought utterly depressed me. I was thankful I hadn't been alone in witnessing Monica standing over Damian's body with a knife. Given our history, my testimony on its own might have been suspicious.

Later, Aunt Kit and I had a light supper of chicken salad with fresh mixed greens. Neither of us had an appetite for a heavier meal. We left soon after eating for a meeting of the Mystery Lovers' Book Club being held at Marshall Library. If I hadn't already invited Aunt Kit to go along, I might have been tempted to stay home—clean the attic, upholster the living room sofa—anything as an excuse to skip it. I was that exhausted.

Since I didn't want to miss the talk my friend and former teacher, Sister Madeleine, was giving on clerical detectives in fiction, I decided to go. It had been Sister Madeleine who had nurtured my friendship with Nita, knowing my life at home was dreary and would be perked up by the loving and fun Romano family. She had also been the one who'd introduced me to mysteries, giving me my first Nancy Drew book. After that, she'd introduced me to books by Mary Stewart, Phyllis A. Whitney, and Helen McGuiness and then more recent ones by Elizabeth Peters and Sue Grafton. We'd bonded over our love of traditional mysteries. Since we were both natural-born problem solvers, trying to solve the puzzles presented in real life also appealed to us.

The parking lot at Marshall Library was nearly filled when we arrived. The book club drew a fair number of people in town to discuss a shared interest and enjoyment of traditional mysteries. A few fans of crime novels, police procedurals, and thrillers also attended. With the topic of clerical detectives in fiction, Sister Madeleine had been the natural choice to give the talk and lead the discussion afterward.

When we walked into the library, Aunt Kit wandered off to scan the bookshelves while I claimed two seats for us. I always felt that Aunt Kit enjoyed her visits to Louiston primarily because of the Marshall Library's wide selection of books. She frequently complained about her local library's small collection and the lack of a bookstore in her village.

When she joined me and plunked down a large stack of books on the table in front of us, my heart sank. She would have to stay for weeks to read all those.

Will Parker sat down near us, and I introduced him to Aunt Kit. He tipped the cowboy hat he was never without. "Howdy, ma'am."

When I discovered Will enjoyed reading mysteries, we had some good discussions about the authors we liked, and I invited him to the library's book club meetings. He had been attending the meetings ever since.

Aunt Kit looked up in surprise at Will's southwestern accent. "What brought you to this part of the country. I would imagine it is quite different from what you are used to."

"You can say that again. Everything is so green here. I settled here 'cause my daughter Claire thought I was getting too old to look after myself. A lot she knows. I think she wanted someone to help her with all those kids she has."

"Whose books do you enjoy, Will?" Aunt Kit asked.

"I'm partial to Tony Hillerman's books. They're set out West in an area I'm familiar with. Sure was sad to learn he'd died."

"But you should know that Hillerman's daughter Anne picked up the Leaphorn and Chee series," Aunt Kit said. That resulted in a discussion of the merits of that series.

While we waited for the meeting to begin, Will and Aunt Kit discovered they were also fans of conspiracy theory books. They quickly became fast book friends.

The meeting began, and after a few business affairs were discussed, the leader of our book group turned control of the meeting over to Sister Madeleine.

On her way to the lectern, Sister Madeleine paused next to my chair and whispered, "Stay after the discussion. I need to talk to you."

What could that be about?

Sister Madeleine gave an amusing and informative talk about

amateur clerical detectives, such as Father Brown, Sydney Brown from Grantchester, Brother Cadfael, Clare Fergusson, Rabbi Small, and others. I never realized there were so many clerical detectives. Sister Madeleine knew her subject and drew on her experience as a teacher to keep certain members of the group on the topic. One member kept trying to steer the discussion to which was better, the books or the TV series featuring the detectives discussed.

Sister Madeleine's presentation captured the groups' interest, and the discussion continued afterward even when members moved over to the refreshments table. It made me wonder why she hadn't tried her hand at writing detective fiction. Maybe she had. I'd have to ask her. She had so many varied interests it wouldn't surprise me.

I left Aunt Kit talking to Will Parker, discussing the latest conspiracy theories, both in fiction and real life, and went in search of Sister Madeleine. I found her sitting away from the other members at a table near the back of the room and took a seat across from her. The look on her face was quite solemn.

Uh, oh. I had a feeling this was going to involve something I wouldn't like and sure enough it did.

Like Nita, Sister Madeleine wasn't subtle and didn't mince words. "You know they've arrested Monica Heller for Damian Reynolds's murder? She didn't do it."

I was too stunned to talk. When I recovered from my surprise, I could barely get words out. "I'm one of four witnesses who found Monica standing over Damian's body with a knife in her hands. I hate to say this, Sister, but she looked pretty guilty."

"Did you see her stab him?"

"No." I squirmed in my seat, remembering the image.

"Then how do you know she did?"

I sighed. "There can be no other logical alternative. We caught her red-handed. *Literally*. As much as you would like to think she's innocent, how can we believe otherwise?"

"Because she told me she didn't kill him."

It took all I could do not to roll my eyes. When was I ever

going to be able to break myself of that bad habit? Sister Madeleine wanted to think the best of everyone, and it was obvious she didn't want to think Monica, one of her former students, could be capable of murder. Nita, Monica, and I had been in the first class Sister Madeleine taught as a young nun. She had a special fondness for us, and as she watched us grow, we became like the children she never had.

"When did she tell you she didn't kill him?" I asked.

"As soon as I heard she had been arrested, I went to see her at the jail. At first, they weren't going to let me in, but I convinced them I was her spiritual advisor, so they relented."

The thought of Monica having a spiritual advisor almost made me laugh. I knew Sister Madeleine had made that up, but it'd worked. It wasn't easy getting into the jail to visit a prisoner, as I'd discovered.

"Monica said she found Damian on the floor and instinctively pulled the knife out. I know what you saw sounds bad, but I believe her."

Sister Madeleine was a much better person than I was. Thinking of Monica being humbled in jail gave me a sliver of satisfaction—though not enough to want to see her convicted of murder.

"Sister, I think people would be willing to give Monica the benefit of the doubt if everyone at the Arts Center hadn't witnessed her argument with Damian and seen how angry she was. The fact that she drove to his house after he had taken her home points to her still being angry and wanting to continue the argument."

"Or perhaps to resolve it?"

"Okay, let's say she entered the house after someone else stabbed Damian. What happened to that person? Did he just walk away with no one catching sight of him? Did Monica see a car leaving? We didn't see anyone fleeing the scene of the crime."

"All I know is what Monica told me. I trust she wasn't lying to me."

"Accused killers lie all the time. Do you think they are going to confess as soon as they are arrested?" I braided my fingers and rested my chin on them.

"Regardless of whether you believe her guilty or innocent, Monica needs help—help you can give her. While she's in jail, her home decorating business is going to suffer. It doesn't take long for a small business to go under when the owner isn't there to run things. It's particularly bad for her because her senior assistant recently moved away. With your talent, you can help keep her business afloat until she's released.

With Monica no longer able to do staging in town, I didn't want to give the impression my business was benefitting from her imprisonment. Still how could I agree to help her?

"Sister, how can you expect me to help Monica? You know how I feel about her. She made my school days a misery. She never tired of taunting me about my second-hand clothing and anything else she could think about."

"I realize that, but that was a long time ago. You are both mature adults now."

"It isn't just that." I hated bringing this up because it embarrassed me that my husband had turned to other women. "I always suspected Monica had been involved with Derrick. The less I have to do with her, the better. His affairs with other women, especially Monica, ate at my heart." Just the thought of Monica and Derrick being together caused me to shudder. I had been making plans to leave him when he was killed in a car crash—with another woman.

I thought I was dealing better with my resentment, but now I realized I'd only buried it, and so shallowly that it erupted easily. "I can't help her."

"What you mean is you won't." Sister Madeleine eyed me critically.

It was mortifying having someone I was fond of witness my refusal to help someone. And all because of my unwillingness to forgive. But I couldn't. Why couldn't Sister Madeleine understand that?

"There's something else." I moved around in my chair, trying to get more comfortable. "Recently some strange things have been happening that have been affecting my business. Trucks we'd reserved getting canceled, bad reviews popping up online about my work, and lots of other little things that I'm starting to link together. When I heard that Monica was moving into the home staging business, I started to suspect she could be responsible for those things. I haven't told anyone else about my suspicions because I could be wrong. And I only mention it to you because I know you won't repeat what I'm telling you."

"Even if that were the case, and as you said, you only have suspicions, I'd hoped you'd have more compassion for Monica's plight now." Sister Madeleine drummed her fingers on the table, which I knew from old she meant, "Let's get on with things."

"There's something else you need to think about." Sister Madeleine gave me the stern look I remembered so well from school. "Whether you help Monica or not, your resentment toward her and your late husband is dragging you down and preventing you from moving forward."

Chapter 17

If a room lacks a focal point, add a console table and a piece of artwork or mirror above it.

Throughout the night, I found myself thinking about my conversation with Sister Madeleine. Her words had stung. Could she be right? My feelings about Monica had been with me for so long I couldn't remember a time when I hadn't felt that way about her. I might have eventually gotten over her school days' taunting if I hadn't later suspected her of being involved with Derrick.

And then there was my resentment toward Derrick. Does a wife ever get over being married to someone as unfaithful—or as selfish and controlling—as Derrick had been? Derrick, with his handsome looks and charming manner, had easily attracted women willing to become involved with a married man. Was Sister Madeleine right and my feelings about him were dragging me down? Could they also be feeding my aversion to handsome men?

Sister Madeleine's words filled my head. It was as though she had invaded my thoughts like the spirit of the dead soldier that invaded Inspector Ian Rutledge's mind in Charles Todd's series featuring the inspector.

It was with those thoughts in mind that I found myself that morning standing in front of the steps leading to the police station to see if I could get in to visit Monica. Sister Madeleine would never know how much my actions were costing me.

I squared my shoulders and started to climb the wide granite steps. When I reached the top step, I abruptly found myself falling toward the steps I'd just climbed. A set of arms caught me before I hit the granite, but not before we both lost our balance and ended up on the steps. Fortunately, my rescuer had twisted his body in the fall so that I landed on top of him. It took me a few seconds to catch my breath and wonder if I had broken something. It was only then that I looked up and realized that I was sitting in Detective Spangler's lap.

If I hadn't been so shaken, I would have sprung up and stomped away with as much hauteur as I could muster. As it was, I could only stare at him, his face just inches from mine.

"Ah, Ms. Bishop, could you move over a bit so I can get up?" A flash of pain crossed his face, and I wondered if he'd been injured in the fall.

Of all the people, in all the world, I had to end up on top of him. I rolled over onto my hands and knees and slowly pushed myself to my feet, accepting the hand he extended to help me.

"I'm sorry, Ms. Bishop. Are you okay?"

He was apologizing? I honestly couldn't say if I was okay or not. It would probably take a few minutes for me to recover from the shock of the tumble to know for sure. When I didn't respond, the detective opened the door to the station lobby and led me to a row of benches.

"I think I'm okay." I sat down as gently as I could. "What happened?"

"We collided. It was my fault. I came out a side door on the landing and dashed around the corner too quickly, apparently just as you reached there." He looked me over from head to toe as though to detect any injuries. "Are you okay?" he asked again.

"I think so. Just let me sit here for a few minutes." I wiped my hands together and then ran them down my skirt to brush any dust away. I did it more out of nervousness than because of any actual dust. Tomorrow I'd probably be covered in bruises.

"What brings you here today?" His dark eyes with those lovely thick lashes studied me with suspicion.

"I hoped to visit Monica Heller. Sister Madeleine asked me to see how she was doing and find out if she needed anything." I was stretching the truth a bit, but he didn't need to know the purpose of my visit.

"Ah, Sister Madeleine—the spiritual advisor."

So he had also been suspicious of the purpose of her visit.

"You know we only allow family members and legal representatives to visit at this point, and if the prisoner agrees." He peered at me intently, probably hoping I would hop up and walk away briskly to show that I changed my mind about seeing Monica. When I didn't, he got up from his seat. "Let me see what I can do."

I was relieved and hoped his guilty conscience about knocking me over was prompting him to help me. If it took a tumble to get in, I'd do it again.

A few minutes later, he returned. "Okay, I've cleared it, and she agrees to see you. If you are feeling okay, go through the doors over there. They'll sign you in and take you back to the visiting area."

He paused and turned back to me. "You aren't going to get involved with this investigation, are you?"

That wasn't my plan.

I gave him an underhanded wave to go away, hoping he would take the hint. As he walked away, I remembered my manners and called out to him. "Detective? Thank you for not knocking me all the way to the bottom of the steps."

He grinned at me and walked through the doorway, limping a bit.

Chapter 18

Certain paint colors can help promote wellness or a sense of well-being. A home stager can help you select those colors.

The visitors' area of the jail, covered in awful green paint, was as dismal as I remembered it. The painters hadn't done a very good job of it either. After I showed my driver's license and signed in, I sat where directed and waited for Monica to be seated on the other side of a glass partition.

After a few minutes, Monica sat down across from me, dressed in an orange uniform that only she could look good in. She didn't look any more excited to see me than I was to see her.

I decided to break the ice. "What made you agree to see me?" It still surprised me that she had agreed to my visit.

"Boredom." She looked nonchalant as though she hadn't anything pressing on her schedule for the day. "I'd been hoping to get away from work this summer, but this place isn't what I had in mind. Not exactly the lovely house on Nantucket I'd planned to rent."

"It could use your touch. Maybe you can give them a few tips while you're here."

Her expression showed me what she thought of my suggestion. "It probably makes you happy seeing me here like this."

"To be honest, a little."

At that, she smiled. "Well, at least you're honest. Did you come to gloat at my situation?"

"No. Not really." And I meant it. Although I did enjoy thinking of her sleeping on sheets that were far from the 600-thread count or silk sheets she was accustomed to sleeping on. "Quite frankly, I came because Sister Madeleine put a guilt trip on me to see you."

"Good old Sister Madeleine. She never gives up on her little chicks. I'm surprised she didn't give up on me years ago." Monica pushed a lock of hair behind her ear. Her less than perfectly coiffed strands were beginning to show darker roots and would soon be announcing to the world that her natural blond hair had darkened with age and needed a little help.

"No, she doesn't." Seeing her touch her hair had me reflexively running my fingers through my long straight hair with added highlights.

"You were always her favorite, you know," Monica said.

"Only because she felt sorry for me. That and because she thought I would be a perfect candidate for the convent."

"I guess you fooled her." Monica laughed and then became somber again. "Strange that I can still laugh. Coming in here, I didn't think I'd ever laugh again."

"Laughter's the best—"

"Medicine? Sometimes. But I don't think it's going to help heal what's wrong with me now."

"It can't hurt."

"So now that you're here, what do you hope to accomplish? Be able to tell everyone how awful I look?"

"Actually, I'm here more to satisfy Sister Madeleine than anything else. For some strange reason, she thinks I might be of help to you—to keep your business from going down the drain while you're here."

At that Monica laughed again. This time not cheerfully. "Right now, keeping my business going is the least of my worries."

Even given our history, I couldn't help but feel sorry for her. "Sister Madeleine believes you didn't kill Damian."

"And after finding me the way you did, you do."

"It looked pretty bad. How could we believe otherwise?"

"But I couldn't have."

"Why?"

Her expression softened. "Because I loved him."

I hadn't expected that. Monica had always been pretty selfish and cold-hearted, and it was rumored her ex-husband had gladly parted with a lot of money in a divorce settlement to be rid of her.

"Hard to believe, huh? But there was something special about Damian. He had a way of bringing out the best in me." She waved her hand in front of her face as though to dry the tears welling up in her eyes—something women did instinctively to keep their eye makeup from running. Although, this time, she had no makeup on to run. Even without it she was still beautiful. Some women have all the luck. Although right now, her stream of luck was drying up.

Either Monica was a very good actor, or she was telling the truth. It was hard to tell. In school, I'd heard her tell some pretty bold-faced lies with an absolutely straight face.

I studied her long and hard. From what I'd read, the truth comes out pretty fast, whereas lies usually take longer. The speaker takes extra time to formulate a lie and think about how they would remember it to retrieve it in the future. Monica was showing no hesitation. But then she'd had time to formulate her story.

"Okay, I know what I saw, but tell me what happened? We heard you and Damian arguing at the Arts Center. What were you arguing about?"

"Damian hired me to decorate the house he had bought. That's how we met. I was immediately attracted to him and was pleased he wanted to make his place comfortable and his own. That meant he planned to stay a while.

"It was exciting working with him. He has—had a terrific eye for color and design. We discovered we had a shared vision for his place, and the design soon became a collaborative effort. He gave me a deposit for the things I was ordering for the place." Her face flushed a bright red. "I got carried away and ordered a lot more than our contract covered. Foolish, I know, but what can I say. I started envisioning it as a place I might someday share with him. Then that night at the Arts Center, he said he'd changed his mind about redecorating the house so extensively. He wouldn't tell me why, only that I should cancel most of the things we had ordered."

"Did you feel he didn't like your designs?"

She looked at me as though I were crazy. Not *like* something she had designed?

"The design was as much a reflection of him as it was of me. He loved everything about it. That's why I couldn't understand his about-face. His canceling the project wasn't only about the loss of money I'd have to absorb. I felt he was rejecting me."

"So that's why you told him that you couldn't let him do that?" I recalled all too vividly her words from that night.

"Yes. I couldn't understand his motives, and he wouldn't explain. After he dropped me at home, I got even more upset—not angry but hurt—and decided to drive to his place to see if I could get him to explain. I needed to know, even if it meant he'd tell me that he had tired of me and wanted to sever our relationship, both professionally and personally. I couldn't accept not knowing why."

"When you arrived, did you see another car or anyone walking nearby?"

She shook her head and then paused. "As I neared his driveway, I saw the rear car lights of a car passing in front of his place. It could have just come down the road, or it could have pulled out of his driveway and turned right onto the road. It was only later that I thought about it."

"What happened when you got there?" I knew what happened, but I needed to hear it again to see if the story differed in any way from what I heard her tell Detective Spangler at the scene. I was learning from Detective Spangler's interviewing techniques.

"It's as I said the other night. The house was dark except for light coming from a side window, which was the kitchen. The front door was ajar. I pushed it open a little more and called his name. When he didn't respond, I pushed it open and went in, thinking he might have been in the bathroom or somewhere he couldn't hear me."

She swallowed several times as though to compose herself. I wondered whether she would be able to continue.

"That's when I saw him on the floor, only a few feet from the door." She stopped and closed her eyes for several seconds. "When I saw the knife, all I could think was to get it out of him. I pulled at it with one hand and then realized that it would take two hands to remove it. Once I got it out, I stood up to phone for help. That's when Nita came in. The rest you know."

I recalled Josh's story about Damian taking some of his own artwork and pieces done by others from his collection for him to sell. If I told her about it, would it make matters better or worse for her? "Do you think Damian could have had financial problems?"

She looked puzzled. "I don't know. Why do you ask?"

"I saw Josh Sheridan recently. He said Damian came into Antiques and Other Things and asked him to sell several pieces of art for him. Josh was surprised and advised him to contact one of the auction houses since they could get far more for the pieces than he could. When Damian declined, Josh wondered if he could be having financial difficulties and didn't want word getting out that he was selling some of his collection."

"Do you think that's why he refused to explain his reasons for canceling the project?" She sounded hopeful and tears began to flow this time. "He wasn't rejecting me?"

We didn't say anything while she wiped her eyes with her sleeve and collected herself.

Good time to change the subject. "Sister Madeleine is concerned about your business while you are here."

Monica closed her eyes, put her head back, and stared at the ceiling. "Things are in such a mess. I became so focused on my work for Damian and began letting things slip. On top of being accused of murder, I have to worry about my business falling apart. Even if by some miracle I'm let out of here, I'll have that to face."

"If I recall, you have a talented staff." I decided not to mention what I'd learned about her doing some home staging in addition to her design work nor my suspicions that she was undermining my business.

"That's the problem. I don't. My most experienced assistant left last month to take a job in Pittsburgh. I take her in and give her the wisdom of my experience, and she up and leaves me." *That didn't surprise me.*

"My other assistant doesn't have the experience to meet our commitments. If I can't get out of here, my business will be ruined."

Monica's business falling apart was the least of her worries.

Chapter 19

Forty percent of paint purchased ends up being the wrong color.
Consulting a home stager about paint color can prevent costly
mistakes.

It wasn't long before Officer Nguyen came and told us that visiting time was almost over. Monica quickly gave me the name of her young assistant and an idea of some of the things I could do to help complete some of her decorating projects. The people she had already contracted with might be inclined to allow her assistant to complete the work, primarily because they had money invested in it, but Monica's business wouldn't be attracting new work while she was in jail.

Again I couldn't believe I was going to help Monica. And I wouldn't have if it hadn't been for Sister Madeleine. I owed her big time for all the things she had done for me throughout my life. Hopefully, working to help Monica would help show her my appreciation.

After leaving the jail, I drove directly to Monica's design studio, Designs by Monica. It was housed in a small, standalone building of white stained cedar with electric blue shutters at each window. Window boxes filled with a profusion of red and white flowers of different varieties added a nice touch, but the flowers were beginning to droop from lack of water and attention.

When I pushed open the door, a bell tinkled, announcing my arrival. A young woman, who looked about seventeen but was probably slightly older, glanced up with an alarmed expression on her face. Was she afraid I was a customer coming in to ask why my project wasn't getting completed? Or worse, was I there to cancel a project?

I decided to put her at ease and let her know that I wasn't there for either reason. "Hi, are you Kimberly Shepherd?" She looked at me with startling blue eyes that looked like they owed their color more to tinted contacts than Mother Nature.

"Yes?" Her response was more question than answer.

"I'm Laura Bishop." I felt sorry for the young woman. Her employer had been arrested, and now she was expected to assume responsibility for a business she didn't have the experience to manage. "You can relax. I'm here to help."

The look of relief on her face was almost comical. I explained that I'd visited Monica and she had given me an idea of some of the most pressing issues they faced. "Why don't you tell me what you are dealing with at the moment and we'll see how I can help?" And she did. An hour later, we had worked out a list of things that were the most pressing and divided up tasks I could handle and those things she would work on. I didn't know how I was going to manage all this with my own work schedule, but I would make it work. At least I hoped I could.

"Oh, and we have a couple of proposed home staging projects we're waiting to hear back about," Kimberly added. "We were busy with our current projects, but since new work coming in had been slow, Monica thought we could line up some home staging to fill in the gaps."

Slow? So that's why Monica had decided to go into home staging. I shook my head and decided to address my suspicions about Monica sabotaging my business with her someday—if she didn't go to prison for life.

One of the most pressing projects was helping Theresa Green, a local homeowner, set up a short-term rental in an area over her garage. Her place was near Fischer College and she planned to rent it to parents of students visiting the college. Theresa had already taken reservations for the place because Monica had assured her it would be done in time. Fortunately, the remodeling work had been completed, so I could take on the finishing details.

"Thank you, Ms. Bishop. I didn't know what I was going to do." Kimberly was sweet, and I was pleased that I could waylay some of her concerns—even if I was the one now feeling overwhelmed. If it would help put my past with Monica behind me, it would be worth it.

Thinking of the past made me wonder about the two recent deaths. If, and it was a big if, Monica was telling the truth and she hadn't stabbed Damian, what could have been in Ian Becker's and Damian Reynolds's pasts that could have contributed to their deaths? Ian hadn't lived in Louiston for about twenty years, and Damian was a relative newcomer to town. Was there any connection between the two deaths other than coincidence? Perhaps the only answer was they'd come into contact with a deranged killer.

I realized that Kimberly was speaking and shook myself back to the present. "Sorry, my mind wandered. Did you ever meet Damian Reynolds?"

"Yes, a couple of times, when I went with Monica to take fabric samples to his house and to take measurements. He was such a nice man." She frowned. "I couldn't say the same thing about his agent, Garrett Fletcher." She grimaced. "Sorry, I shouldn't have said that."

"That's all right. You didn't care for the man?"

"He wasn't nice at all. In fact, he was rude to us, especially to Monica. She later explained that he was very controlling of Damian and didn't like how close he and Monica were becoming. She suspected Mr. Fletcher felt she had too much influence on Damian."

If Monica hadn't killed Damian, then who else around him could have? The only way to find out would be to discover who had been in Damian's life since he came to Louiston.

Where had that thought come from? I couldn't resist a puzzle or mystery, but this was one I needed to stay out of. Or could it be that I was being sucked into this mystery to please Sister Madeleine, who believed Monica?

Kimberly called Theresa Green to set up a time for me to take the items Monica had ordered for the project and start the work.

I would start with the apartment. But first I watered the flowers in the window box.

Chapter 20

To attract buyers, paint with colors that work with cabinets,
flooring, and carpets.

With just enough time before my appointment to have lunch, I called Nita to invite her to join me at Vocaro's.

"We're going to do what?" Nita was incredulous when I told her about my appointment that afternoon with one of Monica's clients. "But Monica is your least favorite person in the whole world. Why would you do that, especially when she is going to prison and her business will be closed anyway?"

I explained to her about my conversation with Sister Madeleine—how she wanted me to help save Monica's business. "And it's not what *we* are going to do, it's what *I'm* going to do. I didn't commit you to this."

"Of course I'm going to help. Monica was my classmate as well. Besides, I could use all the brownie points I can get with Sister Madeleine. If it wasn't for her, Guido and I wouldn't be married."

"What?" First time I'd heard that.

"Never mind. I'll explain someday—maybe."

I was beginning to believe Sister Madeleine had her finger in every pie in town.

When they called the number for our lunch order, I went to the counter to pick it up while Nita read our horoscopes in a newspaper someone had left nearby.

I placed our lunch on the table and sat down. I was hungrier than I realized and took a generous bite of the spinach quiche I'd ordered. "What did our horoscopes predict for today? Anything interesting?"

"Mine wasn't worth getting out of bed for. But yours was interesting. It said Capricorns should beware of people from their past adding to their already heavy burdens."

I tossed a stack of paper napkins at her. "You made that up."

Nita caught the napkins and laughed. "Would I misrepresent what the stars are predicting? Seriously, with all you have on you, you can only do so much to help Monica's business."

"Tell Sister Madeleine that."

We ate quickly so I could get to my appointment on time. "When we helped your niece the other night, she said she had provided admin support to Damian at the college. Do you think she could give us any more information about him?

"We could ask her. What do you want to know?" She took a sip from her coffee and then coughed, probably realizing where this was leading. "*Laura!* You aren't buying Monica's story that someone else stabbed Damian, are you? And please tell me you aren't getting involved in trying to find out who did."

"Frankly, I don't know what to believe. Sister Madeleine is convinced Monica is telling the truth. It's driving me crazy wondering who else would have wanted Damian dead."

Nita shook her head several times. "You are such a sucker for helping the downtrodden."

"You should have seen Monica in that visiting room. All I could think about was what it had been like for Tyrone when he had been accused of a crime and put in jail."

"If you get involved in this case, you wouldn't be doing it because you want to, but because Sister Madeleine believes Monica and not four eyewitnesses—you being one of them."

"I know, but as she pointed out, none of us actually saw Monica stab Damian. If we had, that would be a different story. Not that I believe it, but what if Monica is telling the truth? I'm just trying to puzzle it out."

"Just be careful. Everyone has secrets they don't want revealed, whether they are connected to Damian's death or not."

Chapter 21

To make a small bathroom look larger, go for white tile, cabinets, flooring, and walls.

The Green home was just a few blocks from the college campus and would be a convenient place for parents to stay when visiting the college. The small apartment over the garage was going to be a gold mine for the owners.

I rang the bell, and a petite woman with silvery blond hair opened the door.

"Hi, I'm Laura—

Before I could get my introduction completed, she flung her arms around me. "Laura, I can't tell you how relieved I am to see you."

Well, at least my fears of having to deal with a disgruntled client whose project had been delayed were for nothing.

Theresa stepped back and ushered Nita and me into her house. "Sorry. I shouldn't have done that, but I was so worried this project wasn't going to be completed in time, and I already have the space booked. If I had to cancel, the parents would be really unhappy because all of the local hotels are filled for those dates."

"I understand. I'm sorry you've been worried, but Nita and I are here to complete the work." I introduced Nita, who braced herself for a possible hug.

Theresa walked us out to the garage, which had an outside staircase leading to the apartment above. The area around the entrance was beautifully landscaped and would provide a shaded glen with seating for guests to relax.

"It has a keyless entry, so we don't have to worry about lost keys or keycards," Theresa explained. She gave us the entry code so we could go in and out without a problem. "And we can change it anytime we want to."

After giving us a tour of the surprisingly spacious area, she said she would leave us to our work. I was pleased to see the furniture that Monica had ordered arrived okay and had been put in place. That would help speed things up. Everything she had selected was super durable, including tabletops that wouldn't mark if someone placed a cup or glass on them without a coaster.

I pulled out the folder Kimberly had given me that contained the design drawings and a list of the items we would place inside. Monica had keyed the décor to the historic community around the college. Nita took some before photos. Later she'd take some after shots so I could show Monica. She probably wouldn't be totally satisfied with the job we did, but in her position, she shouldn't complain. And if she went to prison, she couldn't inspect our work.

Once rented, the place would need to be turned over quickly for each new guest, and Monica had designed everything for easy cleaning. The hardwood floors would be easier to maintain than carpeting, and the rugs were all machine washable.

After we carried in everything from my car, including our tool bag, we set to work. Among the equipment we always carried to a home staging was a three-step ladder, which we set up to hang the curtain rods and room-darkening draperies. I noticed the Roman-style shades didn't have pull cords, which could easily become entangled or break. Smart move because over time and with frequent use, they could be broken. They also could present a danger if any guests had young children with them. We hung the draperies and then used a steamer to remove any folds or wrinkles in the fabric.

"I'll give Monica credit. She put a lot of thought into everything," Nita observed. "She even included a laptop workspace and lots of open shelving instead of drawers. That way people won't leave things behind like they do when they put things in drawers."

Monica had provided multiple sets of white linens, which would give the place a spa feeling. Everything was of excellent quality since it would be changed frequently and needed to be durable. She had even included two white bathrobes to give a sense of luxury.

The mention of Monica brought to mind the image of her sitting in that dismal jail. Would she ever be in a comfortable place again with touches of luxury? My momentary satisfaction of seeing her in prison had disappeared to be replaced by feelings of pity. Her situation looked pretty hopeless. I didn't want that to happen to anyone, even my worst enemy.

Nita and I made the bed. Monica had avoided using a cloth headboard to prevent it from getting dirty. The sixty-inch wooden headboard provided a nice focal point for the room.

We positioned two luggage racks in convenient spots, set up a coffee station in a space that had been designed for that purpose, and completed all the other tasks on our list.

Several hours later, Nita plopped down on a two-seater sofa that held a foldout bed. "I'm exhausted. But I must say, the place looks splendid."

I sat down next to her and pulled out the checklist. "Do you think we've forgotten anything?"

"If something is missing, I'm sure the guests will let Theresa know."

As a final act, I spritzed lavender air freshener and then went to get Theresa for her inspection. The place was fabulous as a high-end, short-time rental.

Theresa was suitably impressed and joyfully went around the space inspecting everything. "Oh, it's everything and more than Monica promised. Thank you so much. I know people are going to enjoy staying here."

"It was Monica's design and work. We just executed it." It took us well into the evening, but I was happy the work was completed and we wouldn't have to return tomorrow to finish.

"Speaking of Monica, that was such a shame about her and Damian Reynolds," Theresa said. "Just when we thought he was gaining some happiness in his life after the tragedy in his family."

Nita and I looked at each other. *Tragedy?* "We hadn't heard about that," Nita said. "What happened?" Thank goodness for Nita's willingness to ask pointed questions.

"Oh, dear. Sorry. I shouldn't have said anything. My husband is on the board at the college and was involved in hiring him. Forget I said anything."

I knew Nita would have liked to prod her for more information, but I didn't think we'd get anything further from her, especially since it was obvious she thought she had been indiscreet saying what she had. We'd have to find another source of information.

After we got back into my car, I pulled out my smartphone and did a search on Google for Damian Reynolds. "Nita, you need to see this."

Chapter 22

Studies by real estate organizations show that staged homes sell eighty-eight times faster and for twenty percent more than homes that aren't staged.

Google provided hundreds of links to articles about Damian, reviews of his work, awards he'd received, and lists of dealers selling his paintings and prints. It was a link to a West Coast newspaper article, dated over three years ago, that caught my eye: "Artist's Daughter Lost in Boating Accident."

"That's so sad," Nita said. "Now I know what Theresa meant when she said Damian was finally finding some happiness. How do you recover from something like that?"

We went on to read about Damian and his wife, Helen, being in seclusion at their Carmel estate.

Nita handed my phone back to me. "*He was married?* Poor Monica. Could that be why Damian was trying to sever relations with her? Do you think she knew he was married?"

It was on the tip of my tongue to say that she hadn't had any compunction about getting involved with my late husband, but I thought better of it. Especially since all I had were suspicions.

"For a start, we only know that he wanted to cancel orders related to the redecorating, and that could have been because of financial reasons. We don't know if he wanted to sever his relationship with Monica. Let's not jump to conclusions. How about tomorrow we go see your niece and find out what more she knows about him?"

In the morning, Nita called Jaime and asked if it would be convenient for us to stop by to see her. When we arrived, we found a Hamilton Real Estate vehicle parked out front. The front door of the house flew open as soon as we rang the bell, and Jaime greeted us.

"We have a contract on the house!" The excitement of it almost had her jumping up and down. "Isn't that great? I'm so relieved."

"When did that happen?" Nita and I stepped inside to find Doug Hamilton sitting at the dining room table with a laptop and papers spread out in front of him.

"Doug just brought the offer he received, and we're going over it."

"Hey, ladies." Doug looked up and waved. "Jaime was a bit nervous about selling the house in time, but once I saw the job you did staging it, I wasn't so worried. The place virtually sold itself."

Doug had been involved with the sale of the Denton mansion Tyrone and I had staged in the spring, and he'd helped get the place sold in record time. He was a very pleasant guy, and for a while, I thought there might be something brewing between him and Monica, but that hadn't been the case. Looking back made me wonder if I'd shown more interest, whether Doug and I might have become more than just friends. Maybe, maybe not. It was just as well since I wasn't sure I was ready for a relationship with anyone.

"I can't thank you both enough for all you did staging the house," Jaime added. "Without your help, I'm sure we couldn't have sold it so quickly. Then we would have lost the place we really wanted."

"Is your husband pleased with the offer?" I asked.

"I just spoke to Frankie on the phone, and he thinks it's a good offer. It looks like we're ready to move forward."

Doug motioned Jaime over. "I need to get a signature in a few places and let the buyer's agent know you've accepted their offer. Then you'll be another step closer to moving into your new home." Doug handed a pen to Jaime and turned back to the paperwork. Nita and I went out onto the patio to get out of their way.

A short while later, they joined us outside. Jaime was grinning from ear to ear, and Doug looked relieved. He might have been more concerned about the house selling quickly than he'd let on.

Doug gave us a smart salute, a holdover from his Navy days. "I'll say goodbye since I need to get these documents processed. You ladies take care."

Jaime sank into a deck chair. She looked spent from all the excitement. "I'm so relieved that's over. The couple who wants our place loved it as soon as they walked in the door."

"First impressions are important." I looked through the French doors into the main floor, pleased at how good the changes we made had turned out. No clutter, simple accessories, and a few modern touches really helped to update the place. "It helped that you were willing to make changes that would appeal to others, which is hard to do to your own home."

"I have to admit it was hard," Jaime said. "Especially since this was our first home and we were emotionally attached to it."

I thought of my home and the changes I made to it after my mother died. "Some homeowners aren't willing to change things. They love their pink ruffled curtains, flowered wallpaper, and knickknacks. Buyers can't always see beyond those things."

Nita accepted the iced tea Jaime handed her. "Well now that you've gotten your home-sale challenges taken care of, let's talk about Damian Reynolds."

"What about Damian?" Jaime looked puzzled. "Has this to do with Monica being charged with his murder? That was so surprising considering how crazy she seemed to be about him."

"We read an article online about his daughter being lost in a boating accident. Did you hear anything about that at the college?" I knew there had to have been gossip when a famous artist decided to work at a small college in Pennsylvania.

"That was sad. From what I heard, Damian and his daughter went out on their sailboat and got caught in a squall. The conditions became extremely rough, and she was lost overboard before they could get back to shore. Apparently, he was so affected by it he completely stopped painting."

"Which could account for him teaching art instead of doing it," I said. It probably wasn't unusual following something traumatic for a person to become so blocked they couldn't paint, write, or whatever.

"Yes, especially since his daughter had been a talented artist as well," Jaime added.

"What happened to his wife?" Nita asked.

"From what I heard, she blamed him for the accident since she'd asked them not to go out that day. She couldn't get over it and filed for divorce about a year later."

"So he wasn't still married when he met Monica." For some reason, I was relieved to hear that. We probably would have discovered this if we had done a more thorough Google search.

"No. But I understand she's coming here soon for a memorial service for Damian and bringing their younger daughter. She doesn't live too far from Louiston."

"Why is the service being held here in Louiston?"

"He's being buried here. Apparently, his grandparents came from Louiston, and there's a large Reynolds family plot at Good Shepherd Cemetery. That's why he came to Fischer College. Some family roots here. And Louiston isn't far from where his ex-wife and daughter moved. She came from Pennsylvania too. That way he got to see his daughter from time to time."

Later that evening, I curled up on the sofa with Inky and pulled out my laptop. A search on Google Maps enabled me to pinpoint the town Helen Reynolds and her daughter lived—about a ninety-minute drive from Louiston. Close enough to easily make the drive to Damian's house and back again without being missed for long.

Could she have still been harboring enough resentment toward Damian about their daughter's death to want him dead?

Chapter 23

Add finishing touches like fresh flowers in vases, a bowl of fresh fruit on the kitchen countertop, and plush towels in powder rooms and bathrooms.

With a few hours in between work projects, I'd made arrangements to take Aunt Kit to the Orangery for afternoon tea. With so much of my attention being focused on my staging business and on helping Monica, I felt I'd been neglecting her. I hoped to make it up by taking her to her favorite teashop, a place she enjoyed when visiting Louiston. It was one of my favorite places as well.

The Orangery provided the perfect setting for a cozy get together, so it would be a treat for both of us. Its gentle atmosphere of a traditional English teashop, the soothing tea they served, and the delicious delicacies they were known for did a lot to calm me when I needed a break.

Nita, who was going along, thought it would be a nice gesture to invite Anne Williamson to join us so she could show her appreciation for all Anne had done for the arts festival. Nita also thought Aunt Kit would enjoy having Anne along since the older women had bonded somewhat over their love of art.

Nita and I picked up Aunt Kit at the house. Anne Williamson planned to meet us there.

The woman who met us at the door, dressed in a severe black

gabardine dress with a broach at her neck, looked as though she had stepped off the set of *Downton Abbey*. She had such poise and an assured demeanor she could have been the housekeeper or the lady of the manor. When I told her I had called about a reservation and would be joining someone who might already be there, she escorted us to a cozy nook. A round table was beautifully set with a thick white covering, cloth napkins, and an arrangement of pink tea roses. Delicate cups and saucers covered in floral patterns completed each place setting.

Anne was already seated, and after we got settled and exchanged greetings, she clapped her hands to get our attention. "I have some wonderful news."

Three sets of eyes peered at her intently.

"Nita, your photos from the show sold." Anne's broad smile showed how pleased she was to deliver the news.

Nita's squeal of surprise and delight could be heard throughout the teashop and several heads turned our way. "Oh my gosh. When?"

"I received a call this morning. The photos have to remain up until the end of the show, but after that, they will go home with the new owner. Once the show comes down, I'll process the sale and send you the payment." Anne looked just as thrilled as Nita.

"I can't wait to tell Guido somebody liked my photos enough to pay money for them. That *is* wonderful news, Anne. Thank you."

After the waitress took our orders and then brought us the English breakfast tea we all had agreed on, the conversation quickly turned to the murders that had occurred in Louiston.

"With all that's been happening here, I worry about Laura and Nita." Aunt Kit helped herself to little diamond-shaped sandwiches from a three-tiered tray the waitress placed in the center of the table. "Such a shame about that poor young man who came here from New Zealand to take care of his aunt's estate."

Nita studied the selection of sandwiches. "The police found his cell phone. According to his phone records, he'd made calls to Warren Hendricks, his aunt's attorney, an old girlfriend, and

Anne." She gulped realizing what she had said and probably shouldn't have.

Anne accepted the plate Nita passed to her. "Don't worry, dear, I know about it. A lovely detective questioned me about the call. He asked me how I knew Ian Becker and what had been the purpose of the telephone call."

Detective Spangler, a lovely detective? He was attractive in a rugged sort of way with his dark, thick eyelashes, piercing blue eyes, and dark hair graying slightly at the temples. With the antagonism we seemed to feel toward each other, I don't think I could ever think of him as being a lovely detective. If when using the word "lovely," she meant kind, I couldn't buy that either. Well, maybe somewhat.

Anne paused, and I began to wonder whether she was going to share the reason for the call. After she took another bite of scone and sipped some tea, she began again.

"I explained to Detective Spangler that Ian called to ask me if he could see me while he was in town. We had a lovely chat, and he told me his aunt had written his family over the years and they told him about our friendship. He said he wanted to meet me and express his appreciation for the assistance I'd given her. I hadn't done much, but I told him I would be delighted to meet him. He sounded like such a nice young man."

"Did he visit you?" Nita asked.

"No. Sadly he didn't come before..." She shook her head as though searching for the words.

Nita and I could easily have filled in the blanks, but we didn't say anything. We all understood what she'd left unsaid.

"I was touched to learn Doris thought enough of our friendship to write to her family about me. She was such a kind woman." Anne's doleful look showed how much she missed her friend.

Nita refilled our cups with tea from the teapot and then placed it on the table. "How long had you and Doris been friends?"

"About ten years. I met her when I first moved to Louiston and joined the arts group. When she began having a difficult time getting around and stopped attending our meetings, I started visiting her to help keep her connected to the group."

"That was good of you," Aunt Kit said. "So often older members of a group simply fade away." I wondered whether she was thinking about her own experience. I needed to maintain better contact with her, perhaps influence her to move back to Louiston so I could keep an eye on her.

Anne took another sandwich from the tray. "Doris had been a supportive member of the group for many years, but from what I understand, she never participated in group painting sessions or displayed her work at shows. The poor dear was self-conscious about her artwork, which she viewed as amateurish. But she so enjoyed painting."

"Did you ever see her work?" Aunt Kit asked.

"A few pieces she had hanging in her home." Anne looked at her empty teacup and reached for the teapot.

"And," Nita prompted, "was it amateurish?"

"Let's just say, it was a little simplistic."

We didn't pursue the subject anymore, feeling that we had put Anne in an awkward position commenting about her friend's artwork.

Aunt Kit studied the selection of fruit tarts and took one topped with kiwifruit and blueberries. "What I can't get over is Damian Reynolds being stabbed by his girlfriend. Such a loss for the art world. I have one of his prints hanging on my living room wall."

I hadn't realized Aunt Kit was a fan of modern art, but there were so many things I didn't know about her. I needed to rectify that.

Aunt Kit was on a roll. "Even worse, Nita and Laura walked in and found his girlfriend standing over him—with the knife she used to kill him. And she had been a school friend of theirs."

"That must have been just awful, you poor dears." Anne Williamson said. She and Aunt Kit seemed to be relishing the details.

So much for going to a place that was supposed to be calming. A lot depended on whom you were with and what you were discussing. Aunt Kit and her grim outlook on everything would need far more than a teashop to mellow out. Time to change the subject.

"Nita, why don't you show Aunt Kit and Anne the photos of the short-term rental we completed? It turned out to be a fabulous place." Fortunately, Nita took the hint and started telling them about the apartment and showing them the photos she took.

While she talked, I couldn't help but think of what we'd learned about Damian and the Reynolds family. And then there was his relationship with his agent. What was the full story behind that? Jaime hadn't liked him, and Ron Zigler from the B&B had overheard Damian and his agent having a heated argument while they stayed there. That might be worth looking into further.

Chapter 24

*To prepare a house for sale, clean from the baseboards to the
ceilings and everything in between.*

The next morning, Tyrone and I'd arranged to visit Ron and Geoff
at the B&B on our way to check out the area Josh said might work
as a storage space for our inventory.

"How are you going to feel if you see Ron and Geoff made
changes to the work you did on the house?" Tyrone asked.

I'd been pleased with the way the house had turned out after
we'd staged it. For that project, we'd had virtually free rein to do
whatever the house needed, and it'd needed a lot done to it. Nita's
talented brothers had done repairs and painted the house to make
it attractive to potential buyers. It was our first project, and after it
was completed, we had such pride of workmanship it had been
hard leaving it for someone else to enjoy.

I shrugged. "It's only natural they'll want to put their own
touches on the place. If they made changes and you don't like them,
say nothing."

Tyrone had done preliminary work on the house and had only
seen photos of the completed rooms, so this visit would allow him
to see the completed work. I hoped Geoff and Ron hadn't changed
everything so much that it no longer had our stamp on it.

Tyrone made a locking key gesture near his mouth. I hoped

he'd be able to keep his comments locked up.

We turned onto the entrance of the long drive that led to the B&B. A wooden sign with blue and gold letters identified the Mansion House Bed and Breakfast. The new name paid homage to the house, but I would always think of it as the Denton house.

The large three-storied house of limestone had been built before the Civil War and belonged to the Denton family for generations—until Skip Denton sold it following the tragic death of his ex-wife. It had been a challenge turning the dismal place into an inviting dwelling, but the result had prompted Ron and Geoff to buy the place, with all its contents. Their plan to turn it into a bed and breakfast was the perfect use for the massive structure.

Driving up the long approach to the house, I looked over to where a workman was mowing the grass and was pleased to see Ron and Geoff had kept on Carlos to maintain the lawns and gardens. As we drove by, he looked up from his mowing and waved to us.

We parked in the back near the garage that had once stabled horses and carriages. Earlier Ron had mentioned their dream of turning the structure into additional guest quarters. With the college nearby, they wouldn't have difficulty filling it with guests. I thought of the work we'd done completing Monica's over-the-garage apartment for the Greens. My imagination went into overdrive, and I envisioned us working with Nita's construction family on the project.

When we rounded the corner to the front of the house we found Detective Spangler descending the steps from the large porch fronting the house. He looked as surprised to see us as we were to see him.

"Hello, Ms. Bishop. What brings you here?" His clothing fit him perfectly, and his muscular body showed that he worked out.

"We're here for a tour of the B&B Ron and Geoff promised us. They're going to show us the changes they made." They hadn't promised us a tour, but I was sure they would gladly do so if we asked them.

"What brings you here, Detective?" *Tit for tat.*

"Police business." He tossed his keys in the air, catching them and then tossing them again. He had an annoying habit of fiddling with things, but usually when he was interrogating people—slapping a letter opener into his palm, squeezing a rubber ball, tapping his pen on his notebook, and now tossing his keys. I didn't know whether he was just antsy or he did those things to distract or annoy people.

He nodded at Tyrone and got into his car without saying anything more and drove away.

"From the looks of it, you and the detective seem to have a bit of history." Geoff shook hands with Tyrone in greeting. "Did he break up with you in high school and you're still angry about it?"

That made me laugh. "Not hardly. We had some dealings during Victoria Denton's murder investigation, and we got off on the wrong foot." I needed to be more mature and get over it, and I was getting there—just not very fast.

Tyrone had more reason to be resentful and was dealing with it better than I was since Detective Spangler had arrested him for Victoria Denton's murder. But Tyrone was a much better person than I was.

I climbed the stairs to the porch, noticing that Geoff and Ron had added more rocking chairs, which was a good idea. The position of the porch would give guests fabulous views of the Allegheny Mountains.

Police business. "Are you having problems out here?"

Geoff shook his head. "No, not at all. Besides we have Will Parker keeping an eye on things. Detective Spangler was looking for more information about Ian Becker. Anything we could add about his stay here."

"Were you able to tell him anything?" Tyrone asked.

"Not anything more than we told you before." Geoff grimaced. "That's two of our former guests dead in a week. Rather frightening. We're just relieved that neither death happened here."

I had come to ask them questions about Damian Reynolds and

his stay there. They were going to be inundated with questions about their guests.

"Welcome. Come on inside." Geoff opened the heavy oak door leading into the foyer. "We only have a couple of guests at the moment, but they've gone out to see some of the sights."

We followed him into the massive foyer. A tall hunt table held a guest book and brochures for some of the local sights. The place brought back so many memories of our first visit to the house and everything that had transpired there afterward.

Geoff led us into the living room. "Please have a seat. Ron is in the kitchen cleaning up after breakfast and will join us shortly. He does all the cooking while I take care of bedrooms and baths. He's got the better part of the deal. Since I'm not much of a cook, it's better for the guests that I stick with bathrooms."

"It all depends on how good Ron would be doing bathrooms." I wrinkled my nose. The thought of cleaning several bathrooms a day was more than I wanted to think about.

The living room looked inviting, and after the week I'd experienced, I gratefully sank into a comfortable leather chair, yearning to put my feet up on an ottoman. It was the perfect place to relax. Tyrone sat on a long leather sofa. Seeing the expression on his face and his raised eyebrows, I turned and looked at the direction of his gaze. Sitting on the mantel was a ceramic statue of a pink flamingo, probably something brought back from a trip to Florida. I stifled my urge to laugh, especially given Tyrone's look of horror. It was so out of character with the style of the house. But everyone was entitled to a bit of whimsy.

"Can I get you some coffee?" Geoff asked. He was the perfect host for a B&B.

"Thanks, but we just had some at Vocaro's before we came."

Ron came into the living room, drying his hands on a chef's apron, and greeted us. "Another breakfast finished—hundreds more to go."

I wondered what the breakfast they offered their guests was like. B&Bs could prosper or fail based on the quality of the breakfasts they offered.

"Ron does a bang-up job with breakfast," Geoff said. "You'll have to come up one day and join us. He is always experimenting with new recipes and could use some feedback."

"We'd love that. Can I bring Nita? She knows her pastries and could give you an expert's opinion." Nita would die if she knew I got to have breakfast at the B&B without her.

"Absolutely." Ron waved his arm, gesturing to the room. "How do you like what we've done so far?"

"We haven't seen much yet, but I love the leather club chairs that you've added here."

"Thanks. We got them from Josh. He's going to find us some more. We wanted ones that were a little more broken in than new ones. They're more comfortable and look like they've been here for a while." Ron stood next to the cavernous marble fireplace, the pink flamingo over his shoulder. Tyrone and I grinned at each other.

"Thanks, Laura, for recommending Josh," Geoff added. "He's been great."

I was pleased they liked Josh's warehouses of unusual things but felt the more they visited it, the less the B&B would look as we left it. I needed to learn to separate myself emotionally from the houses we worked on.

"Since Tyrone didn't get to see the final work on the house, we'd love to have a tour if you have time. But first I'd like to ask you a few questions."

"I'd be delighted to give you a tour and answer your questions. What do you want to know—what we changed when we moved in?" The twinkle in Geoff's eye sent a clear message that they had changed things, which could only be expected.

"You've already gotten some questions about your former guests from Detective Spangler. I hope you won't mind a few more. When I spoke to you before, you mentioned that when Damian Reynolds stayed here there was a bit of drama—that he and his agent argued. Can you tell us any more about that?"

Ron and Geoff glanced at each other and shrugged.

Geoff spoke first. "It's been a while. You have to remember, the walls in this place are pretty thick. We could hear raised voices, but not necessarily what they were saying."

"Whatever they argued about," Ron added, "it caused the agent, can't remember his name at the moment, to check out the next morning. He had been scheduled to stay for another night. Geoff, why don't you take them on the tour, and I'll check our records for the agent's name."

Geoff led the way toward the dining room and kitchen. "Eventually we hope to finish the basement. I'd like to add a bar and billiards room, along with a wine cellar. Ron wants a sauna and workout room. I don't know what we'll end up with."

The basement held bad memories for me since that was where I had discovered Victoria Denton's body. They could board up the basement and forget it was there for all I cared. But seeing it turned into useable space made sense.

After seeing the dining room and kitchen, Geoff escorted us up the grand staircase to the guest rooms upstairs and showed us the rooms that weren't occupied. They had added some welcoming touches to each room. "We added more books to the library, and guests are welcome to select a book and relax in there."

When we returned to the ground floor, Ron was waiting for us and handed me a slip of paper with the agent's name printed on it. *Garrett Fletcher.* Now I remembered. That was the name of the man Jaime hadn't liked.

"While you were gone, I had a chance to think more about that evening. I remember one thing I heard, but it wasn't much. Damian kept saying, 'I can't. I just can't.' He almost sounded desperate. And Garrett said something like, 'You must,' or 'You have to.' I can't remember exactly. Is it important?"

"Yes, why are you asking?" Geoff asked. "Is this related to his murder? Didn't they arrest his girlfriend?"

"I'm asking for a friend of mine who won't accept that Monica Heller could have committed the crime. I recalled you mentioned the argument here that evening and thought it might be something that could help with her case. Probably not, but I wanted to be able to give my friend some hope, even if it is a bit misguided."

Ron shook his head. "From what I read, it's going to be hard to dispute the evidence of how she was found."

"I know, but I owe it to my friend to find something. Had Damian and Garrett seemed to be on good terms before the argument?"

"Hard to tell when you don't know people. They'd seemed cordial enough—until their argument that night."

Tyrone, who had his own experience with desperate situations, added, "If you think of anything else, could you give Laura a call?"

"Absolutely." Geoff and Ron followed us as we walked toward the front door."

"Thank you, both, for everything. We appreciated the tour and the information. You never know what can help."

What could Garrett Fletcher have been pressuring Damian to do that he so desperately didn't want to?

Chapter 25

A home stager can stage a vacant house with tasteful furniture and accessories.

After leaving the B&B, Tyrone and I drove to Antiques and Other Things to view the storage area Josh had identified for us. I hoped it would work since Louiston's only self-storage facility didn't have any available storage units at the moment.

I looked around the large space Josh took us to, imagining how it would look once we got shelving and our inventory in. "What do you think, Tyrone?"

"Looks good to me, but it's really big. Do you think we are going to need all this space?"

"It's a big space for the inventory we have now, but it will give us space to grow."

Tyrone shrugged. "I guess you have to think big."

I had always been cautious, sometimes too much so. Now I needed to have confidence that my business would grow and plan for it. And having a place to store the furniture we needed would help us do that.

"I think it'll work quite nicely, Josh."

"I'm glad it will work out for ya'll. How about if I work up a draft lease agreement and we go from there?"

"Sounds good." I could hardly believe it was actually working out. But then I thought of Monica's situation and how quickly a small business could fall apart. I gave myself a shake and decided to think positively—not letting my mother's and aunt's negative views of the world affect me.

Josh closed the metal door behind us. As we walked back to the front entrance, he stopped. "While y'all are here, let me show you the paintings Damian Reynolds consigned with me." He led us to a room with a closed door and pulled out a key.

"How can you sell them if you keep them locked up?" Tyrone asked.

"That's the problem. I don't know how I should handle them. They were valuable when he brought them in, but now that he's dead, they'll become even more valuable. And in all fairness to his family, they need the opportunity to decide whether they want to keep them."

Josh opened the door and switched on a light. He'd hung the paintings on the walls, so we got a good view of them. "The ones on the left are his works, and on the right, works from other artists he'd collected."

Tyrone and I stood stock still taking it all in. I had seen Damian's paintings in magazines, but seeing them in person was quite different. They were impressive.

"Wow!" Tyrone had an excellent eye for color and design, and he was obviously impressed by the pieces in front of us. "These must be worth a fortune."

"Yes, they are." Poor Josh looked wistful, knowing what his share of the sale might have brought him. I'd always felt Josh was an honorable businessman, but this was proving it. He could have sold them and no one would ever have been the wiser.

"That's why I've locked them up." He closed the door behind us and locked it.

"You could always contact his agent. Since Damian was divorced, I don't know whether his ex-wife has any right to them. I read Damian had a teenage daughter. She'll more than likely inherit them."

"I just want to make sure they go where they should and I get them off my hands, with a receipt showing that I turned them over. It makes me nervous having such valuable items here."

"I'll tell you what. I want to talk to his ex-wife and agent about something else. If I'm able to talk to them, would you like for me to get a sense of them and see who you might want to approach about the paintings?"

"If you would, that'd be great." Josh visibly relaxed as though the worry of the paintings had been lifted from him. I just hoped that I'd not taken the worry on myself.

Chapter 26

Clear everything from kitchen countertops except for one or two tasteful accessories, remove magnets and other items from refrigerators, and reduce dishes to best pieces for display.

The next morning at Vocaro's, I knew if we waited long enough, we would eventually cross paths with Warren. He usually came in for coffee, and if he had time, he would sit down and chat with us for a bit. That morning after he ordered breakfast at the counter, I waved at him, and he joined Nita and me at our table.

I moved the work plans Nita and I had been going over to make room for him. He put down a tray laden with an egg-and-sausage sandwich, a bowl of mixed fruit, a muffin, and a carton of banana yogurt. The stress of being a possible suspect in Ian Becker's murder hadn't dulled his appetite.

"How have you been, Warren?" The last time I saw him, he'd been convinced the police suspected him of Ian Becker's murder because his body had been found at the funeral home Warren owned. They couldn't have been serious in that belief because I knew from experience the police don't wait around much before making an arrest.

"I've been better." He took a huge bite from his sandwich and chewed slowly. Hours went by, or so it seemed, before he finally swallowed. "They haven't found out who murdered Ian, so the police may still have me in their sights."

I finished my last bite of croissant in record-breaking time compared to Warren. "Have you thought of anyone else in Louiston Ian might have wanted to see while he was here? What about his girlfriend that last summer? I heard his cell phone showed he'd made a call to her when he first arrived. Did he say anything about her when he called you?"

Warren paused as he peeled the cover off the carton of yoghurt. "Over the years, Ian dated a lot of girls. But that last summer, he'd spent most of his time with one girl—Emily somebody."

"Emily Thompson?" Nita asked. "That was the name on his phone records."

"I think that was her name," Warren said. Even after all he had already eaten, he dug into the yogurt with gusto.

"Did Ian mention her when he talked to you?" I asked.

"No. I can't imagine why he would. Why are you interested?" Warren asked.

Nita went on alert. "We are looking to see if there's a link between Ian's death and Damian's murder."

Warren looked perplexed. "Monica murdered Damian. You think she killed Ian too?"

I glared at Nita. "No. We're looking at both murders to see if the same person could have murdered them—someone other than Monica."

"But you caught Monica standing over Damian's body with a knife in her hands." Warren looked puzzled. "How could you two of all people expect to prove someone else did it? Besides, you and Monica have never gotten on. Why are you trying to help her?"

"Because of Sister Madeleine," Nita said.

I sighed. It did sound impossible. "Not just that. Monica said she didn't do it, and Sister Madeleine believes her. She's convinced me to help Monica with her business while she's in jail. You know Sister Madeleine."

Warren laughed. "Yeah. How well I know Sister Madeleine.

She's a lot like Mrs. Webster—has an iron will and can convince you to do anything. And make you think it was your idea."

"And since she believes Monica is innocent, I'm asking questions to see if she could be right. It may be hard to believe, but when I think about how awful it was for Tyrone to be in jail, and seeing Monica there now too, I'm beginning to feel sorry for her."

Nita snorted. "You are being more considerate of Monica than she deserves."

I ignored her. "Warren, is there anything you can tell us about Ian's last summer here?" I watched as he thought about it, as though searching his memory banks.

"Honestly, I can't remember much. I was working for my dad and getting ready to go back to school. That summer, Ian spent a lot of time with Emily. You might want to talk to her—if she's still in town. I haven't seen her since that summer. She lived somewhere in the outskirts of Louiston."

Warren gathered his trash and got up to leave.

"One more thing, Warren," I said. "Are you handling the funeral arrangements for Damian or Ian?"

"I'm handling them for Damian but not for Ian, especially since he was found at my place. It just wouldn't seem right. His folks are dead, and since he has no other family, his arrangements are a bit up in the air right now. I understand he has an ex-wife, but she doesn't want to get involved with making the decisions about his final arrangements. Probably afraid she would get billed for them."

"She sounds like a nice woman," Nita commented dryly.

"The Reynolds family hasn't made it public yet, but they plan to hold a memorial service for Damian at my place in the chapel. They haven't decided on a date yet."

Good. When the service was held, that would give me the opportunity to possibly talk to Damian's ex-wife.

"Sounds like Damian had a nicer ex-wife if she's arranging the service." Nita took our empty cups and tray over to the collection station.

"Mrs. Reynolds has her daughter to think about," Warren said. "Most of the arrangements are being made by Damian's agent, Garrett Fletcher."

Garrett Fletcher. That was someone else I needed to talk to. Since he would be in town for the memorial service, I'd have to find a way to talk to him too, especially after hearing about his argument with Damian at the B&B.

Chapter 27

Remove excess or oversized furniture to make rooms look larger.

A few days later, Nita and I pulled into the Hendricks Funeral Home parking lot well before the memorial service for Damian was to begin. It would enable us to watch people going in to see who was attending and if anyone acted strangely. But how we would determine what was strange behavior would be anybody's guess.

"Don't you think people will think it's a bit strange for us to be attending this service when we didn't even know Damian Reynolds?" Nita never liked going into funeral homes, but after finding Ian Becker's body in one, she was even more uncomfortable than before.

"He was famous, so there'll be a big crowd there, including other people who didn't know him. Nobody will notice us."

Nita placed her hands over her chest. "My heart is beating fast. I'm feeling faint. Maybe you should take me to St. John's Hospital in case I'm having a heart attack."

"You're not having a heart attack. It's probably a panic attack. Breathe in slowly counting to seven, hold your breath, and then breathe out again. That'll help calm you."

"What'll happen if I get inside and faint?" Nita's eyes widened as though panicked at the idea of being rolled out of there on a stretcher with everyone watching.

"Don't even think about it. We'll sit in the back. If you start to faint, you'll make a spectacle of yourself. We need to fade into the crowd. Drawing attention to ourselves to that degree won't help us."

A black Limousine pulled up and parked nearby. The driver got out and opened the car doors. A man and woman stepped from the car, followed by a young woman. Dressed all in black, they were probably members of the family.

"Please hand me that folder with the photos you downloaded from the Internet." Nita handed it to me. I quickly pulled out the photos and studied them. "That's Garrett Fletcher, Damian's agent. That must be Mrs. Reynolds, but it's hard to tell since her hair looks different. That's Damian's daughter. No mistaking that California beach girl look." I watched as Mrs. Reynolds reached for her daughter's arm and the daughter pulled away. *Ah, some history there.*

"I wonder how Damian's daughter is adjusting to life in Central Pennsylvania?" Nita burst out laughing.

"Be nice. She just lost her father, and before that, her sister. Life has to be rough for her right now, regardless of where she's living."

"Sorry. You're right. It's just such a contrast in lifestyles."

"We didn't do too badly growing up here."

We waited for several more people to go inside before we went to the front entrance ourselves. The flash of news cameras caught us by surprise. Several reporters and cameramen milled about the front entrance. I kept forgetting that Damian had been famous and that photos or live footage of the people going into the service would be on the next news program.

Nita ducked behind me. "If I'd known we were going to be photographed, I'd have worn a better outfit."

"I think any photos or videos of us will end up on the cutting room floor." I patted down my hair just in case they didn't.

Warren Hendricks and an assistant in somber suits with black ties stood inside the main entrance greeting visitors and directing them to the funeral chapel. Seeing us, he quirked an eyebrow as though to ask why we were there. Nita had been right. But hopefully, we'd be lost in the crowd.

The chapel was filling up quickly and few empty seats remained in the pews. Nita and I sat in some folding chairs that had been placed in the back of the chapel in anticipation of a big crowd. Scanning the room, I recognized many people, including Detective Spangler, who looked at us speculatively and frowned. Seeing us there, he probably suspected I was up to something.

A young woman sat down next to Nita. I looked up and recognized her niece Jaime. It was only natural she would want to be there since she had worked with Damian at the college. She hugged Nita and waved at me. Pachelbel's "Canon" played softly in the background, partially covering the murmured whispers around us. It always amazed me the piece was played at both funerals and weddings.

Jaime pointed out some of the people from the college as they came in. Finally, just before the service began, Garrett Fletcher, Mrs. Reynolds, her daughter, and some other people walked in and sat in the front pews.

The service itself was somewhat of a blur since my thoughts were filled with a jumble of images from the past few days. Several people spoke at length about Damian. A cousin recounted some of their adventures growing up, evoking some laughs from those gathered. A former classmate spoke about their college days, and Garrett Fletcher described Damian's early struggles to gain recognition in the art world. Damian's daughter gave a tearful eulogy, recounting some of her happiest memories of her father. How he had tried to teach her to paint and her view that she was hopeless at it. I admired the girl's courage getting up to speak about her father and her ability to get through it.

I looked up to see bowed heads and realized they were saying some final prayers, and it was over. Such a short ceremony to mark the passing of someone who had died all too soon. Thankfully, no one said anything about the way he'd died or mentioned Monica in any way.

Jaime wiped her eyes and turned to us. "Are you going to stay for the reception?"

"I don't think so—"

"Why not?" Nita asked. "It will give you a chance to meet and question Damian's ex-wife and agent."

"Because I don't think it would be appropriate here, especially with so many people trying to talk to them. Besides, I called Ron earlier to see if they were staying at the B&B, and fortunately, they are. First thing tomorrow, I'll take Ron and Geoff up on their invitation to join them for breakfast someday—and if I happen to be there at the same time as the guests are having breakfast, all the better."

"I'm going along with you," Nita said. "It won't look as strange as you being there on your own."

As we got up to leave, Jaime whispered. "See that tall man by the side door—the one with the pink shirt and plaid bowtie? That's Professor Edward Albertson. From what I heard, he was really upset when the college hired Damian."

"Why? Because he wanted the job?" Nita asked, her ears perking up at the idea of another possible suspect.

Jaime shook her head. "No. He's a historian, not an artist. Someone said it was because Damian and Professor Albertson's wife had some history."

As people began spilling out of the chapel, I spotted Helen Reynolds heading to a corridor that led to the restrooms. Perhaps I could casually run into her there. As we both dried our hands at the sink, I could express my sympathy. Later when I questioned her, she might remember me as someone who attended Damian's funeral and be a little more forthcoming.

"Nita, I'll be right back."

When I entered the long corridor leading to the restrooms, I stopped abruptly when in the distance I saw Helen Reynolds walk into the arms of Garrett Fletcher. Their embrace was much more intimate than two people consoling each other.

Chapter 28

Grimy bathroom tile is a turn-off to buyers. Thoroughly clean grout. Replace outdated tile or paint with a special ceramic epoxy covering.

After I arrived home from Damian's memorial service, I thought about the embrace I'd witnessed between Helen Reynolds and Garrett Fletcher. Damian and Helen had divorced long before Damian's murder, but it still made me wonder. Could she have been involved with Garrett while she was still married to Damian? Even now, could Helen or Garrett have had a motive to see Damian out of the picture—one besides Helen's feelings toward him because of the death of their daughter?

I wondered if Detective Spangler had questioned Helen Reynolds. She lived within driving distance of Damian and could have easily gone to his house the night he was murdered and returned home again within a few hours.

Thinking of pictures, I remembered reading that candid photos can sometimes reveal things about people and relationships—children who are always standing away from their parents in family photos, couples who shouldn't be gazing at each other longingly, and individuals who aren't smiling when everyone else in a photo is laughing. Photos sometimes tell a story. Perhaps if I could view photos of Damian, Helen, and Garrett together, they might tell me something. It was worth a try.

I reached for my laptop and searched on Google for photos showing the three of them together. Dozens of photos came up, but I didn't see anything in them that was revealing. That is until I saw a captioned photo that included Edward and Phyllis Albertson. In the photo, Damian had been standing close to Phyllis, with his hand possessively on her shoulder. Her husband had been on the far end of the group.

According to Jaime, Professor Albertson had been upset when the college hired Damian—something about there being a history between Damian and Professor Albertson's wife. Could there have been enough between Damian and Phyllis Albertson that could have driven Professor Albertson to murder? A stretch, but stranger things have happened.

Early the next morning, Nita and I arrived at the B&B, well before the time Geoff and Ron served breakfast. Fortunately, when I'd explained to Geoff and Ron my reason for wanting to be at the B&B that morning, they were more than willing to accommodate us.

The cool early morning air felt wonderful and helped soothe my frazzled nerves. I'd slept poorly the night before, dreading the session with Damian Reynolds's ex-wife and his agent. But we needed to grab the opportunity to see them while they were still in town, and this could be our only opportunity to do so.

We parked in the back of the tall mansion. When we came around the corner of the house to the front entrance, we found Geoff standing on the porch, holding a cup of coffee. The smell of it hit me and reminded me how ready for breakfast I was.

"Good morning, ladies. Glad you got here early. I need to talk to you before our guests start coming down for breakfast."

"Hi, Geoff. What's going on?" Nita stretched her arms out wide and breathed in the fresh mountain air. A look of pure joy filled her face. It was good getting out of town occasionally. We needed to do it more often.

Geoff's expression wasn't as joyful. "Sorry to be the bearer of bad news, Laura. Garrett Fletcher is still here, but Mrs. Reynolds and her daughter decided not to stay another night. They came back after the memorial service and checked out, saying they were anxious to get home. After all that's been happening to them, I can't blame them. I think the daughter was having a particularly hard time of it."

That was disappointing, but it helped take some of the pressure off. I wasn't looking forward to questioning Mrs. Reynolds, especially with an unhappy or sullen daughter nearby. I'd have to find another way to talk to her. I was hopeful that someone else would be identified as Damian's killer before it came to that, especially after witnessing her intimate embrace with Garrett Fletcher.

Geoff looked concerned. Did he think I was going to break into hysterics at the news Mrs. Reynolds had gone home? Asking questions related to a murder was filled with lots of roadblocks. Thankfully, I didn't have to do this as a full-time job. I'd leave that to Detective Spangler. Thinking of him reminded me that I needed to fill him in on what I'd discovered so far.

Geoff opened the large oak front door. "Come on in, and I'll get you some coffee. Ron and I are excited about watching you interrogate a suspect."

My heart sank. This was going to be worse than I expected. "No, Geoff. He isn't a suspect—simply someone who might be able to give us some information. We thought the opportunity to talk to him and Mrs. Reynolds here and away from others would be perfect. It's unfortunate that we won't get to see both of them." I might view Garrett Fletcher as a suspect, but it wouldn't do for Geoff to view him as such.

"Whatever. It's still exciting. You just do your thing. I'll listen in while I serve breakfast. Ron will listen at the door. If you need us to come to your aid, we'll be ready to intervene."

I didn't know what they expected to happen, but I certainly hoped their intervention wouldn't be necessary. It made me laugh imagining Ron bounding out of the kitchen waving a meat cleaver to rescue us. I hoped after breakfast with us Garrett Fletcher wouldn't have reason to demand a refund for his stay.

"Let's go ahead and get you seated in the dining room. Should we pass you off as other guests?"

"No. It's better if we just stick to our original story. We came here to taste test some of your new breakfast items and provide you with feedback. How does that sound? Nita and I will play it by ear and decide how much to say."

Geoff clapped his hands together. "Sounds great. Let me check in the kitchen to see how things are going with Ron."

We took seats at the long dining table that had been set with crisp white linens and lovely bone china. Nita turned over a cup and peeked at the maker's mark on the bottom. Pink and blue hydrangeas from the plants we had passed in the garden filled a crystal bowl in the center of the table. I didn't have any experience staying at bed and breakfasts, but if this proved to be an example of the lovely setting and level of service guests could expect, I'd have to stay at them when I traveled, which sadly wasn't often.

A sideboard groaned under the weight of platters filled with a variety of bread, muffins, and croissants, chafing dishes, and a bowl of mixed fruit. Seeing it reminded me of the description of breakfasts served in English manor homes that were the settings for some of the historical mysteries I read—all the more so with Geoff acting as butler.

Geoff entered the room carrying a china coffee pot in one hand and a teapot in the other. "Coffee or tea?" Ron followed him, carrying a container he placed in one of the chaffing dishes. He winked at us and returned to the kitchen. This was probably the best entertainment they'd had in quite some time.

Oh, the joy of being waited on. I asked for tea, somehow thinking it was more conducive to the setting. Nita opted for coffee. I wondered if it would be as good as the coffee at Vocaro's.

"Today, we have a new mango muffin for you to try and a cheese strata Ron devised. See if you can guess the types of cheese he used." Geoff placed individual dishes filled with pats of butter in front of us. "Anytime you are ready, please help yourselves."

I wondered whether we should wait until Garrett joined us or start eating so we didn't look like we were ready to ambush him. Hunger won out. I went over to the buffet, looked at what was on offer, and began filling my plate. Nita didn't hesitate to follow me.

As we sat down, a tall man I recognized as Garrett from his photos and seeing him at the funeral home entered the room. Geoff greeted him and directed him to a seat near us. We both wished him a good morning and he nodded at us. Not a great start.

Geoff interceded for us. "Mr. Fletcher, please let me introduce Laura Bishop and Nita Martino. They are doing a taste test for us today." I smiled at him, and Nita waved.

Geoff described the dishes on offer, and then told Garrett to help himself. Garrett filled his plate and sat down at the table across from us.

Like guests in those country manor mysteries, constrained by excessive formality, I wasn't sure how to break the ice. Fortunately, Nita didn't feel those same constraints.

"I understand you were Damian Reynolds' agent. His death was so tragic."

He looked up from the plate with barely concealed irritation. It was hard to tell whether his reaction was toward us or being reminded what had happened to Damian.

"Yes, it was tragic." Obviously in his line of work he'd learned to be polite, but just barely.

Nita tried again. "We attended his memorial service yesterday."

"Oh, yes?"

My turn. "We don't believe Monica stabbed Damian, and we would like to try to prove she is innocent." *Nothing like cutting to the chase.*

"And what? Find out who did?" He studied us for a long moment. "Bishop and Martino. Weren't you two of the people who found Monica standing over Damian's body? How can you ignore that? Didn't you believe your own eyes?"

"The thing that everyone forgets is that we found Monica holding the knife. We didn't see her stab him." I couldn't believe that I was coming to Monica's defense. "We've known Monica for most of her life. And even though we found her as we did, she wouldn't or couldn't have killed him. From what we understand, she had come to care deeply for him."

"Care for him or his fame and money?" Garrett asked, with a barely concealed sneer.

That brought out Nita's fighting spirit. "If you were his agent, you are aware of his income from his works. If he had so much money, why was he trying to sell paintings—his own and from his collection—and keep it a secret? Where did all his money go?"

That caught him by surprise. "What are you insinuating? If you are looking at me as a suspect, you can forget it. Damian was my biggest client. I would have been foolish to do anything that would have cut off a major source of my income."

This was going worse than I'd expected. Nita and I were such amateurs at this. Time to change tack. "When you two stayed here before, I understand you had an argument and you left town abruptly. Would you mind saying what the argument was about?"

"Yes, I mind. But I'll tell you anyway so that you two busybodies can look at someone else to suspect. After Damian's daughter drowned, he stopped painting. Not because he didn't want to paint, but because he couldn't. Just picking up a brush caused his hand to shake so uncontrollably he would drop it. That's why he took a job in this Podunk town. If he couldn't paint, he decided to teach. We argued that night because I was trying to convince him to get some counseling, which he refused to do."

"What about Mrs. Reynolds—"

He pushed back his chair, threw his napkin onto the table, and stood up. "This is outrageous. Helen was miles away the night Damian was murdered."

Geoff walked back into the room and received the brunt of Garrett's fury. "I don't know what your purpose was in allowing these two busybodies to be here, but their questioning was not welcome. I'll be checking out—and I won't be back."

After he stomped from the room, Nita eyed his nearly full plate. "Ngaio Marsh! That was a waste of a delicious meal."

I noticed Nita was again using writers from the Golden Age of Detective Fiction for her expletives. I turned to Geoff. "Sorry, I think we cost you a satisfied guest."

"Don't worry about it. It was worth it for the entertainment value. Did you learn anything worthwhile?"

"Just the reason why Damian came to Louiston," Nita said.

"I don't think this was our finest hour."

As we drove home, I pondered what we'd learned. I needed to see Monica again to find out what she could tell me about Garrett Fletcher.

Chapter 29

Colors can evoke different emotions. Warm colors can make a house feel cozy and inviting while cool colors can provide a sense of calm and relaxation.

That afternoon, I found myself again standing in front of the police station, facing a meeting with Monica. I didn't want to visit her again, and the thought of it caused my stomach to clench. But I felt I should give her an update on what Nita and I had been doing related to her business and tell her about the memorial service for Damian Reynolds. Sister Madeleine would expect that of me at the very least. When would I ever learn to resist helping people or simply saying no? I also hoped Monica could tell me something about Garrett Fletcher and Edward Albertson.

I climbed the granite steps into the police station with as much enthusiasm as a novice hiker starting up Mt. Kilimanjaro. The trek up the stairs could be just as dangerous, recalling my collision there with Detective Spangler. I carefully looked for anyone coming around the corner at the landing.

I'd arranged the visit in advance, so Monica knew I was coming. After checking in and showing my ID card, I took a seat and waited to be called. Following my visits there with Tyrone in the spring and now with Monica, the waiting room was becoming all too familiar. Any more visits and the authorities would be issuing me a frequent visitor card.

When Monica appeared on the other side of the glass divider, I took my seat in front of her. She didn't look any more pleased to see me than I was to see her, and we sat staring at each other. It had to be mortifying for her to be seen like this and know that her business rested in my hands.

I decided to be the better person and break the ice. "You're looking well." I knew that sounded inane, but I didn't want to ask her how she was doing. What could I expect her to say: "I'm doing great, how are you?"

Monica ran her fingers through her hair. "I'd look a lot better if you could smuggle me in some hair dye."

I laughed. "And get jailed for smuggling contraband?"

"If I'm here much longer, I'll end up a brunette." Monica sighed deeply, as though she'd brought the exhaled breath all the way from her toes. "And to think I had such lovely blond hair while growing up."

What could I say? If we couldn't discover who'd killed Damian, she could be coming out of prison someday, if she ever got out at all, with white hair.

Monica sat up straighter, possibly to shake off the same thought. "But you didn't come here to talk about my hair. Why did you come?"

"Maybe to console you that your business isn't falling apart—yet." I filled her in on my meetings with her young assistant and all that Nita and I had been doing to help meet deadlines. "The Greens were quite pleased with how the apartment over their garage turned out. It will be a terrific short-term rental."

"That was a cute space and one begging to be used. I'm glad they were pleased."

I contemplated asking Monica about her move into home staging and the things that had been happening to sabotage my business and then decided against it. The incidences had stopped once she had been arrested, so I could only assume she'd been responsible for them. Nothing would be gained by confronting her about them now.

Abruptly, Monica's eyes welled with tears. "Why do things have to change? Damian and I were doing so well together."

That I couldn't answer. Damian and Ian couldn't have anticipated the abrupt changes in their lives. That thought made me think.

"Did you know Ian Becker?"

"Ian Becker? Wasn't he the man who was murdered a few days before Damian?"

"Yes. The one Nita discovered at the funeral home. He used to spend summers in Louiston with his aunt—his last stay was about twenty years ago."

She shook her head. "I don't recall anybody by that name. Why?"

"It's just so strange that both Damian and Ian had been stabbed in the back. With you being found with Damian, the police have no reason to suspect the same person committed both murders. If we could find a link between the two murders, perhaps we can discover who killed Damian."

Monica's face broke out in a wide smile. "You finally believe I'm not guilty of stabbing Damian."

"I'm not going to go that far," I said. "But if you didn't kill Damian, the only way to prove you are innocent is to find out who did."

"Does that mean you're investigating again?" Her eyes widened in surprise.

"Let's just say that I'm asking questions." I didn't want to give her false hope.

"You helped Tyrone—maybe you can help me."

Monica must have become desperate for her to look at me as the solution to her situation.

"What can you tell me about Damian's agent?" I asked.

"Garrett Fletcher? I didn't like the man, and he didn't like me." *Now that was a big surprise.*

"I heard he and Damian had a heated argument while they

were staying at the B&B. Did you know about that?"

"No, but it got to the point where they were arguing quite a bit, so that doesn't surprise me. Garrett represented Damian from the time his work started gaining recognition. He was quite controlling, and Damian let him get away with it. That is until he moved here and we started seeing each other. Garrett saw me as a threat to their relationship."

"Do you think Garrett had any reason to want Damian dead?"

"I didn't like the man, but I really can't see him killing Damian, even in anger. He would be really foolish to do so since Damian was his most successful client."

"Could Garrett have been cheating Damian?"

Monica shrugged. "I don't know. But since you said Damian had consigned some of his art collection to Josh's business, something had to account for his financial problems."

"It could be as Garrett said—Damian stopped painting. That would have started drying up a major source of his income. You don't make a fortune teaching at a small college."

Monica's forehead furrowed as though deep in thought. "Damian didn't say much about it, but I got the impression the divorce settlement with his ex-wife was huge. That could have taken a bigger toll on his finances than he expected."

"Do you have any reason to think there might have been anything between Garrett and Helen Reynolds?"

Monica eyes widened in surprise. "I don't know. I never met her, and Damian didn't say anything about that. Why do you ask?"

"I'm trying to consider anything that could have a bearing on Damian's death—even if farfetched."

Monica seemed to mull that over but didn't add anything more.

"What about Professor Albertson at the college? Do you know anything about bad feelings he harbored about Damian?"

"Are you talking about that old story about Damian being involved with Edward Albertson's wife?"

I shrugged.

"Damian said he was surprised to discover Edward Albertson was a member of the Fischer faculty. He'd known him from somewhere else—I don't remember where. Edward was pretty unpleasant to Damian when we saw him at functions. When I asked him about it, he said Edward long ago had accused him of being involved with his wife. Damian denied it." Monica laughed. "After seeing Phyllis, I believed him." *Typical Monica.*

I didn't mention the photo I had seen of Damian with the Albertsons. Monica was probably as gullible as I was occasionally, wanting to believe him.

Time to change the subject. "I also came today because I thought you might like to hear about Damian's memorial service."

Monica nodded slowly, so I went on. "Nita and I attended the service. The chapel at Hendricks Funeral Home was filled to capacity. Family and friends talked about his school days and how hard he'd worked to get a foothold in the art world."

Monica dabbed at her eyes that were starting to fill with tears again. "Did anyone mention that Damian's father had been angry he didn't go into engineering and join his firm? He predicted Damian would become a starving artist." Monica paused. "I wish his father had lived long enough to see how successful Damian had become."

"It was a moving service," I said.

When Monica's chin began to tremble, I decided it was a good time to leave.

As I walked away, I heard a faint "Thank you."

Now that I'd gotten Monica's hopes up, how was I going to deliver on finding out who'd killed Damian?

Chapter 30

New stainless steel appliances will scream new kitchen.

The next morning, Aunt Kit sat at the kitchen table while I prepared breakfast for us, wholegrain pancakes with ground almonds. While I cooked, I filled Aunt Kit in about my meeting with Monica.

"I don't know if there is any hope for her," Aunt Kit said, shaking her head.

I worried about the same thing. After serving Aunt Kit, I took two pancakes and poured a small amount of maple syrup over them, skipping the butter in an attempt to eat somewhat healthy. I took a bite, enjoying the crunch the almonds provided.

"What do you have planned for today?" I asked Aunt Kit.

"Anne Williamson and I are going to see an art display in the lobby of the medical center. They are supposed to have some nice pieces done by local artists." Aunt Kit dug into her pancakes. She enjoyed anything that resembled dessert.

"You and Anne have been spending a fair amount of time together." I reached for more maple syrup, thinking I should have added the butter.

"It's nice sharing my interest in art with someone close to my age—someone who can understand where I'm coming from."

My sense of guilt for not spending more time with Aunt Kit

during her visit made me cringe. Could her statement have been aimed at me? "Why don't you stay longer so we can visit some of the places you haven't been to for a while."

"That would be nice. What about you? Do you have a place to stage today?

Just then, I heard a knock on the door and went to answer it, finding Nita standing there with an arm full of folders and a laptop. We had planned to work on several things that morning, including updating our webpage. We decided we would have far fewer distractions at my place than at Vocaro's.

A surprise to us both, Nita had turned out to be a wiz with the technological things that were *supposed* to help us with our business. I was thankful that she had taken right to it since the devices that were supposed to save us time took far too much of our time. With my background in IT, I could have handled it but was happy not having to.

"Hey, Nita. You're just in time for breakfast."

"You fixed breakfast? That's a new one." Nita put her things down.

"It's a special treat for Aunt Kit."

Aunt Kit called from the kitchen. "Nita, I'm glad you're here. Laura and I have been talking about Monica's situation." *Situation* was definitely a euphemism or polite way of saying she was in jail and accused of murder.

When we reached the kitchen, Nita hugged Aunt Kit and then leaned over to pet Inky. He had positioned himself under the table ready to snatch a piece of bacon if someone, namely Nita or Aunt Kit, offered it to him.

After Nita sat down, I handed her a plate of hot pancakes and bacon I took from a warm oven. She accepted it with relish. Everyone seemed to love pancakes.

Sitting down again, I eyed my now-cold breakfast. "I was about to tell Aunt Kit about my visit to see Monica yesterday and that we haven't discovered anything that could remotely help her. It's so frustrating. With us finding her over Damian's body, it's hard to prove someone else could have killed him.

Nita poured syrup liberally over her warm pancakes. "Sister Madeleine will be happy if we can discover anything that could point to someone other than Monica. She truly believes Monica is innocent."

"Let's think about it." Aunt Kit seemed to be mulling it over as she put English breakfast tea into a warmed teapot, poured boiling water over it from the electric kettle, put the lid on the teapot, and covered it with a tea cozy to keep it warm. She was a stickler for making sure the tea was made properly. "Doesn't anyone think it's strange there were two murders in town within a few days of each other—both murdered similarly. Monica looks pretty guilty about the one, but is there anything connecting her to the other?"

I shrugged. "Monica said she didn't know Ian. I don't know much about him myself. Poor guy. He comes to town to settle his aunt's estate, which we all assumed to be a modest one, and then is murdered. For all we know, his aunt could have been the millionaire next door no one suspects of having any money."

"Could that have been the case?" Aunt Kit sounded almost envious. I wondered again about how she was doing. Could she be having financial troubles?

"You never know," Nita said. "She could have been left a fortune by her parents and never spent much of it."

"Let's be realistic." I reached for the last piece of bacon that I wasn't going to share with Inky. "It would be somewhat improbable that the motive for Ian's death was related to a huge inheritance. But even if she had been as rich as Andrew Carnegie, who in town could benefit from Ian's death? Ian didn't have any other connections here other than his aunt and a few friends he hadn't seen in twenty years—Warren being one of them. It's unlikely anyone here would have benefitted from his death."

"Maybe someone from New Zealand followed him here and murdered him," Aunt Kit said.

Nita and I both laughed at that one. Aunt Kit, like Will Parker, enjoyed bizarre mysteries that were way out there. Next she would be on the lookout for a Chinese man to show up as a surprise suspect as they often did in movies from the 1930s—a device used so often that Ronald Knox in his Ten Commandments of Detective Fiction admonished writers not to use it.

"Don't you think it was suspicious that Ian was murdered in Warren's funeral home?" Aunt Kit added. She loved conspiracy theories.

"I don't suspect Warren of killing someone he hasn't seen in twenty years." But I'd been wrong in my judgment of people before. In Warren's case, I hoped not. "Warren would have been more likely to bore him to death telling him every detail about his upcoming stage production than to have stabbed him."

Aunt Kit reached over and took another pancake, which surprised me since she usually ate so little. "Who else might have known Ian was in town—or would have remembered him for that matter?"

"Remember what my cousin Neil said about one of the calls on Ian's phone records being to an old girlfriend? Maybe the girlfriend is worth looking into."

Aunt Kit pondered that for a minute. Being a real fan of mysteries, she loved trying to solve the puzzles they presented. Perhaps I had inherited my sense of inquisitiveness after all. "I still think the police should continue looking at what could've connected Damian and Ian. Something they may have had in common?" Aunt Kit shared her piece of bacon with Inky.

"They both stayed at the B&B," I said. "But at different times."

Aunt Kit's frown told me I wasn't taking this seriously enough.

"Okay, let's consider this," I said. "Damian was about ten years older than Ian. Before coming to Louiston, Damian lived in California, Ian in New Zealand. To the best of my knowledge, neither had been in Louiston at the same time until recently. Damian was an artist and was teaching at the college. I don't know what Ian did for a living, but we probably could find out."

Aunt Kit sat up abruptly. "Maybe that's the connection."

"What?" Nita was wide-eyed and anticipating a revelation.

"Art," Aunt Kit said.

"I never heard Ian was an artist," I said. That was something else I needed to check into.

"No, but his aunt was." Aunt Kit waved her fork at us as if for emphasis. "Maybe it's far-fetched and a pretty weak link, but so far that's the only link between the two men."

That was a real stretch, but I didn't want to tell Aunt Kit that. She looked as satisfied as if she'd just uncovered the solution to a major case and delivered it to Perry Mason in the courtroom herself.

Aunt Kit poured us cups of the brewed tea, which I was more than ready for. "All I'm saying is think about that connection," she said.

"I will, I will. But if we are going to look into Ian Becker's death, it might be important to talk to the old girlfriend he called."

"And don't forget his aunt's attorney," Aunt Kit added. "He could be hiding the money she left."

"No, that won't be the case." Nita put down her cup abruptly. "Her attorney was my cousin Ted. He wouldn't steal from anyone. You don't know Ted. He is so straitlaced the family is still surprised he didn't go into the priesthood."

Aunt Kit was adamant. "I still think you need to look at the art link."

Maybe Nita and I should turn our search for information over to Aunt Kit.

Nita nodded. "We should look for who might inherit Doris Becker's money since Ian is no longer around. Maybe someone else was named in the will."

"You have to see the will," Aunt Kit said.

"I wish I knew how we could do that." I refilled everyone's teacups and sat back down.

"Let me think about it." Nita scrunched up her face in thought. "I may have a way we can find out."

Oh no, another one of Nita's ideas. Her ideas once nearly put us in jail.

I couldn't believe this. Now we were delving into *two* murders. It was difficult enough trying to make sense of one, but two separate murders with no obvious connection were enough to make me reach into the cupboard for the bottle of Harvey's—and it was only breakfast time. How did I get myself pulled into these things?

Chapter 31

Make sure every area of the house is spotless. Cleaning things like the top of the hot water heater shows buyers that the house has been well-maintained.

While Nita and I worked that morning, I was able to get our minds off murders, wills, and huge inheritances. Hours flew by, and we made good progress.

Nita snapped her laptop closed and stretched. "We now have an updated web page and a new Facebook page. But we have to keep posting to make them worthwhile."

"Nita, you are a jewel—in more ways than one. I hope Guido appreciates how wonderful you are."

She smiled. "Thankfully he does. And if he forgets, I don't hesitate to remind him."

"Next we have to work on updating our inventory system. At the rate we're accumulating things, if we don't work on it, the system will be woefully out of date."

"Yeah, but first we have to think of a way to find out who else might have been named in Doris Becker's will." She picked up her things and walked to the door.

"That may be a challenge," I said.

"No, it won't." Nita gave me an amused and calculated look. "I've worked out a plan. Meet me at my house tonight at nine and wear something old. Oh, and bring your vacuum cleaner."

Just before nine that evening, I pulled up in front of Nita's house. She stood by the curb, wearing a baggy pair of jeans and a brown plaid shirt that hung almost to her knees, probably borrowed from Guido. In one hand she held a bucket with a mop inside it—the long mop handle resting on her shoulder.

What in the world did she have in mind? Her crazy ideas had gotten us into trouble in the past, and I feared this was going to be another one of those occasions.

"Did you bring the vacuum cleaner?" she asked.

"It's in the back. Nita, what is this all about?" I opened the back of my car and she deposited the bucket and mop.

"We're going to get into Ted's office and search for that will."

"What? Nita are you crazy?" Nita's cousin Ted Wojdakowski was handling Doris Becker's estate.

Nita got in the front seat. "I didn't want to say anything earlier and give you time to think about it. Ted isn't going to tell us anything, so that's the only way we can find the information we need. We aren't going to take anything. We are merely going to look and then leave. And we won't disclose what we've learned unless it's absolutely necessary."

I stood on the curb, not knowing whether to run away and leave her sitting in my car or go along with another one of her hair-brained ideas.

Nita waved at me. "Come on, get in the car."

"And end up sharing a cell with Monica when we're arrested for breaking and entering?" Of all the people in the second grade I could've made friends with, I picked the certifiably insane one. It was all Sister Madeleine's fault—both for encouraging my friendship with Nita and for putting a guilt trip on me to help Monica.

Nita held up a set of keys. "Who said anything about breaking and entering? We'll go in looking like cleaning personnel, search, and get out of there. Easy."

"Where'd you get those?" I asked, eyeing the keys.

Nita put them back in her pocket. "Let's just say it's good to have sympathetic relatives."

I got in my dented Corolla that had once belonged to my mother and started the motor. I still missed the Volvo I'd sold to help finance my staging business. What a stupid thought to come to mind—missing a luxury car when I wasn't going to need one in prison.

"You know where Ted's office is?" Nita asked. "It's in the professional building just down the street from the police station."

"That'll make it convenient for the police to nab us in the middle of our search. Did you think to inquire if there are any alarms we need to turn off once we're inside?" What was I talking about? Could I possibly be agreeing to this caper?

"Alarm? Are you kidding? This is Louiston, not Manhattan. Pull into the parking lot in the back, and we'll go in through the rear entrance."

As cleaner number one, I unloaded my vacuum cleaner, all the time wondering what the sentence was for unlawful entry.

"Just act like a cleaning crew member who is going in for a scheduled cleaning," Nita said.

"And just how am I supposed to act, never having been the member of a cleaning crew?"

"I don't know. Try to look like you should be here and like you've had a hard day."

"The hard day part won't be difficult." The vacuum cleaner weighed a ton and I decided it would be easier if I wheeled it across the lot instead of carrying it.

The rear parking lot was empty. "It looks like everyone's gone. That's good. With any luck, no one will be coming back this late at night." Nita retrieved her bucket and mop and followed behind me.

I looked up at the two-story building. "Some lights are still on."

"Those are the lights in the corridors."

When we reached the door, Nita inserted the largest of the keys into the lock. I kept hoping it wouldn't work, but she turned it with little effort. I looked up to check for surveillance cameras that could be pointed at us. I then realized that wasn't a smart thing to do. If there were cameras, they now had a clear view of my face.

Nita held the door open while I dragged my vacuum inside, wishing mine was a lighter one. The only vacuum I had was my mother's old Kirby, which was all metal and heavy. When the door closed behind us, all I could think of was the clang a jail cell makes as it closes behind a prisoner.

When we arrived at Ted's office, Nita again easily unlocked the door. I held my breath waiting as the seconds clicked away for an alarm to go off. When one didn't, I released my breath, suddenly feeling faint. Nita had gotten us into some strange escapades, but this one had to be the worst.

Nita switched lights on in the outer office.

It was the first time I'd been in Ted's office, and I wasn't impressed. It was as basic as Sam Spade's office looked in the movie version of the Dashiell Hammett's *Maltese Falcon*. I put down my vacuum and eyed with distaste the thick border of dust around the edge of the carpet. "Whatever cleaning company Ted is using, they aren't doing a good job. Look at how dusty the furniture is. Perhaps we should give it a cleaning, and if anyone finds us here, we could say we were doing it as a surprise for your cousin."

"This isn't the time to be evaluating the place." Nita grabbed a rag from the bucket she had left by the door and tossed it at me. "Here, you start dusting, and if anyone comes in unexpectedly, they'll catch you in the act of cleaning, and we can then bluff our way out. I'll search. Fortunately, Ted doesn't have a huge practice, so it shouldn't take long."

Not ready to leave the searching to Nita, I went over to the secretary's desk looking for a folder marked "Becker." As I searched, I brushed away the crumbs that had accumulated on the desktop. Whoever the secretary was, she ate at her desk. And from the looks of it, she did that a lot. As I worked, I forced myself to resist the urge to straighten things a bit. My desk was covered with papers, but it never looked as bad as this.

Just then, I heard the sound of the nearby elevator doors open. My heart started to beat wildly. "Nita, I think someone's coming."

She stopped what she was doing, gently pushed closed the file drawer she had been going through, and grabbed another cloth. For all her bravado, she looked as nervous as I felt. To think we were going through all this for Monica, who had been hateful to us all our lives. Sister Madeleine would tell us that we were building up treasure in our treasure chest in heaven for helping others. Of course, I don't know what she would say about our illegal search of Ted's office.

A few long minutes later when the elevator sounded again, I let out a sigh of relief. "It could have been a night watchman making rounds."

Nita switched off the lights in Ted's office. "I don't know what to say. I couldn't find a folder of any kind for Doris Becker. Did you find anything?"

I shook my head. "Maybe he has a vault somewhere else in the building where he stores documents. If that's the case, we'll never be able to get to them." I drew the line at safe cracking.

The window in the outer office looked out over the rear parking lot. We heard what sounded like a small panel truck pulling into the lot. My mouth went dry.

Nita turned off the overhead light and peered between the Venetian blind panels. "A panel truck just parked. Oh my gosh. It's another cleaning service. Let's get out of here."

I switched off the one remaining light, and we grabbed our equipment, heading for the door. Nita locked it behind us, and we rushed to the stairs to avoid passing anyone coming up in the elevator.

After lugging the heavy Kirby down to the ground floor, my arms ached, and I resolved to get a cleaning service so I'd never have to handle a vacuum again. *Well, maybe someday when I could afford it.*

We waited in the stairwell on the ground floor until we heard the whoosh of the elevator going up. We then raced down the hall to the rear entrance. When we reached the door, we forced ourselves to slow down and not look suspicious as we left the building and casually walked across the parking lot—or as casually as I could with the heavy Kirby in my arms.

Once we loaded our equipment into my car and got in, every part of my body began to shake so much I wasn't sure I'd be able to drive home. "I don't care what they say about orange being the new black. I just wouldn't look good in it."

"You worry too much," Nita said, but I noticed that she looked a bit flushed.

"I'll remind you of that when Bruiser Betty pins you against a cell wall."

"No folders. You know what that means, don't you?"

I moaned. "We have to ask Ted about the will."

Chapter 32

Store away bills, private papers, and valuables before potential buyers start touring your house.

The next morning, after our fruitless search of Ted's office, Nita and I stood in front of his office building again.

I checked my watch for the third time. We were early for office hours, but if we could catch Ted before his clients started to arrive, we might be able to get into see him and, with any luck, get the information we needed. "I have a feeling this is going to be a waste of time, just like last night. Ted probably won't tell us a thing about what's in the will."

"It's not like it's a state secret." Nita chewed on her thumbnail, something she only did if she was nervous or embarrassed. "If somebody else had a copy, they could tell us, without breaking client confidentiality. Unfortunately, Ted had always been close-mouthed, even when we were kids. Must come from the Polish side of his family."

"Who else could have a copy? Maybe Ian? If so, it might have been among the things he left at the B&B."

"Unfortunately, his things are no longer there. Neil said Detective Spangler sent him out there to get Ian's belongings. Maybe you could ask Detective Spangler if he found a copy of the will."

I grimaced. "We can forget that. Even if he did, could you in your wildest dreams imagine Detective Spangler letting me read it?"

"Maybe, if you two got along better." Nita shook her head as though it was a mystery to her why I didn't get along with Detective Spangler.

It wasn't a mystery to me, especially after I couldn't convince him Tyrone was incapable of murdering someone. I kept thinking of all those days Tyrone spent in jail.

"I don't think Ted is going to tell us anything. And your stupid idea of us getting into his office last night had to have been your worst idea yet."

"Well, you went along with it. If we'd found the information we needed, you would now be thinking it was a terrific idea." Nita began chewing on her other thumbnail. She must be feeling more nervous than she was letting on.

"I went along with your idea only because we were desperate," I admitted. "Now we still have to convince Ted to share the information with us."

Nita pondered that for a few seconds. "That may be difficult. Even as kids he wasn't good at sharing."

I threw up my hands, wanting to give this up as a lost cause.

"Okay, let's go." Nita started toward the front entrance of the building. "We'll just have to brazen it out with Ted and see what he'll tell us. Too bad I don't have some family history to blackmail him with. He was always so proper."

Reaching the second floor, we turned the corner only to find Ted standing at the door of his office. He must have come in from a back entrance. With his key in hand, he was ready to unlock the door.

"You guys are up early. What brings you here?" Ted unlocked the door and switched on the lights. "My secretary hasn't even arrived yet." He looked around him, as though noticing something was different but unable to put his finger on what. Probably the fact that his secretary's desk was no longer covered in food remains.

Nita didn't waste any time. "We wanted to see you before you got busy. Do you have a second?"

Ted eyed us suspiciously. "Why do I think this is going to give me heartburn, even before my first cup of coffee?"

We followed him into his office, which looked all too familiar. I spotted a rag we had dropped there the night before and used my foot to push it under a chair. Could the police find fingerprints on cloth?

"Sorry to bother you, Ted, but we are looking for some information. You've heard about Damian Reynolds's murder? Nita and I want to help Monica Heller, who's accused of his murder."

A pained look crossed his face. "Yeah. Heard you guys caught her in the act. Sure am glad I'm not representing her." Ted put his briefcase on his desk, switched on his desk lamp, and sat down. We took the two seats in front of him.

I sat forward in my chair and was sorry I did when it emitted a loud squeak. "We didn't see Monica stab him. We only saw her with a knife in her hands. But that's beside the point. To help her, we need to see if there's a connection between Damian Reynolds's murder and Ian Becker's murder."

Ted put his head back, stared at the ceiling, and then sighed. The sigh of someone who wanted to tell us we were crazy but too polite to do so.

"Why do you two keep getting involved in things like this? There is no connection."

Nita huffed. "Maybe there is but no one has made that connection yet."

I hoped if I could get his attention focused on me, he would forget the antagonism he and Nita had built up as cousins. "According to his phone records, Ian called you when he got into town. Can you tell us what he had to say?"

"Yes, he did. But we only talked long enough to set up an appointment for him to come in. But he never came."

I sensed Ted was going to be out of patience with us soon. "Let's make it simple. All we want to do is find out who else was named in Doris Becker's will and if someone could have benefitted from Ian's death. Then we can follow the trail to see if there could be a link between the two murders."

"A will names the beneficiaries. But it depends on how a will is written as to who would get his portion if he died—his heirs, if any—or if his share is to be divided among any other heirs named in the will. And that's all I'm going to say." His face reddened when he realized what he had just insinuated. So there had been more heirs named. But that still didn't help us know who they were.

Nita went in firing both guns. "Come on, Ted. You always had a thing about Monica. Don't you want to see her proved innocent?"

"I didn't—"

"You did." Nita looked smug. She'd found something to use. "When we were in school and you drove me anywhere, how was it we always passed Monica's house on the way?"

I almost felt sorry for him. Having Nita as a cousin couldn't be easy. "Ted, you've got to help us so we can help Monica."

Ted reached for his briefcase, opened it, and pulled out a folder. "I'd like to help you out, Laura." Ted tapped on the folder. "But what's in Doris Becker's will is confidential."

So that's where the will had been. He had taken it home the night before. No wonder Nita and I couldn't find it.

I tried to hide my frustration. "Yes, but your client is dead. And her nephew, Ian Becker, is dead. The information will eventually be made available to the public when probate is filed. Couldn't you just speed up the process so we can see who the beneficiaries are now?"

"Think of Monica sitting in jail—wearing orange and not looking her gorgeous self." Nita was digging deep.

We heard a door close outside Ted's office.

"Excuse me for a minute. I need to see if that's my first appointment." With that he got up and left the room, closing the door behind him.

Nita jumped up and reached across the desk for the folder.

"Nita! You can't do that."

"Watch me." With that, she opened the folder and flipped through the pages, paused, and then just as quickly returned the folder.

She'd barely sat down again when the door opened. For a second I was certain my heart had stopped beating, and I wasn't sure it would start again.

"Okay, guys, I've got a client waiting, so I need for you to leave. Sorry I couldn't help you."

"Ah, Ted, think of Monica." Nita was such a natural actor. She really should try out for the Louiston Players.

"Come on, Nita. Ted's a busy guy." I rushed her out of the office. "Thanks for your time, Ted. If you change your mind, please let us know."

We raced down the steps to the lobby, not waiting for the elevator.

"Nita, you nearly gave me a heart attack. What if Ted had come in and found you going through the folder?" I was out of breath and about ready to faint.

Nita started to giggle. "What are you so nervous about? If Ted hadn't wanted us to look at that folder, he wouldn't have left it there. As I said, he always had a thing for Monica. He'd do anything to help her, even if she didn't know he was alive. Men."

"What'd you see?"

"You aren't going to believe this. In addition to Ian, Doris named two other people. Emily Thompson and Brandon Thompson."

Chapter 33

A master bedroom should be gender neutral to appeal to both sexes. Remove floral patterns and NASCAR posters. Select neutral colors for walls and bedding.

After Nita and I left Ted's law office, we stopped at Vocaro's, where Tyrone made us our favorite coffee drinks—cappuccino for me and a macchiato for Nita. I probably should have ordered chamomile tea instead to calm my frazzled nerves. Had Ted really left the folder out so we could see the will? If so, he must still *really* have a thing for Monica.

We got our drinks and took a table in the back to discuss what we'd learned related to what we already knew. I tried to absorb the information. As we had learned before, Ian Becker made four calls on his cell phone when he arrived in Louiston, and one of them had been to Emily Thompson—his girlfriend twenty years ago. Could he have called her because he wanted to talk about their times together or because of the will? Had Ian been aware his aunt had named Emily Thompson and Brandon Thompson, whoever he was, in her will?

For once, Nita didn't have a theory about it. "I don't know Emily or Brandon Thompson. We'll have to do some investigating."

"Before we do that, we have to focus on our work." We went over our list of activities for the day and the remainder of the week.

Working things into our schedule to help Monica's business and fulfilling our own obligations kept us quite busy. No wonder Agatha Christie's Hercule Poirot had been able to solve so many cases. It was his full-time job.

Nita took off to meet with a potential client about staging a house for sale. As I headed for the door, a thought occurred to me, and I stopped at the counter to talk to Tyrone. Fortunately, the early morning rush was over and he was free to talk.

"Hey, Tyrone, I have a question for you. Do you know Emily or Brandon Thompson?"

Tyrone wiped the counter with a damp cloth and pondered that. "I don't know an Emily Thompson, but Brandon Thompson was in one of my art classes—the one with Damian Reynolds. I think he was also taking some private lessons with Damian. He was that good. Why?"

"I can't say now. I'll explain later. Thanks."

Hmm. Brandon was a college-aged young man and possibly a protégé of Damian. Interesting.

I headed to Mrs. Webster's house with a carload of fabrics. One of the projects I had taken over from Monica's assistant involved installing new window treatments and throw pillows in coordinating fabrics for one of Monica's customers. Since her usual seamstress was overwhelmed and putting Monica's projects last, probably thinking Monica wasn't coming back, I had arranged with Mrs. Webster to handle the work. She was an excellent seamstress, and when I explained what Nita and I were trying to do, she grumbled about Monica but agreed to make the draperies and pillow covers. It would help Monica's business, and the fee for the work would help Mrs. Webster financially. She would probably try to refuse payment to help Monica, but I would insist she take the payment.

After making two trips to the car to retrieve the fabrics and pillows Monica had ordered for the project, I entered the house through the screen door Mrs. Webster held open for me.

"Girl, get in here. It's hotter than blazes out there today." She firmly shut the front door behind us, preventing anymore hot air from getting in. The cooler air inside made me shiver. I hadn't realized how hot the day had become. It made me think about how much harder life had been before air conditioning.

"Where should I put these?" I looked around for a place to drop the fabric bolts, which were getting heavy.

"Take them into the dining room." She led the way, carrying the pillows I'd left on the porch. "I've turned it into my temporary sewing room. The dining room table makes the perfect place to lay out long drapery panels."

I followed her into the dining room and placed the bolts on the table along with the other items she had brought in from the porch.

"This sure is beautiful fabric," Mrs. Webster said as she stroked a bolt of celery green velvet. The colors for the various rooms were ones I'd love to have in my own home but couldn't afford.

"These fabrics will make gorgeous draperies." I handed her a folder. "Here's the information you'll need. I double-checked all the measurements in case you're wondering." The folder contained the window measurements and other guidelines, along with photos of the windows the draperies were intended for.

"I wouldn't doubt you did. You're pretty thorough. We wouldn't want to have them wrong and have Monica blame us." She took the folder and placed it on the table. "Come into the kitchen and have a seat. How about some iced tea? I just made some."

"That would be wonderful, thank you." I followed her into the kitchen and took a seat at the kitchen table.

Mrs. Webster poured us large glasses of tea and placed a slice of coffee cake in front of me without asking if I wanted some. "So tell me, what's been happening since we last talked?"

The cake looked very inviting and I dug in. I'd given Mrs. Webster a brief outline of my activities when I called to ask her about helping with the draperies. Now with more time, I filled her in on my efforts to find out more about the deaths of Ian Becker and Damian Reynolds.

"Why do you think the deaths are connected?" She refilled my now empty glass of iced tea and added more ice. Condensation dripped down the side of the glass.

"It's more wishful thinking. If they are connected, maybe then we could buy Monica's story about only pulling the knife from Damian's body and that somebody else was responsible for both killings. We need to find a link to prove that."

"Have you found a link yet?" Mrs. Webster held up the cake plate as though offering me another slice. As tempted as I was, I shook my head.

"Not really. Aunt Kit suggested a link, but it's a weak one."

"Which was?" Mrs. Webster perked up, thinking this was going to lead somewhere.

"That they both were involved in art."

"Was Ian Becker an artist too?" Mrs. Webster asked.

"That's why the link is so weak. As far as we know, he wasn't. His aunt was a member of the local arts group and dabbled in art. From what I heard, her work was rather simplistic."

"Yeah, that's a pretty weak link." She took a sip of iced tea.

"We have nothing else to go on—only a suspicion that Damian's agent Garrett Fletcher is hiding something."

I told Mrs. Webster about what Nita and I had discovered about Doris Becker's will. "Two more people were named in the will. If they knew about it, it could have given one or both of them a motive in Ian Becker's death. That is, depending on how the will was written."

"That sounds more like something out of a Margery Allingham novel. I always did like those writers from the Golden Age of Detective Fiction."

"I wish I had the experience those old writers and their detectives had. Next I need to talk to Emily Thompson, and it isn't something I look forward to."

I gathered up our dishes and took them over to the sink ready to leave.

"How is your Aunt Kit doing? Are you getting along?" Mrs. Webster asked.

That made me laugh. "You know Aunt Kit—always sees the glass half empty, just like my mom."

"People like that are fearful—braced for the worst to happen. They feel if they become the least bit optimistic they'll be disappointed. They expect the worst and then they aren't disappointed. The important thing isn't whether a glass is half full or half empty but that it can be refilled."

"That's a good thought. Aunt Kit worries about me too much. But I know she loves me and means well."

"You know, I always suspected that she was secretly in love with your father."

"It wouldn't surprise me." My father's handsome looks and charm attracted everyone to him. "I often wonder what happened to him. After my parents divorced he faded away from my life. It always hurt that he didn't try to see me."

"Why don't you ask your Aunt Kit about him. Perhaps she knows something."

"I'm not sure. My mother would get upset if I even mentioned him, so I learned not to raise the subject." Would Aunt Kit react the same way?

Chapter 34

*Make sure switch plate and outlet covers match and look new.
Consider adding mirror switch plate and outlet covers to
bathrooms to add some sparkle.*

Sunday morning as I left church and rapidly walked away, I heard hurried footsteps behind me. I'd purposely gone to an early service so I wouldn't run into Sister Madeleine, and my instincts told me I was about to have the meeting with her that I'd been trying to avoid.

"Laura, wait up."

I turned to see the small slender figure of Sister Madeleine huffing and puffing as she tried to catch up with me. I felt guilty that in my desire to avoid her, I'd caused the older nun to chase after me. I knew she would be hopeful I'd heard something that might help Monica, and I didn't want to disappoint her with the little I had learned.

There I was a grown woman in my early forties, and just hearing her call my name catapulted me back to the second grade in seconds. "Good morning, Sister Madeleine."

"When were you going to tell me about your visit with Monica?"

I hadn't told her I'd broken down and gone to see Monica, especially since I'd only done so to assuage my sense of guilt for initially not wanting to help her. How had she learned that I'd visited Monica?

"I can tell from your face you didn't know I was aware of your visit," she said, bending over, trying to catch her breath. "Monica told me you had been to see her. It quite surprised her."

"I don't know that my visit accomplished much."

"On the contrary. She said you offered to help keep her business going. That was quite generous of you considering how busy you are with your own work."

How like Sister Madeleine to make it sound as though it'd been my idea and not because she'd prodded me into it.

"I met with her assistant to determine the most pressing work—things that need to be done to meet deadlines. Nita and I've been managing." *Just barely.*

"Have you been hearing anything that could help Monica's case?"

"Nothing that would prove her to be innocent. But I learned some things that point to other possible suspects." I told her about our disastrous meeting at the B&B with Garrett Fletcher, Damian's agent. "He said Damian was his most successful client and he would be foolish to cut off the income he earned from representing him. That's true, but he could have murdered Damian in a rage and then later regretted it because of financial reasons."

She pondered that. "Could he have been mishandling Damian's earnings? Maybe Damian found out and Fletcher didn't want to be exposed."

"That's always a possibility." Something important to consider.

"What about his wife? The spouse is usually the first person the police look at."

I told her about Damian's daughter drowning and his wife subsequently divorcing him, and that she lived within driving distance of Louiston. I also told her of the scene I'd witnessed at the funeral home when I saw Damian's ex-wife and agent embracing.

"That's interesting. But it's unlikely she would have murdered him years later. She has her other daughter to think about. We can't discount that. Have you spoken to her?"

I hunched my shoulders, feeling like I did when I hadn't completed my homework. "No. I'm hoping something will come to light and it won't be necessary."

That seemed to satisfy Sister Madeleine.

"There's another biggie. Nita and I discovered Ian's aunt, Doris Becker, left part of her estate to Emily Thompson, Ian's old girlfriend, and Brandon Thompson."

"Now that adds some spice to the brew." Sister Madeleine looked almost gleeful as though I'd pulled a diamond from a bag of coal.

"Tomorrow, I'm going to visit Emily to see what I can find out. It's difficult questioning people when you don't have any authority to do so." My blood pressure felt like it was rising just thinking about it.

"Did you ever think you might have more luck assisting the police in their investigation rather than going it alone. And it would be safer. What about working with Detective Spangler and sharing information with him?"

That made me want to hoot with laughter. "If there were any sharing of information, it would be one way—from me to him."

"Perhaps if you befriended him you might get more cooperation. If you remember from Ellis Peters' medieval mystery series, Brother Cadfael was able to accomplish far more in solving the mysteries facing him because of his friendship with the Shrewsbury sheriff, Hugh Beringar."

Befriend Detective Spangler. That would be the day. "Detective Spangler views me as a busybody." My cheeks burned at the memory of being called a busybody by Garrett Fletcher. Did other people view me that way as well?

"There's a difference between being a busybody and an astute observer of people. Agatha Christie's Miss Marple was considered by some to be a busybody, but it was her observations of people that made her so successful in solving mysteries."

"Okay, I'll try. But don't expect Detective Spangler and me to have the same kind of relationship Brother Cadfael and Hugh Beringar had."

"All you can do is try," Sister Madeleine said and turned away.

I walked the short distance home deep in thought. I'd promised Sister Madeleine I would try working with Detective Spangler. I didn't say when.

Chapter 35

Pay as much attention to the outside of your home as the inside.
Trim shrubbery, plant flowers, and lay mulch.

It didn't take long to find an address for Emily Thompson. The
question was what excuse could I use to talk to her? What approach
could I use? Would I find her at home? If I called before I went to
see her, she would have time to prepare for my questions and raise
her defenses. Or she might refuse to talk to me. But she could also
shrug and say it was nothing to do with her.

I drove up steep winding roads onto Miller's Mountain until I
found the turn-off to the Thompson place. A large red barn stood in
the distance. Nearby, a woman on horseback galloped across a
broad pasture.

I parked my car next to the barn, and after not seeing anyone
else around, I walked over to the fenced pasture, watching in
amazement as the rider and horse jumped over stacked bales of
hay. When they turned in my direction, I waved to the rider, who
guided her horse toward the fence. I stepped back from the fence,
surprised at how tall the horse was and how high up the rider sat.
The rider slowly slid from the horse and landed with a thump,
raising a cloud of dust. I was a city girl and found the dust and the
smell of hay and dung somewhat overpowering.

The woman took off her helmet and shook out her long brown

hair. She looked to be in her early forties or perhaps younger. It was hard to tell. If she'd spent time working out of doors, and with the toll the sun can take on your skin, she could have been much younger than she looked. Either that or she could have had a hard life.

The woman walked over to the fence railing close to where I stood. "Hi, there. Can I help you?"

"Hi, I'm looking for Emily Thompson." I tried to sound friendly and buoyant so as not to put her on her guard.

"You found her. If you're looking to board a horse, I'm full up at the moment, but I may have space in a few weeks." Her long legs were clad in faded jeans, which were tucked into high riding boots that had seen hard service. If riding a horse accounted for her slim figure, I would have to consider trying it.

"Uh, no. I don't own a horse." Rarely venturing from town, I hadn't known the surrounding area had enough horses to need places to board them. I wondered if Will Parker, a retired rodeo star who had come east to live with his daughter and her family, knew about this place. For that matter, I didn't know if he even still rode. I made a mental note to tell him about this place.

"I'm Laura Bishop from down in Louiston. I'd like to ask you a few questions if you have some time."

Emily opened the gate and led the horse from the field. "If you can wait a few minutes until I can get Gertie here cooled down and fed, I'd be happy to talk to you." She patted the horse on the neck and fed her a carrot she took from a pocket. "She hasn't been exercised as much recently as she should have been, so I gave her more of a workout than usual. I'm going to walk her for a few minutes and then hose her off. You're welcome to follow me unless you'd rather wait here."

I eyed the back of the large horse, reluctant to get closer, barely avoiding being hit in the face by a swishing tail. My approach to questioning Emily might be more casual if she were occupied caring for Gertie.

"Sure, I'll follow along."

"Okay, but watch where you step." I looked down and saw why she had warned me. Ugh.

I followed Emily into what I assumed was a paddock where she led Gertie around for several minutes to cool down. Again I was struck with how big the horse was and how easily Emily guided it to where she wanted it to go. She then led Gertie to a water trough, where the horse took a long drink of water and then shook her head, spraying me with drops of water.

Minutes before I had been neatly dressed and sitting in an air-conditioned car. I pulled a piece of straw from my hair. Now I was sweaty, covered in water, and wearing good sandals that were covered in dirt. I looked down at the ground around me. Hopefully, by the time I left there, my sandals wouldn't be covered with anything else.

Emily led Gertie into the barn. Her hoofs beating on the ground made clopping sounds. I followed, continuing to look down at where I stepped, and once inside, studied the variety of equipment hanging on the wall. Most of it was made of leather and brass. With half of my mind always on my business, I couldn't help but think how perfect some of the pieces would be as wall décor in a home of horse lovers.

Emily tethered Gertie to a post, and then unfastened, removed, and stored the saddle. Muscles she'd developed over years of doing hard work were evident in her arms. She was extremely fit. She then took a hose and showered Gertie with a gentle spray of water. The day was hot and the spray looked inviting, I was tempted to step into it myself. Gertie stood patiently as Emily brushed her with a pad or some type of brush, using long and short strokes. Seeing Gertie's contented look, I felt I had stepped into a horse spa.

Watching all that Emily was doing for Gertie proved so fascinating, I completely forgot about my plan to question Emily as she worked.

After Emily completed her chores, she walked over to a small sink and washed her hands. "Sorry. That was probably a lot longer than you wanted to wait, but I didn't want to leave Gertie's cool down until later, especially on such a hot day."

"It was interesting. I didn't realize horses needed so much care."

"We run a good place here, and the folks who leave their horses with us know that we'll take proper care of them. Lots of places only do a halfway job of it."

She pointed to some bales of hay, and we both took a seat.

"So Laura, what'd you want to talk about, if not about boarding a horse?"

I took a deep breath and then wished I hadn't. The odor of horse, hay, and manure was beginning to overwhelm me. How to proceed?

"I know this is going to sound strange, but I'm here because I'm trying to help a friend. And to do that, I need to ask some questions you might rather I didn't ask."

That caught her attention, but so far she hadn't darted from the barn. I couldn't believe I had used the term friend for Monica, but what the heck.

"You may have heard that Monica Heller was arrested for the murder of Damian Reynolds, an artist teaching at Fischer College. To help in her defense, a friend and I are looking at anything that could raise doubt she did it."

"What's that got to do with me? My son had him as an instructor at the college, but I didn't know him."

This was the hard part. "With his death occurring so close to that of Ian Becker, and with both of them being stabbed, we're looking into both of their deaths to see if there could be a connection. I know it is a stretch, but we want to consider anything that could help us in Monica's defense."

Emily's open expression changed as soon as I mentioned Ian Becker. I couldn't tell whether the look on her face expressed anger, pain, or desolation. She didn't say anything, so I continued.

"I'm very sorry about Ian's death. I was one of the people who found him in Hendricks Funeral Home."

"Again, why are you coming to see me about this?"

"The police discovered from Ian's phone records that you were one of the people he telephoned when he arrived in Louiston. I also heard that you and Ian dated the last summer he spent here with his aunt."

Her expression became mulish. Would I be able to get anything from her?

After several long seconds, she responded. "Yeah, he called and left a message on the answering machine. Said he wanted to see me—probably for old times' sake. A police detective came to see me about the call, and I told him the same thing."

Detective Spangler had already been there. That was no surprise.

"So you didn't talk to Ian?"

"No. I didn't particularly want to see him, so I didn't call back. It'd been a long time since he was here, and my life has gone on."

"That's all?"

From behind us, a voice shouted. "Tell her. Tell her that he got you pregnant with me and then ran off—out of the country and didn't look back."

I turned to look behind me. A tall blond young man of about eighteen or nineteen stood in the opening to the barn. Dressed in old, dust-covered jeans, he looked as though he had spent the day working outside. His face was flushed and one of his hands was curled into a fist. In his other hand, he held a rake.

A shocked look crossed Emily's face. "Brandon, stay out of this."

"Why are you keeping this a secret? He's dead. He didn't care anything about us, or he wouldn't have fled the country and left you as he did."

The anger the young man felt toward his absent father was visible on his face, which held a scowl. Had Brandon been angry enough with Ian to want him dead?

"Leave now, before you make this worse." Emily stood and pointed to the large barn doors behind us. I thought for a second he was going to refuse, but after glaring at his mother for what seemed like minutes, he thrust away the rake he'd been holding and stomped away.

Emily sighed, sank back onto the hay bale, and covered her face with her hands. "Why did Ian have to come back?"

Perhaps she was fortunate Ian hadn't come back before. Since having a son and an elderly aunt who had helped raise him hadn't been enough reason for him to come back in twenty years, they might have been better off without him. It was only when Ted had notified him that he was the executor of his aunt's estate that he bothered to return. What kind of a father would he have been if his only motivation to come now had possibly been because of money?

"Ian was such a charmer. I should never have gotten involved with him, but he had been so different from the boys I had grown up with. When we met, I think he was attracted to me. But when he discovered we had horses, he flipped. He loved to ride. You could say I came with benefits." At that, she laughed. "It was a toss-up as to what he found more irresistible—me or the horses."

"Did he know you were pregnant?"

"Oh, yes. I told him right before he was to join his family for their move to New Zealand. His father had accepted a job there and would be gone for a few years, so Ian and his mother went too. When I told him, he couldn't leave the country fast enough. I never forgave him for that."

"When he called you, was that the first time you heard from him in all these years?"

"That's right. You can imagine what a shock it was hearing his message. When I had to tell my dad about the baby, he got in touch with Ian's aunt. Dad made it clear that Ian should be held responsible, but she convinced him that nothing good would come of it and that she would help us financially. She said she could more than afford to do so. Ian was very immature, and quite frankly, a little odd. Maybe she was protecting us. From what she said over the years, he never really grew up. Ian was someone with, what do you call it, a Peter Pan syndrome. He was happy to surf, have fun, and live off his father's money."

"What about Brandon? When did he discover who his father was?"

"I told him when he turned fifteen, thinking at that age he would be old enough to understand. I should never have told him. It would have been better if I had listed Father Unknown on the birth certificate and left it at that. He demanded to know more about Ian and asked where he could find him. It got worse after my father died and there was no longer a father figure around. Fortunately, I didn't have an address for Ian, but Doris did.

"How did he know of Doris?"

"He found a check Doris sent me and asked about it. He's a pretty smart kid and put it all together. I hadn't wanted to accept money from her, but she insisted. She said Brandon deserved it, and if nothing else, I could save it for his college expenses. And that's what I've been using it for. I think she felt guilty that she hadn't kept better tabs on Ian when he stayed with her. As if that would have mattered. He'd always run wild. I think his parents were happy to shunt him off to her each summer."

"Brandon seemed pretty angry at Ian."

"That's because he wrote to Ian, but Ian never wrote back. Brandon convinced Doris to give him Ian's address. Her health was beginning to fail and it was easy to get it out of her. If she had been in better health, she might not have given it to him."

"Did Brandon know Ian was in town and called you?"

"Brandon heard the message Ian left."

The look on her face said volumes. She was terrified Brandon had killed Ian.

Brandon knew Damian Reynolds and was connected to Ian Becker. Perhaps Emily Thompson had reason to worry.

Chapter 36

Unpleasant odors can put off prospective buyers. Remove carpets and rugs that are stained and can trap offensive odors.

During dinner that evening, Aunt Kit proved to be a great sounding board. Of course, it came with the usual warnings about dire consequences.

"Have you reported anything you've learned to the police? You need to involve them in this. It was one thing for Sister Madeleine to want you to help Monica's business while she is in jail, but it's a completely different thing for you to be asking questions about Damian's murder."

"Well for a start, I'm only asking questions. We haven't learned anything the police probably don't already know, and they don't want people getting involved in their investigations. I'm simply making inquiries and taking an approach the police may not be taking."

"Do you think the police are inept?"

Wasn't that always how the amateur sleuths in the mysteries I read frequently viewed the police? "Of course not. I may not be crazy about Detective Spangler, but I respect him for his abilities. It doesn't hurt for citizens to assist the police. They don't suspect a link between Ian and Damian's deaths. Primarily because we caught Monica over Damian's body, so she looks pretty guilty. Also, there's nothing that shows a motive for her killing Ian."

"What about Emily and Brandon Thompson?"

"That's a hard one. I think eventually over the years Emily was happy to have Ian stay out of her life and didn't want anything more to do with him. It helped that Doris helped them financially, so she hadn't built up resentment because they had to struggle financially. But I'm not sure about Brandon. He's filled with anger. Now whether he was angry enough to stab Ian in the back, that's another thing. I can't see that, but who knows. He took classes from Damian Reynolds, but I haven't heard anything that would point to a motive for Brandon to kill him."

Aunt Kit picked at the sautéed chicken I'd made especially for her. The one with mushrooms and Harvey's cream sherry she liked. When she finally took a bite, she chewed it for so long I worried it might have become too dry for her to swallow. If Aunt Kit choked when swallowing it, would I be able to do the Heimlich maneuver on her?

"I wonder how much of a relationship Doris had with Emily and Brandon, especially since Brandon was her grandnephew?" I held my breath, watching Aunt Kit continue to chew.

She finally swallowed. "Anne Williamson was a good friend to Doris. I'm going to have lunch with Anne tomorrow. I'll ask her what she knows. By the way, is this a new recipe? It's a bit dry. You might want to add a bit of Harvey's next time you make it."

What? Nita had been right. I should have added a double measure of it to her food.

"Also, how about Damian's agent?"

"As far as I know, he wasn't in town when Damian was murdered. But who's to say he couldn't have come into town without anyone knowing it, got into another argument with Damian, and stabbed him in anger. But he made a very good point. If he had killed Damian, he definitely would have cut off a major source of his income."

"People have done stupider things than that. Who else do you have to look at?" Aunt Kit took another bite of chicken, and again I held my breath.

"Nita's niece said that one of the professors at the college held a grudge against Damian—something about his wife having a history with him. Then there's Damian's ex-wife. She held him responsible for their daughter's drowning—enough so that it resulted in their divorce. I'll probably leave that one until last." With any luck, I wouldn't have to talk to her.

I cleared the table, ready for dessert, which I knew Aunt Kit would have no trouble swallowing—strawberry shortcake. With ice cream.

Aunt Kit surveyed the room, looking around her. "You've done a lovely job brightening this place since your mother died. You didn't get your decorating talent from her, that's for sure."

"Thanks. The brighter yellow paint gives the place a completely different feel from when I was growing up." When my mother lived there, the house had been very gloomy, which pretty much matched her outlook on life. Now might be the perfect time to ask Aunt Kit about my mother and dad.

"Speaking of Mom, I can't help but wonder what happened to my dad. I only saw him a few times after they divorced, but then he stopped coming to visit me. When I asked her about him, she said that he'd moved away from the area and didn't want to see either one of us. Later when I asked her again, she said he had died and then quickly changed the subject. Even as young as I was, I didn't quite believe her. When I was older and had the wherewithal to search for him, I was so hurt that he'd turned his back on us, on me, that I decided I didn't care and didn't want to know.

Aunt Kit frowned as though the memory of my dad was a painful one, and it made me wonder about Mrs. Webster's suspicion that Aunt Kit had been in love with him. But from what my mother had said, many women had been enamored with him. At least that was what she believed.

"Your parents were terribly mismatched. Unfortunately, your mother never saw anything but doom and gloom, and your dad was just the opposite. I give him a lot of credit living with her for as long as he did."

"She said she divorced him because he had been unfaithful. Was that true?"

"She believed he'd been involved with another woman. He could have been, but I don't know if that was the case. He was utterly handsome—and charming in a nice kind of way, so it wouldn't have surprised me if other women hadn't come on to him. As to where he is, I don't know. I never heard that he was dead, so that story surprises me. But after all these years, he could be."

"I should have tried harder to find out about him. But after I married Derrick and came to know of his affairs with other women, I couldn't tolerate the idea that my dad had been the same way, and I didn't want anything to do with him. I came to understand better why my mother was so bitter, but that doesn't explain why he didn't want me in his life."

Aunt Kit stopped eating her shortcake and ice cream and looked at me with gentle eyes. "Your father loved you very much."

"Then why hasn't he tried to contact me after all these years? He could have another family now and might not want to hear from me."

"Well, then, you won't know unless you try." Aunt Kit added another scoop of vanilla ice cream to her bowl.

"I'll think about it. Right now, I have to focus on my business, Monica's business, and trying to convince the police to further investigate the link between Ian and Damian." If that were possible.

Chapter 37

Add seasonal scents. In the fall and winter, simmer apple cider with cinnamon. In the spring and summer, add a vase of fragrant lilacs or roses.

There was no way I could avoid it. I needed to talk to Detective Spangler about Monica's case. Even at the risk of being called a busybody twice in one week. But rather than going to his office, I decided I might have better luck meeting him away from his turf and on neutral territory. I knew from the past he frequently went to Hibbard's Bakery in the morning, so early the next day I waited outside the bakery in my car, hoping he'd show up.

There were pros and cons to that plan. If I waited until he got inside, it might appear I was following him. If I waited inside, he might grab something and be out the door before I could catch him. Amateur sleuthing could be exasperating.

When my car got too hot without the air conditioner running, I broke down and decided to wait inside. The lure of coffee and freshly made donuts and pastries helped. The donuts wouldn't be nutritious, but I needed a reward for my efforts.

Just as I reached the door, Detective Spangler came from the other direction. I couldn't have planned it any better.

"Well, Ms. Bishop, we continue to collide in doorways."

"Good morning, Detective Spangler. In need of coffee?"

"Always."

He opened the door and allowed me to enter first, which meant I could be first at the counter to place my order. Good. That way I could sit down and it would be up to him to join me or not. I gave myself a good mental shake. This was beginning to feel like being back in high school and plotting to run into a crush.

I took a seat in a back booth, unwrapped my English scone with butterscotch chips, and took a bite. Heaven. I then took a sip of coffee and tried to look nonchalant—or as relaxed and unconcerned as I could, which wasn't easy when facing a talk with Detective Spangler. We always seemed to be on opposite sides of a discussion.

"May I join you?"

I looked up to see Detective Spangler. "Please do."

He sat down and unwrapped a giant bear claw pastry and took a big bite. That gave me a chance to speak while he had a mouth full.

"I'm glad I ran into you, Detective. I've been meaning to talk to you about Monica Heller."

I waited for him to finish chewing and swallow, which seemed to take forever. I seemed to be spending a lot of time recently watching people chew. What was with these men and their big bites? Didn't they know you can choke on a bite that size?

He then slowly took a sip of coffee. "You're going to say she's a friend of yours and she could never have killed someone. Is that it?"

That was far from the truth. "Not really. My relationship with Monica has never been a friendly one and, given half a chance, she might stab me in the back. Figuratively, not literally. But I can't believe she stabbed Damian." Perhaps I should have said Sister Madeleine couldn't believe that. I still had my doubts.

"Figuratively, okay. What did you want to say about her?" He finished the bear claw in about four bites.

This was going to sound just about as stupid, but I decided I might as well just jump right in. "You know we never saw Monica stab Damian. She swears she only removed the knife."

"Yes, she's stated that, but there's nothing to prove it. No other suspect, no one seen running from the scene of the crime by you or anyone else. We see this all the time. We catch someone with a smoking gun. When we ask, 'Is that your gun?' we get a response. 'Not my gun.' As though it had just appeared out of thin air. Do you have anything concrete you can present to prove Ms. Heller didn't stab Damian Reynolds?

"No, but that's what I want to get to. I think you need to look more closely at a possible link between Damian's murder and Ian Becker's murder."

He took a long swallow of coffee and eyed me over the rim of his cup. "Ms. Bishop, give us some credit. Don't you think we've already done that? Other than both victims being stabbed, we found no other link. What possible link do you think there could've been?"

"Maybe art? Ian's aunt was a member of the local art group." It still sounded pretty weak.

His eyes narrowed and he slammed his coffee cup on the table. "Please don't tell me you've been questioning people about these cases."

"No, not really...well, maybe a little. When you are in business, you come into contact with people."

"And someone told you because Ian's aunt dabbled in art she might have had some connection to a *world-famous artist*?"

"My Aunt Kit suggested—"

He groaned, the equivalent of rolling his eyes. "Suggested what? That because they both had lifted a paintbrush there was enough reason to connect the murders?"

"Wait. There's more."

"Please tell me. I can't wait to hear what other reasons you have. When you were younger, did you want to be a police officer?"

There was no warming up to this guy, regardless of how attractive he was, and single. "Did you know that Ian's aunt, Doris Becker, named two local people in her will and that one of them was Ian's illegitimate son?"

"But how does that link the two murders? In one of those mystery novels you read, that might've been a motive in Ian's murder. But considering Doris Becker left little to any of them, that's not enough to suspect them of killing Ian."

"There's always that possibility. Ian's son Brandon was really angry at his father for deserting them when he went off to New Zealand."

"Angry enough to want to kill him as soon as he arrived in town?" He paused. "We've already questioned Emily and Brandon Thompson. I didn't learn that Brandon had tried to contact his father, so I'll look at him again. Even if it were true and Brandon was responsible for Ian's death, that doesn't link him to Damian's murder."

"Did you know that Brandon took some classes from Damian at the college?

Detective Spangler pressed his lips into a thin line. "No, I didn't know that. And you think what, that he could have taken revenge on Damian for giving him a less than desirable grade?"

I gave him a withering look. "Don't you see? He could be the link between Damian and Ian."

"Okay. I'll check it out."

Maybe another tactic might work. "Did you know that Damian's ex-wife blamed him for their daughter's drowning? She lives only a couple hours' drive from here. And he was unable to paint because of the trauma of the accident."

"Yes, we know all that."

"And that Damian and his agent argued? And his agent resented Monica."

"Yes. Anything more?" He wadded up the paper wrapping from his bear claw, preparing to leave.

"Okay, here's this: Did you know that Professor Albertson's wife and Damian had a history and the professor resented him because of it? Professor Albertson is on the faculty at Fischer College

"You've got me there. I didn't know that, but I'll check it out."

He stood up, ready to leave. "Did you hear me? I'll check it out."

"Can you let me know what you learn?"

He groaned again. "Ms. Bishop..."

"Yes, detective?"

"Stay safe." With that, he walked away.

Drat! I forgot to ask him about the knife used to stab Damian. If it had been one from his kitchen, whoever killed him could have become enraged and reached for it. If however, the knife wasn't one of his, the killer must have brought one with him. That could prove the murder was premeditated. The same thing could've been said about Ian's murder. What about that knife?

Monica said she went to Damian's house to find out why he wanted to cancel the decorating orders. She probably wouldn't have gone armed with a knife for that discussion. Would she?

Chapter 38

A home for sale as-is can sit on the market months longer than homes that are move-in ready.

It was one thing trying to solve the mystery of two murders, but it was another thing trying to do it while attempting to make a living. Fortunately, we had been getting calls from people who'd picked up our flyers at the Small Business Fair. I'd spent the last two hours doing a consultation with a man who wanted to sell his home and move to Florida. I didn't realize it would be just him there. And although he was a nice man, I decided in the future I would take Nita or Tyrone along on calls from men. You just can't be too careful.

After I had gone over his home and made recommendations, we stood on his porch talking. "Since my wife has gone down to Florida to take care of her mother, that leaves all this staging to me. Sometimes I think we should ship everything to Florida and sell the house as it is."

"That's entirely up to you. But with vacant homes, buyers are in and out within minutes and make quicker decisions. They'll stay longer in a furnished home, and the longer they stay, the more likely they are to imagine themselves living there. If you'd like to move your things sooner than later, we could always bring some furnishings in to make your home look lived in. Also, be aware that if you sell it as-is, it could sit on the market for a while. We could help you get it in condition to sell."

"All at a cost?"

"Yes, but within your budget. The staging cost will be far less than your first price reduction if it doesn't sell right away."

"Yeah. Furniture or no furniture, it needs to sell fast. The house across the street will be going up for sale soon, and I don't want to be competing with it. I thought it would go on the market by now, but the nephew of the woman who owned it was murdered. I don't know what'll happen to it now."

"Murdered?" I looked at the large Victorian home. "Was that Doris Becker's house?"

"Yeah, it was. Did you know Doris?"

"No. I just read about her nephew in the paper." It didn't serve any purpose telling him that I'd been one of the people who found him.

He slowly shook his head several times. "Sure was a shame about him. He used to spend summers with her when he was a youngster."

"Did you know Doris Becker well?"

"Not really. She kept pretty much to herself. But the times I talked to her, I found her to be a real nice lady. She was a painter, but we never saw anything she painted. Too afraid people would laugh at it. Darn shame she developed dementia. Got to the point where she didn't know who we were."

I looked over at the house with its large wrap-around porch and a huge turret. With all that natural light, the turret must have been a lovely place for Doris to paint.

"Sad she lived there all alone for so many years." I felt a pang thinking about how lonely she might have been. It made me think of Aunt Kit growing older and living alone in another town.

"She used to have friends come and go, but over the past few years, the only person I saw was that woman from the arts group— Anne somebody."

"Anne Williamson?"

"Yeah. That's right. We'd see her going in a couple of times a week. She'd carry in groceries and occasionally bring things out. I went over once to ask if I could give her a hand loading up her car, but she said she was managing fine. Said she was taking some of Doris's things down to the Salvation Army to donate. I have to give it to her. For a woman her age, she didn't have any problems carrying that stuff. Awfully nice lady to help Doris as she did."

The grand old Victorian house had seen better days. The shrubbery was overgrown, the paint was chipping off, and one piece of decorative grillwork around the top of the porch was barely hanging on. "The house could use some work." I wondered what it looked like inside.

"That's another reason I'm anxious to sell soon. The more neglected that place becomes, the harder it'll be to sell. And it'll affect prices around here."

As I drove back home, I used my cell phone to check in with Kimberly, Monica's assistant, and made arrangements to see her tomorrow about another project. Just as I hung up, I received a call from Nita.

"Did you schedule an appointment to meet with someone this afternoon?" Nita asked.

"I don't believe so. Or if I did, I don't remember it. Everything has been so chaotic. Why?"

"We received a message on our website confirming your appointment with an M. Cassatt at two."

"Oh, dear." Great for business, but not great for my schedule. I pulled over to the side of the road and entered the address Nita gave me into my phone. Looking at my watch, I had just enough time to get there.

"Thanks, Nita. It would have been embarrassing if I'd missed that one. I'll check in with you when I've finished there."

I drove to the address Nita had given me and parked in front of the mid-century modern home with a large For Sale sign hanging out front. M. Cassatt must be a real estate agent I didn't know. *Thank you, Nita, for alerting me.* I didn't want to miss an appointment with an agent since they referred work to us. Finding a better method for keeping track of appointments needed to go on my to-do list.

No other cars were parked nearby, so thankfully, I wasn't late and had arrived before Mr. or Ms. Cassatt. That would give me time to evaluate what attention the outside of the house might need. As I got out of my car, I looked toward the house and saw the front door was open. That was strange. Perhaps M. Cassatt had parked in the back.

I knocked on the door, and receiving no response, pushed it open further. "Hello, anyone here?" Still no response. Perhaps the agent had left the door open for me to get in and would be back. Well, if nothing else, it would enable me to look at the house and be better prepared to discuss a staging approach. I pulled a notebook from my canvas tote bag ready to make notes.

The home was empty, so we wouldn't have to deal with furniture that might not be in good shape or attractive—or with furniture not in keeping with a mid-century modern home. Homeowners frequently selected furniture so out of character with the style of their homes. I could never understand why someone would buy a modern home and then fill it with Victorian furniture.

I noted the terrazzo floors in the living and dining rooms and then headed down a long hall toward the bedrooms. I scrunched up my nose at the musty smell that permeated the house and pointed to a need for a good airing—or maybe something more drastic. I made a note about needing some charcoal air filter bags to help with the musty odor.

I turned into the first bedroom and gave it a quick look. The carpet was a bit worse for wear and would need to be replaced or pulled up. With any luck, terrazzo flooring would be under the carpeting.

The master bedroom was a good size. As I stepped into the room, suddenly something dark flapped over my head and strong arms wrapped around my middle. Before I could react, I felt myself being pushed forward into the nearby closet. I hit the closet wall and felt pain shoot across my shoulder and down my arm. My knees buckled and I collapsed onto the floor with a thud.

The door slammed behind me, and I found myself enveloped in darkness. Once I had gotten over the shock, I realized that I still had some type of cloth or blanket covering my head. I struggled with it and once I got it off, I could see a thin band of light at the bottom of the door.

When I could get my wits about me, I stood and tried the door handle. It turned easily, but when I pushed against it, it wouldn't budge. I pounded on the door. "Help. Let me out." A lot of good that was going to do. Whoever had locked me in wasn't going to respond to my pleas for help.

In the struggle, I'd dropped my bag and along with it my cell phone. All I could do was hope the person who'd locked me in the closet was satisfied to leave me there and that was all. I shuddered to think for what purpose?

Chapter 39

Packed closets will give the appearance of limited storage space.

Hours later, or what seemed like hours, I was hoarse from yelling for help, thirsty, and desperate to use a bathroom. The air conditioner was running in the house, but not enough to reach the confined area of the closet. I was dripping with perspiration.

Each time I heard a car drive by, I shouted for help, but to no avail. My hands ached from pounding on the door. Then I thought of my little Inky and hoped Aunt Kit was home and would feed him.

I couldn't believe I was locked in a closet. What would possess someone to do that? Did that person plan to come back later to let me out, or worse? I took in several deep breaths and let them out slowly, trying to stave off a panic attack. I tried to center myself as I had learned to do taking Yoga.

At the last house I'd visited, I thought it probably wouldn't be a good idea to go alone to houses unless there was a woman there. Now I'd have to take someone with me to empty houses. Was there any place safe for women these days?

A car door slammed. I pounded on the door and shouted, "Help! Help me!" Then it occurred to me that it could be the person who imprisoned me who had come back, and I started to shiver all over. Still, I shouted.

I heard a faint voice calling my name. I kept shouting for help, but being inside a closet, it would be difficult for someone to hear me. Fortunately, the house was a rambler, and the bedroom was on the ground floor and faced the street.

"Laura? Are you in there?" It was Tyrone. Thank God.

"Yes, yes. I'm in here." I shouted as loud as I could and pounded on the door. "I'm locked in a closet."

Tyrone's voice got louder. "Hold on, I'll try the front door."

"Forget the front door. Break the window." Mrs. Webster was there with him. I sent up a double thank you.

"Okay, Laura, stand back. I'm going to throw a rock through the window," Tyrone called.

Since I wasn't anywhere near a window, that made me laugh. It felt good to laugh considering how desperate my situation had been.

I heard a crash and then the sound of glass falling—followed by another crash. Mrs. Webster must have thrown a rock too.

"I've got it, hold on," Tyrone called out. "It's a crank out window."

Seconds later, the door opened and Tyrone stood in the opening. Fresh air filled the closet and helped revive me. "Hold on Tyrone. I'll hug you once I've gone down the hall."

I finished in the bathroom and when I came out, Tyrone and Mrs. Webster were waiting for me. I hugged each of them. "I don't know what brought you here, but thank you."

"It was Nita," Tyrone said. "When you didn't call her back or answer your cell phone, she got concerned. She called to ask me if I had heard from you."

"Girl, you had us good and worried, especially when we pulled up and saw your car parked in front and everything locked up." As strong as Mrs. Webster usually appeared, she looked shaken. "We decided to circle the house and heard your cry. If the bedroom had been on the second floor, we probably wouldn't have heard you."

"But how did you decide to look here?"

"Nita said you had an appointment at two at this address. I had just picked Gran up from one of her church group meetings and was heading home. I told Nita we would drive by here on our way. We thought maybe your meeting had taken longer than expected, and with your history of not having a cell phone that always gets reception, we figured you might not have thought to or been able to call Nita to check in as you'd said you would."

"That was my old phone. My new one gets good reception, but I dropped my bag with my phone in it when someone grabbed me."

"Who was the rascal that locked you in there? Are you hurt?" Mrs. Webster picked up my bag from the floor and handed it to me. I was thankful it was still there.

"I never saw anyone. I found the house unlocked and went in thinking the agent had left it open for me to view and would be back. I thought perhaps the agent had gone for coffee or something. If I had been smart, when I saw that no one was here, I would have called the agent listed on the For Sale sign. Life learned the hard way."

Tyrone's face was creased in anger. "I can't believe someone locked you in that closet. How'd that happen without you seeing who it was?"

"After I walked into the master bedroom, I no sooner entered when someone pulled a blanket over my head and grabbed me. Before I could react, he shoved me into the closet. It all happened so fast." I rubbed my shoulder.

"Let me see that." Mrs. Webster gently extended my arm and rotated it. "Does that pain you?"

"It's sore from where my shoulder hit the wall, but I can move my arm okay."

Sirens sounded in the distance and kept getting closer. When they stopped in front of the house, I turned to Mrs. Webster and Tyrone. "Are the police coming here?"

Mrs. Webster held up her cell phone, which I didn't even know she owned. "As soon as we realized you were locked in that closet, I called 911. We didn't know how we would find you, and we needed to report this crime."

Tyrone had opened the door from the inside after he had

climbed in through the window and let Mrs. Webster in, so the door was open when the police officer and EMTs arrived.

An officer I didn't know came in. "Are you hurt, ma'am?"

"No, I'm just banged up a bit."

"But what about that?" He pointed to drops of blood that had landed on the floor near our feet.

I looked at it puzzled.

"Oh, that's me." Tyrone held up his right hand. "I cut it on the glass when I put my hand through the window to unlock it and crank it open. It's just a scratch. Sorry, I forgot about it."

Mrs. Webster, always the nurse, grabbed his hand and examined it. "I think you may need a few stitches there." She reached into her large purse and pulled out a wad of tissues and pressed it against the wound. "Hold this against it until we can get you to the emergency room."

"Oh, Tyrone. I'm so sorry you were hurt," I said.

I looked up to see Detective Spangler coming through the doorway. "We meet again, Detective." I spoke with more bravado than I was feeling. Anger began to build up in me the longer I thought about the person who had locked me up and because Tyrone had been injured as a result of it.

Detective Spangler studied me closely. "Are you okay? When I heard the call go out, I followed, not knowing what we'd find."

"My shoulder is a bit sore, but other than that, I'm okay." I told him everything that happened.

"It sounds like someone purposely lured you here. You have nothing to go on except for an email from an M. Cassatt?"

"That's all. I thought it was strange that we received a reminder for an appointment that none of us remembered making, but at the time I figured one of us forgot to mark it down." I paused. "Sorry, one second. Mrs. Webster, could you please let Nita know that I'm okay."

"I already have. She's madder than a wet hornet."

I followed Detective Spangler down the hall to the master bedroom and stood aside as he perused the empty room. Empty except for a pole-like device lying on the floor. He took out a white cloth handkerchief and used it to pick it up. "It's one of those devices you put under a door handle to secure it when you don't have a door lock or you want additional security in a door with a lock. People frequently use them when staying in hotel rooms."

"Since the house is empty, someone brought it to lock me in that closet?"

"Afraid so." His expression was grim. "The question is who did you rile up enough to do that. The fact somebody contacted you to get you out here shows that it wasn't a random act—someone seeing you enter an empty place and taking advantage of the situation."

"But there was nobody here, or I didn't think anyone was here."

"Obviously someone was waiting for you behind the door. But the question is who and why? I'll have an officer visit the other houses on this street to see if anyone saw someone going into the house. But since it was midday, no one may have been home."

"Detective?" We looked up to see a uniform office standing there.

"Yes, what is it?"

"The back door was jimmied open."

Tyrone jumped from where he had been sitting on the floor. "You mean I went through that window when the back door was open the whole time?"

When the detective walked away with the officer to investigate the back door, Tyrone leaned toward me and whispered. "Do you think I could be charged for breaking that window and entering?"

"I don't think so. Not in an emergency." But given Tyrone's experience with the police when he had been charged with murdering a homeowner, I could well understand his concern.

Detective Spangler came back into the front room. "Looks like whoever attacked you got into the house through the back door. It was definitely a setup. I've called the real estate agent who will notify the homeowner. The agent said he'd be right over to secure the place."

I suddenly felt weary. "Can we go now? We'd like to get Tyrone to the emergency room. Mrs. Webster said his hand might need stitches, and the EMTs who were here confirmed it."

Mrs. Webster, who had been sitting on the floor as well, stood and came over to where we were standing. "I'll go with Tyrone to the hospital. You go on ahead home."

Detective Spangler looked up from the notebook he was making notes in. "Wait a few minutes and I'll drop you at your place. You may not want to drive after your experience."

"Thank you. I'd appreciate that. Aunt Kit and I can come back for my car tomorrow."

I said goodbye to Mrs. Webster and thanked Tyrone again for his heroic effort in rescuing me. I didn't know what I'd do without the people in my life who frequently came to my aid.

Now I had to face a ride to my home with Detective Spangler.

Chapter 40

Shine a light on dark areas of the house. Increase light by replacing dim light bulbs with high-wattage or LED bulbs.

Being enclosed in a vehicle with Detective Spangler proved to be awkward. He vibrated with anger, and I could almost feel it bouncing off me. The vein on the side of his neck began to pulse.

After minutes of stony silence, he cleared his throat and finally spoke. "I don't know what to make of you. I know you want to help your friend, but don't you realize when you start asking questions of people who could be connected to a murder victim or involved in the crime you could be endangering yourself?" His carefully controlled tone said more than if he had shouted at me.

"Do you have any idea how lucky you were? If the person who attacked you had been involved in one of the murders, you could now be dead. Why that person only locked you in a closet, I'll never know. Perhaps it was a warning. But whoever it was took a big chance giving you that warning. Next time you may not be so fortunate."

"We don't know for sure what happened today was connected to my asking questions. It could simply have been someone who was looking for an easy target." Even as I said those words, I didn't believe them myself.

I shrank further into my side of the front seat, duly chastised.

Abruptly I sat up. "Wait a minute. If someone was giving me a warning, that means that person could've been the one who killed Ian or Damian, or both of them."

"If you've been asking around about Ian Becker's murder, perhaps so."

Several more minutes went by without either of us saying anything. Then we both started speaking at the same time.

"Ms. Bishop—"

"Detective—"

"You first," he said.

"Thank you for coming to my aid."

"I'm glad I was available to respond to the call. Can you think of anything, anything at all you remember from the attack? I know it might be painful to mentally relive it, but take your time and think about it. A good technique is to think about it using your five senses."

I thought about it for a few minutes related to my senses. "I didn't see anything when I went into the bedroom. And once the blanket came down over my head, I absolutely didn't see anything. As to my other senses, I can't remember feeling anything other than the roughness of the blanket and the strong arms of my attacker.

"I didn't taste anything." *Except maybe fear.* "The door slamming behind me was the only sound I heard. That leaves the sense of smell. The blanket smelled old and musty. That I remember, especially since it took me a while to get it off my head.

"Wait. When I walked into the room, I vaguely remember smelling a light scent—spicy like aftershave lotion or cologne. Very light as though the person had applied it hours before and the scent had faded." I tried to remember anything else. "Sorry, that's all I remember."

"Sleep on it. When you're rested, something else may occur to you." He continued staring straight ahead as though trying to avoid eye contact with me.

We lapsed into silence again. When we pulled up in front of my house, I looked up to see Aunt Kit standing in the doorway.

He finally turned toward me. "For your safety, stay out of this. Next time you may not be so lucky."

"That's why we have to find that person—so there isn't a *next* time."

"There is no *we* about this." He nearly shouted. "Stay out of this and leave it to the police."

I opened my mouth to speak and then closed it again. As I reached for the door handle to leave, he placed his hand on my arm. "Laura, please."

Aunt Kit grabbed me when I walked in the door and hugged me hard. "Are you okay?" She stepped back and studied me closely. I was surprised to see tears well up in her eyes.

"I'm fine." But I began to shake as I said it.

"Sit down, and I'll bring you a nice cup of tea."

I collapsed on the sofa and pulled an afghan over my legs. Inky must have sensed that I was distressed because he jumped on me and curled up in my lap. His warmth and purring helped soothe me.

I thought of Detective Spangler's warning and then remembered his use of my given name—a first.

"This will fix you right up." Aunt Kit handed me tea in a cup and saucer, instead of the mug I usually used. It made it feel like a special occasion. "Unless you want something stronger."

This clearly was an occasion for Harvey's Bristol Cream, but I decided to stick with the tea. I needed a clear head. Usually, I don't take sugar in my tea, but since Aunt Kit fixed it for me that way, for medicinal purposes, I decided to say nothing about it.

Aunt Kit took a seat in a chair next to me. "Do you feel up to talking about what happened? Tyrone called to tell me you were okay. He was concerned Nita may have called, asking if I knew where you were and that I would be worried."

"That was good of Tyrone. He's always so thoughtful."

"Do you think you're getting too close to whoever is

responsible for the murders?" She leaned over and tucked the afghan over my legs.

"It might be wishful thinking, but I'd like to think I am— enough to shake up whoever it was that struck out at me. But then, it could have been someone totally unconnected to the murders who lured me to that home."

"It's not safe for women to go anywhere alone these days." Aunt Kit pursed her lips and shook her head.

"It's important to be careful, but we can't live in fear." Although right now I was feeling pretty fearful.

"Of the people you questioned, which one do you think could have attacked you?"

"Any of them—male or female. Whoever it was caught me off guard, so it didn't take much effort to get me into that closet. Once that blanket went over my head, I was disoriented."

Someone knocked on the front door, causing Aunt Kit to jump up. "I'll see who's there. Maybe I should take a fireplace poker with me in case I have to defend us."

She returned with Nita and Guido trailing behind her.

"Tyrone said you were okay, but we weren't going to be satisfied until we saw that for ourselves." Nita reached over and petted Inky.

Again, I was comforted I had such good friends who cared about me—and came to my rescue.

I ran my fingers through my unruly hair, realizing that I hadn't brushed it since the blanket did a number on me. "I look a dreadful mess, but I'm fine."

Guido leaned over and hugged me. "You look great. Any clues as to who attacked you?"

I shook my head. "Detective Spangler told me to think of my five senses to see if they'd trigger a memory. I didn't see, hear, feel, or taste anything, other than the blanket that was thrown over my head. It smelled awful." Could it have come from someone's trunk or Emily Thompson's barn? "I remembered smelling an aftershave or cologne as I entered the room. Now all I have to do is come in contact with everyone in Louiston to see if I recognize that scent on someone. It could be one used by half of the people in town, so it might not be a viable clue."

Nita frowned. "I can't believe someone did that to you. Are we going to have to do a background check on potential customers before we meet with them?"

"We'll have to be careful about who we meet and where in the future. If in doubt, we'll go in pairs."

"If this is linked to one of the murders, you must have riled someone," Guido said. "Next time you need to go somewhere that might be questionable, call me and I'll go along. You can't be too careful."

"Thanks, Guido, you're a gem."

"Laura, have you recorded somewhere everything you've learned so far?" Nita asked. "It might be a good idea to list everyone you've questioned and what your conclusions are so you have a record of it. That way, if anything—"

"You mean if anything happens to me, you'll have a record of what I learned?"

"Well..."

"You're right." I held up a spiral notebook. "I made a few notes earlier, but I plan to add to it. Aunt Kit, I'm leaving it here for you to find if something happens to me."

Aunt Kit's eyebrows shot up. "That's supposed to comfort me? I knew nothing good was going to come from you getting involved in this. I'm not going to let you out of my sight until this whole issue is resolved."

Chapter 41

Check out resale shops, antique stores, and garage sales for items to help in staging.

I spent half the night writing down everything I could remember since I started digging into both Ian's and Damian's deaths, filling page after page in my notebook. Reviewing what I'd written, I still didn't get a clear picture of who could have committed the crimes or how they could be linked.

Checking the time, I saw it was getting late, and I needed to focus more on my home staging business and less playing amateur sleuth. Nita and I had the staging work we'd scheduled, plus the work we had committed to doing for Monica's business.

Since Aunt Kit had been staying with me, I'd been having breakfast with her instead of meeting Nita at Vocaro's. Some days it was the only time we had together. She had been busy meeting old friends and spending time with Anne Williamson, who had taken a shine to Aunt Kit. They must think alike.

I plopped my notebook on the kitchen table. "I've recorded everything I can remember since I got involved in this. There are plenty of suspects, but nothing that clearly points to who committed the crimes or if they are linked. It's getting harder to prove Monica didn't do it."

Aunt Kit reached for the notebook. "Do you mind if I read your notes? Maybe another set of eyes will help."

"Please do. I'm open to suggestions. By the way, I'm heading out to visit some resale shops this morning."

Today was my day to go scouting for goods. Every week I took time to do a quick walk-through of the local resale stores like those run by the Salvation Army, St. Vincent de Paul, and Goodwill, looking for items to add to our inventory. They were excellent sources for the furnishings and accessories we used in staging. People frequently donated quality items that I could pick up for a song. Purchasing items from these organizations was a win-win situation. It enabled me to expand our inventory and helped the organizations raise money for their programs. On the weekends I hit the yard sales and estate sales, always finding something we could use. Then there were Josh's warehouses. But I needed a full day there.

"Do you think it's wise for you to go out, considering what happened to you yesterday?" Aunt Kit asked. Concern was written all over her face.

"I have a business to run. I can't cower indoors afraid someone might be lying in wait for me."

"Then perhaps I'll go along with you."

"What, and trail behind me as a bodyguard?" Thinking of my older aunt jumping out to protect me made me laugh. "You already have plans today with Anne. I'll be careful. Besides, the only trouble I can get into at the resale shops is buying too much."

Aunt Kit didn't look convinced, but she didn't say anything further. I was touched by her concern.

The morning sped by quickly as I went from one resale shop to another. I was on the hunt for attractive lamps, artwork, decorative items, and anything I thought we could eventually use to make an empty home attractive to buyers. The trick was picking up things when I saw them. If I was doubtful about an item and left it, it probably wouldn't be there if I went back later.

At my last stop, while walking through the kitchenware area, a knife set in a wooden block caught my eye. The handles were brushed metal with a black ring around the edge. I froze in place looking at the set. The knife handles looked identical to the one I'd seen in Ian's back when we found him. Examining the set, I saw one knife was missing.

Surely the knife used to kill Ian couldn't have been from this set. People lost knives in sets all the time. But the design of the knife used to kill Ian was unusual and matched this set. Could it be the same set? It would be really strange for me to come upon the knife set owned by the murderer. Stuff like that only happened in movies. Or did it? It would be a weird coincidence. But stranger things in life happened all the time.

The knife used to kill Damian had been different. Otherwise, the police would have linked the two murders.

If the knife that had killed Ian had come from this set, how had it ended up here? Could the killer's prints still be on the knives or the holder? Surely the person who got rid of it would have wiped it clean of any fingerprints. Or could the killer have been so arrogant as to think no one would find the set or connect it to the murder?

The set could be evidence. Thinking about how Detective Spangler would react to my showing up with it made me cringe, but I would put that worry aside for the moment.

First I had to purchase the set. What a conundrum—having to purchase possible evidence. My chances of convincing the woman at the counter I was confiscating the knife set as evidence in a murder case seemed remote.

If I picked it up, I'd be adding my fingerprints to those left on it since the killer had dumped it. Maybe I could ask the woman at the counter for a plastic bag to put around it. But I didn't want to leave the set there in case someone walked off with it.

A stack of cloth napkins lay among a jumble of linens on a nearby table. I grabbed two and carefully wrapped them around the wooden block and took it to the checkout counter.

"Excuse me, could you ring this up without handling it?" I asked the clerk.

The woman looked at me like I was trying to conceal the price. "Sure, but I need to see the price tag."

I carefully held the block with the napkins and turned it over to show her the price tag on the bottom.

"That will be sixty-five dollars. Do you want those napkins as well?"

Yikes, that was a lot, especially since one of the knives was missing. What brand was it? Oh, well. This wasn't the time to haggle over the price. "Ah, no. I'll take the napkins back. I didn't want to risk cutting myself. Can I use them first to put the knife set in a bag?"

She offered to wrap the set in paper, but I didn't want her handling it. Again she looked at me like she was taking a chance selling knives to a nutcase like me.

"Do you have any idea who donated this?" I asked.

She shrugged. "All the donated items come in through the loading dock. You can check with Pete back there. He's here most days. But it's pretty doubtful he'll remember who brought it in."

I paid her, slid the knife set and wooden block holder into a plastic bag, and took my receipt from the clerk, who still eyed me suspiciously.

"I'll return the napkins to the table where I'd found them."

She took them from me. "I'll take them back."

What did she think I was going to do—stuff them in my bag? How embarrassing to be viewed as a potential shoplifter.

I thanked her, took my bag, and slunk away, looking around for the door to the loading dock. I could have asked the clerk for directions, but I'd wanted to get away from her as soon as I could. I located a door marked *Do Not Enter*, figuring it would lead me to the storage/sorting room and loading dock. I pushed the door open and entered a large room piled high with every kind of item imaginable.

Near the tall doors opening to the loading dock, two men sat in bentwood chairs. The younger of the two, who looked to be in his early twenties, lounged back with his chair tilted against the wall.

As I approached, he quickly drained a Pepsi in a glass bottle, lost his balance, and his chair legs abruptly hit the floor. A much older man sat with his feet firmly planted on the grimy floor. His gray hair and stooped shoulders a sign he'd spent a lifetime carrying heavy loads. Both men looked up as I approached.

"Hi. Is one of you Pete?"

"That's me." The older man said. "What can I do for you?"

"I just purchased a set of knives in a wooden storage block. Do either of you remember who donated the set?" I held open the plastic bag.

The gray-haired man looked in the bag and scratched his head. "People bring lots of stuff in here. Impossible to remember who brings what."

The younger man leaned over and peered in the bag. He scrunched up his face in deep concentration. "I vaguely remember that set." He sat for a few minutes pondering the item. "That mighta been the set a fellow dropped off last week. Said he saw it in a dumpster and pulled it out. I remember 'cause he yammered on about what the world was comin' to when someone threw out a perfectly good set of knives 'cause one was missing."

"Did he say where he found it?"

"He mighta said, but I don't recall. Is it important? The knives weren't stolen from you were they?"

"No, they weren't mine." Disappointed I couldn't find out more, I pulled one of my business cards from the bottom of my canvas bag and handed it to the young man. "You've been very helpful. Thank you. If you remember anything more, could you please call me? The information could be vital to a murder investigation."

Now I needed to get the evidence to the police.

Chapter 42

Hang new house numbers or polish existing ones, and ensure they can be seen from the street.

Leaving the shop, I drove immediately to the police station. I decided against going inside since I knew I couldn't carry several knives in with me. I also didn't want to explain to the officers at the desk why I needed to see the detective.

Instead, I pulled out Detective Spangler's card and punched his number into my cell phone. He answered on the third ring.

"Spangler."

"Ah, Detective Spangler, this is Laura Bishop. I have something I think you need to see. I'm in my car in the lot outside. Can you come down and take a look at it? I can't bring it into the station."

He covered his phone, but I still could hear murmuring in the background. "Can you wait for a few minutes? I'm in the middle of something, but I might be able to get away shortly."

It was a pleasant day, so I got out of my car, reached into the backseat to retrieve the bag containing the knife set, and walked over to stand in the shade of a large maple tree nearby. Anyone seeing the detective meeting me in the parking lot would assume our meeting was personal, but I didn't care. I wanted to hand him the knife set and get back to my business. Besides, I didn't want him looming over me as I sat in my car.

About ten minutes later, he walked up to where I stood. "What do you have there?"

"Good morning to you too, Detective."

"Sorry, it's been a hectic morning. I ducked out of a meeting to see what you have. I hope it's important."

Annoyed that he thought I might have stopped by just for a chat, I picked up the bag at my feet and thrust it to him. "Careful. It's a knife set. Don't reach inside the bag."

He looked puzzled, opened the bag, and peered inside. "A knife set?"

"Not just any knife set. Look closely at the handles. Look familiar?"

His eyes widened. "Yes, they do. Where did you find this?"

"At the resale shop down on Main Street. If you look closely, you'll see one knife is missing. One of the employees at the shop said a man brought it in last week. Said he'd found it in a dumpster. The employee said the man told him where, but he couldn't remember. I asked him to give me a call if the location came to mind."

"The knife handles have an unusual design. I'll give you that." He rubbed his chin with his hand.

"Exactly." I was starting to feel hopeful.

"But other people in town could have the same set, and plenty of them with pieces missing. I don't know what we gain finding this."

"But why would someone throw out an expensive set of knives?" I wasn't giving up easily.

"You got me there."

"If this is the set, it helps narrow the number of suspects in Ian's case. And once we can identify his killer, we might be able to link his murder to Damian's."

"There you go again with the *we*."

"Don't you agree it narrows the search—even if only a little? If someone came from out of town intending to murder Ian, that person might have brought a knife but not a whole set. It must have been someone who lives locally." There goes the theory that someone could have followed Ian from New Zealand. "It also shows premeditation. If Warren didn't have a set like that at the funeral home or in his apartment upstairs, the killer had to have brought the knife with him."

"You are still going under the assumption that the knife came from this set. Have you considered someone could have owned a single knife with this design without owning a whole set? We have nothing to link this set to the murder. With a pretty questionable chain of custody of the evidence, I'm not sure the evidence would be admissible."

"What about fingerprints on it?"

"Okay. Say the knife came from this set. Even if we got prints from it, unless we have prints in our system to match them against, they wouldn't do us much good. We'd have to fingerprint every person in Louiston, searching for a match."

"You could start with the other people named in Doris Becker's will," I said.

He leaned his head back and expelled a long, drawn-out breath. "Are you trying to tell me again how to do my job?"

"If it would help solve two murders, yes."

He shook his head as though in disbelief, tucked the bag under his arm, and walked away.

I thought about the sixty-five dollars I'd paid for the evidence. With my tight budget, I started to pull the receipt from my purse and chase after him but decided against it. I couldn't ask him to reimburse me for the cost of the evidence. That might look suspicious. Once Monica was set free, I'd collect it from her.

I felt in my bones that we were getting close to discovering something—at least about Ian's death. But when it came to Damian's death, would we discover something that would help free Monica or confirm her guilt?

Chapter 43

Make minor repairs. Buyers noticing small things that need to be repaired will wonder how well the house has been maintained.

The rest of the week passed quickly. I worked with Monica's assistant on several projects, while Nita helped a homeowner with an occupied staging, using the homeowner's furnishings. Unfortunately, the homeowner's living room furniture was well-worn and outdated. Prospective buyers seeing tattered upholstery would wonder what else in the house needed attention. Evidence of deferred maintenance caused more lost sales than anything else. Nita solved the problem by convincing the homeowner to purchase inexpensive covers, which made a huge difference.

At the end of a particularly busy day, Nita dropped me at my house. I looked forward to a relaxing weekend.

"I hate to remind you of this, considering how exhausted you must be, but we promised to help take down the art exhibit at the Arts Center tomorrow. We have to have everything out by tomorrow afternoon."

I groaned. There went my restful Saturday. "Okay, what time do you want me to be there?"

We made arrangements to meet the next morning bright and early so we could finish and still have part of the day to rest. "I'm picking up Mrs. Webster, so you won't need to get her. She wants to come. Tyrone has classes tomorrow and won't be able to give her a ride."

The next morning, the Arts Center hummed with activity with artists retrieving their artwork, patrons claiming the pieces they'd purchased, and volunteers dismantling display boards. The various exhibit rooms were filled with everyone taking a final look at the exhibit.

We all had our assignments, and for a while, it seemed like controlled chaos.

"Anyone seen Anne Williamson?" someone called from across the room.

"She's back in the room where they did the dance exhibits," another volunteer responded. "If you need to talk to her, better catch her right away because she's leaving today to go on vacation. Otherwise, talk to Nita. She's handling the takedown."

With responsibility for the takedown resting with Nita, she was dashing from room to room responding to questions and directing volunteers who needed guidance on what they should be doing. I was impressed with how well she was handling it.

A few minutes later, we took a break and walked into the room devoted to photography to admire the *Sold* signs on her photographs.

"Stand in front of your photo," I motioned to Nita. "I want to get a snap of you with your award-winning photos."

"It was only an honorable mention." Nita stood between her two photos.

"Still award-winning." I pulled my iPhone from my bag and looked for the camera option.

The small room was filled with people trying to get a last look, so it took me a few seconds to be able to step back enough to fit Nita and her framed photos into the camera view. When I finally snapped the photo, I froze. A spicy scent floated across the room, paralyzing me. For a brief second, darkness descended over me and

I was back in a closet, wondering about my fate.

"Laura? Are you okay?" Nita was staring at me, her face creased with concern.

Dizziness overcame me, but I forced myself to look behind me to see who was wearing a scent I would never forget. But the small room had cleared of everyone except for a young mother with a baby in a stroller and a toddler who was holding her hand. I ignored Nita's question and moved closer to the woman and sniffed several times, hoping she wouldn't notice me. Unfortunately, she did. She leaned over the baby in the stroller and sniffed. Glaring at me she pointed the stroller to the door and dragged the toddler from the room.

"Laura, what's gotten into you?" Nita came up behind me.

"I smelled it. The fragrance worn by whoever locked me in that closet."

"Someone who was here?" Nita looked around her at the empty room.

"Either that or someone who walked by the entrance. Did you recognize anyone in here?"

She shook her head. "Sorry. I was focused on my photos and then posing for you."

"Hurry. Let's go into the main hall so I can see who's out there." I grabbed Nita by the arm and raced through the doorway.

The room was filled with people. I rushed through the crowd, sniffing so much I was getting lightheaded. I couldn't find the now-familiar fragrance and felt deflated.

Mrs. Webster grabbed my arm as I walked by. "Calm down, girl. You look frantic. What's going on?"

I explained about catching a whiff of the aftershave or cologne worn by the person who had attacked me.

Nita came up behind us. "Even if you find someone here wearing that scent, it wouldn't prove that was the person who attacked you. Lots of men, or women, could be wearing it."

"I don't think so. It seemed distinctive, as in expensive, and I don't recall smelling it before the other day."

"So now you're an expert on aftershaves and colognes?" Nita said.

"Of course not. But smells evoke memories more so than anything else. I don't think I would've reacted as I did to a different scent."

Mrs. Webster scanned the main display room, which was slowly emptying of people. "Short of lining everyone up and you sniffing each one, which they probably would object to, I don't think there is anything you can do. Besides, lots of folks have already gone."

Nita and Mrs. Webster were right. It would be a wasted effort trying to find my cologne-wearing attacker here. My head began to pound. I was certain if I ever smelled the fragrance again, it would make me ill.

Mrs. Webster scrutinized me as though wondering if she should push my head between my knees to revive me. "Are you okay?" she asked.

I nodded.

"Then I need to get back to the front desk. I'm helping to check off the names of the artists as they take their works out."

"You go ahead. I'll be fine. Thank you for your concern."

Mrs. Webster headed to the front desk but kept looking back at me as though to make sure I hadn't collapsed on the floor.

Nita handed me a glass of water. "Here, drink this. It's hot in here, and it's easy to get dehydrated."

"And you're thinking dehydration sent me a bit crazy?" I took the glass from her.

"No. I believe you. It's too bad you didn't see whoever it was wearing the scent."

I didn't know what I would've done if I'd found that person. Make a citizen's arrest? It was too late to worry about it now. "Come on," I urged Nita. "Let's get back to work. We still have plenty to do."

Later, most of the artwork had been taken down except for some large pieces. We found Mrs. Webster staring at the piece painted by Anne Williamson, which had been sold and was waiting to be claimed by the buyer. It was a brilliant piece of art. A young woman, dressed in a flowing gown with slashes of black, purple, and lavender, stood in front of a portrait of a haggard old woman in the same dress. It reminded me of Oscar Wilde's book *A Portrait of Dorian Gray*, which told the story of a young man who sold his soul to the devil to stay eternally young, while a painting of him aged in the attic.

"That's a fabulous painting," Nita remarked to Mrs. Webster.

Absorbed in studying the painting, she didn't respond.

Her eyes widened, and she reached out and took my arm to steady herself. "Remember I said there was something about this painting? It was something I couldn't put my finger on. Although it seemed familiar, I couldn't remember why. I kept thinking about it, wondering where I could have seen it before. You know how you get something in your head and it won't let go."

I nodded. It was the same with trying to solve these murders. The details kept churning around in my thoughts, and I had little peace of mind.

"It's taken me a while, but now that I've seen it again, I know where I saw it before."

"Where?"

"At Doris Becker's home. It was years and years ago when I first started doing home nursing. I cared for her when she recovered from surgery."

I blinked and looked at the painting again studying it closer.

Nita looked puzzled. "But I heard Doris never let anyone see her paintings. She didn't think they were any good. How did you get to view any of them?"

"Seeing it again today, it finally clicked, and I remembered where I saw it. While caring for Doris, I went into a room adjoining her bedroom looking for extra blankets. She must have used the room as an art studio, and it was there."

"In the turret room?" I asked.

"Yes. The room was round with lots of windows."

When I saw her house, I'd wondered if she'd used that room to paint in.

"The painting rested on an easel in the center of the room, so I couldn't miss it. But afterward, I got busy caring for Doris and didn't think about it again, until now."

I was puzzled. "Why would Anne's painting be at Doris Becker's home?"

"That's just it. Anne Williamson couldn't have painted it. She didn't move to Louiston until years later. Doris must have painted it."

"What?" I was confused, trying to absorb what she said. "But Anne said Doris's work was simplistic. There is nothing simple about this painting."

Nita shook her head. "We only have Anne's word about Doris's work. From what I heard, Doris was extremely private about her painting. She didn't think her work was good enough to display, so no one ever saw it."

I couldn't understand it. "She must have had high expectations if she didn't think this was any good. Look how much it sold for."

"And sold by Anne Williamson as her work. She must have taken this painting from Doris. And perhaps all the other ones she sold. Did anyone ever see Anne working on a piece—perhaps at a group painting session to know what her work looked like? To compare?"

"I don't think so. But don't forget I haven't been a member of the arts group for long," Nita said.

"What about Doris? Did anyone ever mention seeing her paint, perhaps in a group session?" Mrs. Webster continued to stare at the painting.

"As I understand it, Doris enjoyed being a member of the group," Nita said. "When she could no longer attend the meetings, the members tried to keep her involved. She was getting very forgetful. Anne befriended her and used to visit her often."

"But how did Anne see Doris's paintings?" I asked.

"Probably when she visited Doris," Nita said. "If Doris was

developing dementia, I bet it was easy for Anne to see what paintings Doris had in her house."

"Used to visit her and took her paintings, a few at a time," I said indignantly. "Her neighbor said he saw Anne loading her car with some of Doris's things. She told him she was taking things Doris wanted to donate to the Salvation Army."

Mrs. Webster grunted. "I always wondered about that woman."

"But if no one saw Doris's paintings, how do we prove she painted them and not Anne?"

I gasped. "Aunt Kit was a genius."

"What's this got to do with Aunt Kit?" Nita asked.

"She said art might have been the link between Ian's and Damian's deaths." I turned to Nita and Mrs. Webster, who looked at me as though I'd lost my mind. "I thought Aunt Kit was totally off the mark, but she was right. Don't you see? The only person possibly familiar with Doris's paintings had been gone for over twenty years and didn't seem like a threat. That is until he showed up to settle his aunt's estate. One of the calls on his phone, when he arrived, had been to Anne. Ian would have been in a position to question what had happened to his aunt's paintings."

Mrs. Webster walked up to the painting and studied the price tag on it. "If what you say is true and Anne has been selling Doris's paintings as her own, she's made a tidy sum from her ill-gotten gains."

I nodded. "And we don't know how many more paintings she smuggled out of Doris's house and may still have. She couldn't afford to have Ian raise the alarm about them."

"So she stabbed poor Ian to keep him quiet?" Nita asked.

"I think that's the only explanation." I hoped I was right.

"How is this linked to Damian?" Nita asked. "He didn't know Doris and hadn't lived in Louiston for very long. He wouldn't have known anything about Doris's paintings." Nita, trying to take it all in, looked puzzled.

I looked at the painting as though trying to absorb its role in two murders. "The night of the awards ceremony, I was standing next to Anne and we both watched Damian studying her painting. He stood there for some time and even got up close to it as though studying the brushstrokes. I think Anne wondered about his scrutiny of the painting and was worried he was suspicious of her. I'm guessing she couldn't take a chance and decided to get rid of him just in case. She killed once to cover her trail, so it probably didn't take much for her to kill again."

Nita looked somber. "Anne must have seen Damian and Ian as threats to her reputation and income flow."

I peered up at the large painting and shook my head, remembering Damian's close examination of the painting that night. "After Anne saw him inspecting her painting, or I should say Doris's painting, she must have gone home and decided she needed to act right away—before Damian had a chance to say something to anyone else about the painting. If Monica hadn't been arrested, Anne might have gone after her too, guessing that Damian had said something to her on the way home."

"Being in jail could have saved her life," Mrs. Webster said.

"If nothing else, Anne needed to go home to grab a knife. After she stabbed Damian, she got away just before Monica arrived." I shook my head. "She cut it pretty close."

"Wicked woman," Mrs. Webster said. "The world gets worse every day."

"How do we prove any of it?" Nita asked.

"I don't know. We need to give this some thought. If we rush into it, we could blow the whole thing."

Chapter 44

Make sure all locks and doorbells work.

Nita drove Mrs. Webster home and planned to join me at my house so we could grab something to eat quickly and plan our next steps. It was never good to make important decisions when starving.

Entering the house, I called out to Aunt Kit but didn't get an answer. Instead, Inky came running to greet me. After the shock I'd received that morning, it was comforting to have his affectionate greeting.

I made a pot of tea and quickly pulled leftover Chinese from the refrigerator to heat in the microwave. What did we ever do before microwaves were invented?

While waiting for Nita, I opened the notebook I'd left on the kitchen table and recorded our recent findings with a notation to possibly scout out Anne's house.

I had just finished recording my notes when Nita tapped on the door and I let her in.

"That smells wonderful. I thought we'd be having something fast like cheese sandwiches. What is that?"

"Leftover Chinese. Even faster than making sandwiches."

We dug into the selection of dishes from the night before, both of us deep in thought about what we could do next.

I reached down and fed Inky a piece of chicken, something I

didn't usually do from the table. "If we could find some of Doris's paintings at Anne's house, it would be evidence pointing to a motive for the murders."

"What if all the paintings have Anne's signature on them?" Nita dug into the bag of chocolate chip cookies I set on the table.

"Anne probably painted over Doris's signature and signed her own name. If so, I'm sure there's a way an art expert could get below Anne's signature to find Doris's signature. That is if Doris wasn't too modest to sign her paintings. If that's the case, I don't know if there is any way to prove Doris painted them."

"With any luck, some are still there with Doris's signature. Then we'd have something concrete to report to the police." Nita took our dishes over to the sink. "All we have now are guesses. We need to find some of those paintings."

"What excuse can we use to get into Anne's house?" I asked.

"Bring your vacuum cleaner and we can offer to clean her house." From the twinkle in her eye, I knew Nita was kidding.

"Whatever we do, we need to get there soon. If Anne is leaving on vacation, we just may catch her. I wish Aunt Kit were here. She and Anne have become chummy, and if she were with us, it wouldn't look as strange as our showing up on her doorstep alone."

Why don't you call Aunt Kit and suggest she meet us there?" Nita picked up her purse, ready to leave.

"It wouldn't do any good trying to call her. She never turns her phone on except to make a call. Says it saves the battery." It annoyed me to no end and made me wonder how I would get in touch with her in an emergency—like now.

"Why are we always plagued with cell phone problems?" Nita asked, reminding me of the problems I'd had in the past with an old phone and poor connectivity.

"Come on, let's think of an excuse to visit Anne on our way there." We stepped outside to discover that it had started raining, and the temperature had dropped considerably. I grabbed a jacket hanging on a peg near the back door and offered one to Nita. She declined, saying she had one in the car.

When we pulled up in front of Anne's house, we saw her car was gone. "Don't tell me we missed her!" Nita groaned.

"Let's knock. She may be parked out back somewhere." We ran to the house to avoid getting wet in the drizzly rain. Stepping onto the porch, I twisted the old-fashioned door ringer built into the middle of the door. When we didn't get a response, I tried again. The ringer's grinding noise would have woken anyone sleeping in the house.

"Nita, look at this." We peered through the window in the upper half of the door and I pointed to the two large suitcases sitting just inside.

Nita grinned. "Good. She hasn't left yet. Maybe she went for gas or something. Do you think she's going on vacation or escaping before things get too hot for her to stay here? Maybe she's going on the lam."

"I don't know. If she's going on the lam, as you say, the police might never find her. This could be our only opportunity to gather the evidence and catch her before she leaves."

Nita tried the doorknob. It turned easily. "Since Anne didn't answer, do you think she could be inside sick or injured? Maybe she hurt her back lifting those suitcases and is lying upstairs helpless? We should go inside and check on her."

"Wouldn't that be unlawful entry?" I asked. Between the two of us, I was the one who adhered to the rules more often.

"She could be dying in there. Do we quibble about it being unlawful to go in and check on her when she might need help?"

The thought of Anne getting away was more than I could bear, especially if she had packed any of Doris's remaining artwork in her car. "Okay, but only to check to make sure Anne is okay."

Nita pushed open the door and went in first, with me following. "What do you notice?" I whispered.

"Spicy cologne. Was that what you smelled before?" Nita asked.

"I could never forget it. Now I know we're on the right path."

Nita tiptoed further inside. "Anne, are you here? It's Laura and

Nita. We didn't get an answer to our ring, and we want to make sure you're okay."

We got no response. "It doesn't appear she's here. Why don't you check upstairs to see if she is lying on the floor up there, and I'll search around down here? Oh, and check the closets and under the beds."

"Closets and under the bed?" Nita asked, looking perplexed.

"For any artwork," I whispered.

"Oh, right." With that, she tiptoed up the stairs. "Anne, are you up there?"

After searching the living room, peering behind and under the sofa and chairs and not finding anything except dust bunnies, I quickly searched the dining room and kitchen. No signs of any paintings. I peered out the back window. No garage out back, so there wouldn't be any paintings stored there. That left the dreaded basement. I doubted she stored them in a damp, cold place, but I couldn't risk missing them if they were there in a humidity-controlled storage cupboard.

I pushed open the door and peered down into the basement. The musty odor from stale air and dampness hit me. I hated basements—especially basements in old houses. It brought back the memory of my experience staging the Denton mansion. My first instinct was to close the door and run, but I couldn't leave without making sure we'd checked the whole house. We needed those paintings to prove Anne Williamson had been stealing them from Doris.

Anne could say Doris had given them to her, but that would be hard to prove, especially since Anne had signed her name to them and been passing them off as her own. If we could prove that, we might be able to prove she had a motive to murder both Ian and Damian to keep her secret.

From the top of the stairs, I looked around for a light switch. When I didn't see one, I looked on the wall outside the basement door and found a switch on the kitchen wall. I flipped the switch and saw a single bare light bulb illuminate. It hung from the ceiling at the bottom of the stairs, spilling a weak circle of light that was just enough illumination for me to find my way down to the cement floor. The homes in this area of Louiston were about a hundred and fifty years old, and electricity had been added to them well after they had been built. It wasn't unusual to find very little lighting in the basements.

As I started down the stairs, the sudden drop in temperature sent shivers over me. I wrapped the front of my jacket across my chest, thankful I'd grabbed something warm to wear earlier when we'd dashed from my house.

As I slowly made my way down the stairs, I reached out to steady myself and felt the cold foundation that consisted of stacked rocks. The rocks in this house had been whitewashed, which helped make the basement feel less like a dungeon—but not by much.

At the bottom of the stairs, I scanned the area looking for places Anne could have stored any of the paintings—if she still had some in her possession. The basement felt cold and damp, even in summer. The rain earlier hadn't helped.

I couldn't imagine Anne would store the paintings down here given the damp conditions, but she could have if she were desperate enough to ensure no one saw them.

From where I stood, I could see a wide-open area filled with a haphazard collection of things that must have been stored there for years. It was covered not in dust but grimy soot. Two old-fashioned wooden highchairs stood in a corner, surrounded by galvanized buckets, wooden crates filled with colored soda bottles, and a wooden ice cream churn. Various pieces of lawn and gardening equipment filled one end of the basement, which meant there must be an exit to the backyard. But I didn't see one.

I looked around for more light switches to help me find the outside door, or perhaps some ceiling lights with pull chains or cords. Not finding any, I opened a wood-paneled door, and from the dim light near the stairwell, saw a furnace and water heater. There must be lights around here, but not knowing where they were, I couldn't find them to turn them on. The grimy walls in one corner showed that coal had once been stored there. That meant this area faced the street, where the coal would have been unloaded.

Finding nothing stored there, I turned to leave and ran into long cobwebs hanging from the wood beams overhead. They stuck to my face and hair. I hated cobwebs. And even though I knew they were harmless, it was all I could do not to screech.

Nita called from the doorway. "You okay down there?" She started down the steps. Perhaps she didn't have the aversion to basements I had.

"Yeah. I just ran into some cobwebs. This place is pretty well locked up. I don't see any windows or doors to the outside."

Nita joined me in the furnace room. "The windows were probably covered over to keep people from breaking in through the basement."

"Could be. I also didn't see any exits to outside," I said. "But it's so dark a door to the outside could be here, but I just don't see one."

"Did you find any paintings? There weren't any upstairs. Maybe we are on a wild goose chase."

"So far, no paintings down here either."

We left the furnace room and started to the other end of the basement, where I could see a large metal cabinet.

Just then I heard footsteps overhead. My heart skipped a beat. Before I could react, the basement door slammed closed, and the light went out. Weak as the light had been, it had still been better than nothing. We found ourselves enveloped in total darkness. My pulse quickened, reminding me of the growing panic attacks I'd experienced when facing unreasonable deadlines in the corporate world, and I reminded myself to stay calm.

"Beatrix Potter!" Nita gasped and reached out and grabbed me. It wasn't only the blackness around us that frightened me. An unnatural stillness filled the house. If we couldn't hear much from outside, would anyone outside be able to hear us if we shouted for help?

My first instinct was to remain silent. Perhaps Anne shut the door and turned off the light thinking that she'd left them that way earlier. If so, she might not realize we were down there.

"Nita, are you okay?"

"I guess. But what do we do now?"

"Stay calm. Maybe we can bluff our way out of this." Who was I kidding? Anne probably knew somebody was down here. If not Nita and me, then somebody else.

The darkness was so total I couldn't see my hand in front of my face. I was disoriented and unsure of what direction I was facing. As my eyes started to become more accustomed to the dark, I could see faint light coming from beneath the door at the top of the stairs leading into the kitchen. Not a lot of light, but enough to guide us to the stairs.

"Stay here for a sec. No sense both of us falling down the steps."

I carefully felt my way up the staircase, holding on to the railing on one side and the whitewashed stone foundation on the other. At the top, I turned the door handle. It turned easily. But when I pulled, the door held firmly closed. A lock on the handle wasn't keeping it from opening. I tugged again and the door gave way slightly but still didn't open. Then I remembered seeing a hook near the top of the outside doorframe. Once fitted into the eye on the door, it would hold the door firmly closed.

The thought of being imprisoned caused my body to quiver. What would happen if we couldn't get out? Who would take care of Inky?

No more waiting for Anne to leave. I pounded my fist on the door and shouted, "Hello! Anyone there?" No response. I pounded louder until pain shot through my hand and radiated up my arm.

That's when I heard a light knock on the door and a familiar voice.

"Hello, Laura. You really should have minded your own business."

Anne? I decided to play the innocent. "Hi, Anne. It's me,

Laura, down here with Nita. We came looking for you and decided to see if you were down here. Can you please let us out?" I tried to keep my tone light. "Maybe we can have that cup of tea together we've been meaning to have."

"Now, Laura, you and I both know I can't do that." Anne sounded so normal and not the least like a cold-blooded killer.

I tried to sound just as normal and not like a trapped prisoner possibly left here to die. "Sure you can. Just unlock the door, and when we come out, we can talk about this."

"Sorry, dear. As soon as I finish packing my car, I'll be on my way. You really should have stayed out of my affairs. This is most inconvenient."

I heard her footsteps as she walked away. "Drat."

Earlier we'd seen suitcases in the hall. We knew she was planning to leave town. Could she be so coldhearted as to leave us prisoner in her basement? The answer to that was pretty evident. She had killed two men without a qualm. Would two more people make any difference to her?

I began feeling like a character in Edgar Allen Poe's "Cask of the Amontillado," when a man tempts his rival into a cellar with the reward of a fine cask of sherry and imprisons him there. Was that what was happening to us? We were being imprisoned, and we didn't even have a bottle of sherry to warm ourselves. Why, oh why, had we left our bags locked in Nita's car with our cell phones in them?

Drat, drat, drat. And we hadn't told anybody where we were going.

Chapter 45

Empty basements, attics, and closets as much as possible to show ample storage space.

"What are we going to do now?" Nita called from the bottom of the steps. "She's going to get away, and we can't do anything to stop her stuck down here."

I had to face the direction of Nita's voice since I couldn't see her or anything else for that matter. Nita was worried about Anne getting away, while I was worried about us being imprisoned in a cellar, in an empty house, with no one knowing where we were.

"Right now, finding a way out of here is far more important than catching Anne."

"Don't worry, I'll simply call Guido and tell him we're here."

I sat patiently waiting for Nita to reach into her jacket pocket and discover her cell phone wasn't there.

"I can't find it. I must have left it in my bag. Oh, no. I left it in the car. Please tell me you have yours."

"Nope. I left my bag locked in the car along with yours. Remember we decided to leave them there?"

"Georgette Heyer!" Now she had gone to romance writers. "Laura, you got us into this. Now what are you going to do to get us out of here?"

"I got us into this?" The stress of being locked in a basement, that was every bit like a dungeon, was starting to get to us fast. At this rate, how long would we stay sane? "You were the one who thought we should search the house using the feeble excuse Anne might need our help."

I was irritated Nita was blaming this on me. "Maybe we should try sending telepathic messages to Madame Zolta and have her come rescue us." Madame Zolta was the local psychic Nita had brought to the house of a local homeowner who had been murdered to sweep the house of negative energy. Long story.

"That's a great idea." She paused. "Do you think that'll work?"

"Of course it's not going to work," I said, more caustically than I intended. Nita made no response. She was fond of Madame Zolta and believed she had abilities most mortals don't have. I knew I'd hurt her feelings.

"Sorry. I was being sarcastic and shouldn't have been." I started slowly walking down the stairs, holding tightly to the railing.

"From what I remember before the lights went out, there are no windows, or they are boarded up. There may be a door to the outside, but I didn't see one. Our only option is trying to break down the door going into the kitchen."

"With what?" Nita asked.

"Whatever we can find down here."

When I got to the last step, I reached out to determine if Nita was close. "I'm here. Take my hand. We'll use the wall as a guide and make our way around the basement and search anything we come in contact with."

We felt along the stone foundation until we came to a metal cabinet. My hand came into contact with some handles, and I gently pulled the doors open. I didn't want anything to fall on us. I stuck my hands inside and felt shelving. Starting with the top shelf, I slowly moved my hands along the edge, coming in contact with dusty jars with lids. Filled canning jars. They must have been there for years from the feel of the grime on them. The other shelves contained jars as well. No luck there. "I feel canning jars. Full ones.

Depending on the condition of what's in those jars, we might not starve for a while."

We continued to feel our way along the wall. My knee struck something hard. "Ouch!" I stopped and rubbed it. With each minute, I gained even more respect for Helen Keller.

My knees began to wobble and I felt as though my system was shutting down. We had just eaten, so it more than likely wasn't a low sugar drop. If it wasn't a sugar drop, then it must be the early signs of a panic attack. I couldn't let that happen when I needed to keep my head clear and my body functioning well. "Why don't we sit down for a while?"

We sat with crossed knees on the cold floor. The cold bypassed my flesh and went straight to my bones. I began to shiver. The rain and drop in temperature earlier in the day made the basement feel even colder than it would have felt this time of year.

"I'm sorry. This is my fault," Nita said, her teeth beginning to chatter. "I shouldn't have convinced you to come in here."

"No sense placing blame. I could have said no."

We sat quietly for a while. "What if we never get out of here?" Nita said with a shaky voice.

"Don't talk like that. We'll get out—eventually. Guido will be looking for you and someone will eventually notice that Anne has left town and wonder why."

"What if we don't get out? Nita asked. "It's times like this that make you evaluate your life." She paused. "Do you have any regrets?"

I thought about her question for a long minute. "Lots. But I particularly regret having an expired passport without a single stamp in it."

Nita laughed—a good sign she wasn't panicking. "I regret that I left Guido with a huge stack of dirty laundry. Oh, gosh." Nita jerked upright. "I forgot to give Guido the new password to our bank accounts. I just changed it."

"Relax. You can give it to him when we get out of here."

I heard Nita settle back down. "I'm getting really chilled."

"I know what you mean." I thrust my hands into my jacket pockets, glad I had worn it when I left home. In one pocket, I felt my car key and pulled it out. I stared at it. Why hadn't I thought of it before?

"Look, Nita." I held up the key, and then realized she wouldn't be able to see it. "I found my car key in my pocket. If I trigger the panic button, it will set off the car horn and someone might come to investigate, especially if I keep doing it." I held the key high over my head, pushed the button, and waited for the car horn to start sounding outside. Nothing. I tried again. Still nothing.

"We're too far away from your car for it to work," Nita said, disappointed.

"Well, it was worth the try." I put my hands back in my pockets. My fingers came into contact with something in my other pocket. I pulled it out, examining it with both hands. It felt like two small boxes of some sort. I held them up to my ear and shook them. Match boxes. How had they gotten into my pocket? Then I remembered Josh had given the matches to me the day I'd visited his shop with Geoff and Ron. I could hardly believe my luck finding them. Good old Josh. Had he foreseen my need for them?

I slid one of the boxes open and pulled out a match. My hands shook so hard I could hardly strike it.

Nita started at the erupting flame. "What the heck!"

"Matches Josh gave me." The flame burned down close to my fingers, and I blew it out before it could burn me. "Nita, I'm going to light another one. When I do, quickly look around us to see what you can find. If we can't find any old candles, look for an old broom or even a stack of newspapers."

I struck several more matches in a row while Nita scurried around searching the basement close to where the matches illuminated.

"Here's a broom. What do you want me to do with it?"

"Break off a handful of the bristles. I'll set them alight. They'll give us a burst of light but will burn out fast. When I set them alight, look around to see what you can find."

I touched a match flame to the bunch of broom bristles. They flamed up quickly and put off a burst of light. After a few seconds, I dropped them to the floor and stamped out any embers with my shoe. "See anything?"

"Here, I found a rake. We can try using that to break down the door. And I found a stack of old newspapers."

"Great. Give me the papers, and you get ready to run up the stairs when I light some." I took wades of paper and rolled them tightly to form a torch. "See if you can get the teeth of the rake between the door and the doorframe."

I lit the paper roll and Nita ran. I stood there like a torchbearer, wondering if any of the characters from my favorite mystery series ever faced such a bizarre situation as this. When the paper flared up too much, I dropped it on the floor and stood back and let it burn out. Thankfully, nothing was close enough to catch fire.

Nita yelled from the top step. "The rake teeth won't fit between the door and the frame. I'm going to try wedging it under the door."

I heard a loud crack.

"Christopher Columbus!"

Uh, oh. Now she had gone to historical figures. A sure sign her stress levels were escalating.

"What happened? Are you okay?" I felt my way over to the bottom of the stairs.

"The handle broke off."

"It was a good try. I'm going to light another torch. Come back down and let's think about what we can do next. I'm getting thirsty. Did you see a deep sink down here?"

Nita came back beside me. "Didn't see one."

I dropped the torch and let it burn out. We sat down again, the air around us smelling of smoke.

I tried to get comfortable on the hard floor. "One thing is certain. These old houses were well built. It would probably take a bulldozer to break down that door."

Nita laughed. "Yeah. Too bad we didn't bring a truck. We

could've attached a rope to the door handle and had the truck back up to pull the door open."

"All we're missing is a truck—and a rope long enough to reach the street. We should have planned better." At least we hadn't lost our sense of humor.

A truck in front of the house. That triggered a memory. I recalled telling Tyrone about some of the features in these old homes. How they originally had coal furnaces. Workers would back a truck up to a house and dump a load of coal down a chute into the basement.

A coal chute from the sidewalk to the basement. Could we be that lucky?

"Nita, when I walked around the basement before Anne turned off the light, I saw the walls in the corner of the furnace room stained with coal dust. That means this house used to have coal stored here and must have had a coal chute. It may still be here."

"So?" She said it as though wondering what that had to do with the price of tea in China.

"The chute goes from the street to the furnace room. If we can find it, we may be able to climb up the chute and push the cover off at the top. If that doesn't work, we can yell from there and maybe someone going by will hear us."

"How are we going to climb up a chute?"

"They don't go straight up and down like a laundry chute." I shivered thinking about my experience with one before. "They slope from the street into the basement, going under the porch. I remember watching workmen deliver coal to my grandparents' house when I was a kid. The chutes aren't that long or that steep. It might be worth looking for it."

"I'm game to try anything that'll get us out of here. What direction was the furnace room?"

I lit a match and looked around to get my bearings. "In that far corner. Think you can find your way there in the dark? We're getting low on matches, and I want to reserve a few."

Holding onto each other, we slowly made our way across the

basement, bumping into a crate of empty soda bottles that rattled. Eventually, we made it to the entrance of the furnace room. The wooden door screeched when I pulled it open.

The coal storage area was located in the far corner. Using the wall as a guide, we made our way to the corner. I ran my hands over the wall in that area feeling for whatever covered the chute. My fingers came into contact with what felt like a piece of plywood pushed up against the stone foundation. For the first time that day, it seemed as though things might be going our way.

"Nita, give me your hand and I'll guide you. Do you feel the edge of this board?" I positioned her hand against it.

"Yes."

"I think it covers the entrance to the chute. See if you can get your fingers along the edge. When I say go, pull it as hard as you can."

"Go." We both pulled, and it gave away so easily we landed on our bottoms with a thump.

"Well, that wasn't a challenge at all," Nita said.

I felt along the entrance to the chute and was relieved to find that it hadn't been filled in. "The challenge will be climbing up the chute." I rubbed my sore bottom. First my knee and now my bottom. By the time we escaped, I was going to be one big bruise.

I pushed my head inside and was relieved to see a few pinpricks of light at the top.

"Can you tell how long the chute is?" Nita asked.

"Not really, but I can see a little light, so we're not too far from the street. The chute's probably the same width as the porch. With any luck, it's only about fifteen feet—maybe a few more feet because of the slope of the chute.

"Okay, let's give it a try. I'll go first. Wait here until I get a feel for how it goes." I breathed in slowly through my nose and exhaled out through my mouth, trying to calm myself. Feeling a little calmer, I put my knee on the lip of the chute, stooped over, and pushed myself inside. The chute was wide enough for me to fit inside okay. Grime covered the inside, and it felt creepy. Between the dark and the grime, this must have been what it was like during the Victorian Era when young children had been stuffed inside chimneys to work as chimney sweeps. If our lives weren't at stake, no amount of money would have convinced me to go inside the chute.

At first, I tried to climb using my knees but found there wasn't quite enough room for that, even with me stooped over. Crawling on my stomach and using my forearms to propel myself forward seemed the only option. The chute wasn't as I had imagined it would be—smooth metal like a children's sliding board. It had been heavily dented from years of coal landing on it and each ding was encrusted with bits of coal. The smell was awful, and I could feel gritty bits of coal dust and dirt, and things I didn't want to contemplate, in my nose and on my tongue. I started to cough.

"Are you okay? Want me to give it a try?" Nita's voice sounded muffled, as though coming from a great distance, not the few feet that separated us.

"Yuk. It's disgusting in here. I think I swallowed some coal dust." I started coughing again.

After my coughing jag stopped, I pulled myself forward a couple of feet and just as quickly slid back to where I started.

"This isn't going to be as easy as I thought. Bits of coal are digging into my arms and body."

"How about if I push you?" Nita suggested.

"Thanks, but I don't think you'd be strong enough to do that." Sweat began dripping into my eyes, and I wiped my face with the backs of my grimy hands.

"I'll tell you what. I'm going to scoot up a bit. When I do, climb in behind me. Stretch your arms and legs out to the sides of the chute as though to anchor yourself. Maybe with you there, I won't slide backward, or at least not as far."

Nita clambered in behind me. "Okay. But be careful where you put your feet. I don't want a flattened nose. It's not the greatest nose, but I'm rather attached to it."

I started to laugh and cough at the same time, nearly causing me to slide backward again. It was easy to laugh now that we had found an escape route. But we weren't there yet. I used my forearms to pull myself forward again, occasionally stopping to gasp for air, trying not to breathe too deeply and get coal dust in my lungs.

A thick coating of coal dust now covered my tongue. This must have been what coal miners experienced down in the mines. I wanted to spit it out but didn't want Nita coming behind me and putting a hand in it.

As I continued wiggling forward, Nita scooted behind me. I prayed we wouldn't both slide backward with me landing on top of her.

Just a few more inches and I would be able to reach the cover to the chute. I started to slide again, but I felt Nita's hand on my leg holding me firm. Again I dug my forearms in and scooted forward. My outfit would now be ruined, and it had been one of my favorites.

What a time to think of ruined clothing. Better to have it ruined by going up the chute than to have it clean and covering my dead body in that dungeon of a cellar. How long would it be before someone entered Anne's house again with her gone? Weeks? Months? If we couldn't escape through the chute, would we look like mummies when they found us?

Chapter 46

Box up items like seasonal clothing and Christmas decorations and move them to a storage unit.

With one final lunge forward, I was within reach of the cover. Now all I had to do was get enough leverage to push the door out. I hoped it didn't have any kind of lock on it. I wedged my knee under me and shoved my shoulder against it.

The cover fell forward and bright light hit me—along with some gloriously fresh air. It had stopped drizzling and the sun had come out. I tried to pull myself out of the chute and looked up to see the stunned faces of Aunt Kit and Mrs. Webster. I don't know who was more shocked—them or me.

Aunt Kit grabbed my arms and helped work me out of the chute. Coal dust covered me from head to toe, some of which had now come off onto her.

I pointed behind me. "Nita is still in there."

Mrs. Webster took hold of my arm to steady me. "Girl, what in tarnation is going on?"

"Let's get Nita out and then I'll explain."

Nita, with Aunt Kit's help, came tumbling out of the chute and collapsed onto the grass. "Am I ever glad to see you two," she said.

"How did you come to be here?" I asked them, still astounded to find them just when we needed them.

Aunt Kit answered first. "When I didn't find you at home, I sat at the kitchen table to have some lunch and found the notebook you were using to record your findings. Since you said it would be okay, I read your notes and was stunned to see what you had written regarding Anne and your plan to check out her house. When you didn't answer your cell phone and then neither did Nita, I got concerned. I called Mrs. Webster to ask if she had seen either of you. I told her I was coming here, and because she was alarmed, she insisted on coming with me. I picked her up on the way. We thought you'd come and gone when we saw Anne's car driving away."

Mrs. Webster frowned and looked disapproving. "We were trying to decide what to do next when you popped out of the earth. I've never seen such an entrance."

"You just saw Anne driving away?" I couldn't believe she hadn't taken off earlier. With us being imprisoned in the basement, she didn't need to rush to get packed and away. She took her time, thinking she had gotten away with theft—and murder.

"Did you see what direction she headed?" I looked up and down the street.

"She turned right at the end of the street. That would've put her going in the direction of the Interstate," Aunt Kit said.

We couldn't let her get away. "Quick. Maybe we can cut her off before she gets to the Interstate. I know a shortcut over the mountain."

We scrambled into my little car. I started the engine and checked my rearview mirror for cars coming down the road behind us. That's when I saw my reflection in the mirror. My hair was coated with coal dust, and dark streaks covered my face where I had wiped it with my grimy hands.

No time to worry about that now. I glanced over at Nita, who was equally as dirty.

"Nita, find your cell phone and call Detective Spangler. Tell him our location and that we're chasing Ian and Damian's killer." I took a left turn at the end of the street and headed in the opposite direction Anne had taken. With any luck, we could make it to the Interstate before she could get there.

"Aunt Kit, what color and type of car did Anne have?" I went careening around the next corner.

"A silver Lexus."

Anne must have been doing well with those paintings.

I could hear Nita talking into the phone while I focused on driving. "This isn't the greatest route, but it cuts off a lot of miles. We should get to the road leading to the Interstate before she does." At least I hoped so.

Aunt Kit had a death grip on her bag. "That's if we get there in one piece."

Mrs. Webster looked like she was having the time of her life. "Can you please tell us now more about what's going on? Why did you come out of the basement the way you did?"

"Yeah and looking like escapees from a coal mine?" added Aunt Kit. "I don't think you're ever going to get your upholstery clean again."

Good old Aunt Kit, worried about my upholstery as we chased down a cold-blooded killer.

"After Mrs. Webster recognized the painting, we suspected Anne of stealing the paintings and murdering Ian Becker and Damian Reynolds to cover her trail. When someone said she was going away, we knew we needed to act fast to find evidence of the painting thefts. If we could, we might be able to connect Anne to the murders."

"In case she was going on the lam," Nita added.

"We found Anne was gone and the door unlocked, so we went it. Anne came back, locked us in the basement, and turned out the lights."

"That must mean Anne was the one who attacked you at the empty house?" Aunt Kit seemed stunned by all these revelations about Anne, especially since she had been spending so much time with her recently. "Now it makes sense why she was always asking me about what you and Nita were discovering with your investigation."

"I'm thankful that she didn't stab Laura like she did the other two." Mrs. Webster said.

Nita gasped. "She might have if Aunt Kit hadn't befriended her. Maybe she has some redeeming qualities after all."

Aunt Kit grunted. "She sure had me fooled. Frankly, I think anyone who could kill two people in cold blood and rob a helpless woman is a bit insane."

Mrs. Webster grabbed the back of Nita's seat as I navigated another sharp bend in the road. "Watch it girl." She straightened her hat, which had fallen over her face. "Anne fooled most people with her sweet and helpful manner. It goes to show you people are willing to commit serious crimes regardless of their age. She didn't hesitate to take advantage of Doris's increasing dementia."

"I still can't get over her locking us in that cellar, in the dark, without anyone knowing where we were." Nita was still outraged. "Fortunately, Laura remembered those old houses had coal chutes. If it weren't for her, we'd still be down there."

"There's the highway," I said, pointing ahead. When we reached the intersection, I stopped at the stop sign. We either had missed Anne or she would be coming along anytime now. No cars were behind us, so we were able to sit and wait. I drummed my fingers on the steering wheel, impatient for Anne to drive by.

"There's her car," Aunt Kit shouted, pointing to a silver vehicle.

I saw it pass in front of us and quickly turned to follow it. "Nita, please tell Detective Spangler that we have Anne in our sights near the intersection of Adams Road and the highway. We are heading east toward the Interstate."

We stayed a couple of cars behind Anne. She wouldn't have any reason to recognize my car, but I didn't want to take any chances. Besides, she thought Nita and I were tucked away nicely in her basement and wouldn't suspect we were right behind her.

Nita sat forward in her seat. "She's put her right turn signal on. We aren't near the Interstate yet. Where could she be going?"

"I don't know, but we're following right behind her." I slowed down to stay out of sight.

Mrs. Webster hit the back of my seat with her hand. "She's signaling a left turn now." The excitement of the chase was getting to her. I had to admit it was rather like being in a movie.

As we got closer, we saw Anne pull into a self-storage facility. She stopped at a metal gate, lowered her car window, and looked like she was entering a code. The gate slid open and she drove inside with the gate closing behind her.

"After her," urged Mrs. Webster. "She probably has the rest of the paintings stored in there. We can catch her red-handed."

"We can't get in there without a code." Mrs. Webster probably was right and the paintings were stored there. Anne wasn't leaving the area without them. I was even more determined now to prevent her from getting away.

"She may have gotten in, but she won't be getting out." I pulled my car in front of the gate and blocked the exit.

Nita's cell phone rang, and she answered it. "Yes, we know where she is. We're at the self-storage facility just off the highway. Yes. Okay." Nita hung up. "Detective Spangler said they're on their way."

We sat in place for about ten minutes, impatiently waiting for Anne to come out.

"Here she comes," Mrs. Webster said, spotting the Lexus approaching the exit.

I opened my car door. "Get out quick in case she decides to ram the car." It wouldn't surprise me at all if she did. We all jumped from the car and stood beside it, facing the gate.

The metal gate slid open. Anne started to move forward and stopped when she saw my car blocking her exit. That's when she spotted us standing close by. The look on her face was worth crawling up the coal chute for. It would have been impossible for her eyes to widen any wider than they did.

Anne opened her car door and stepped out as though to get a better look and confirm it was us blocking her path.

"You again," she screeched and then said something I wouldn't repeat. She looked around her as though searching for a weapon. Finding nothing, she removed one of her shoes and threw it at us. It bounced off the hood of my car leaving a ding. Now she'd really made me determined to get her.

Chapter 47

Remove vehicles or anything blocking a clear view of your house. At night, turn on outside lights so an interested buyer who drives by at night can see it.

Three police cars with flashing lights pulled in front of the storage facility. Detective Spangler and several uniformed police officers jumped from their cars and came toward us.

Anne Williamson saw the police and ran toward the back of the facility, limping with only one shoe on.

Detective Spangler pointed to two officers nearby. "Go after her. And be careful—we don't know if she's armed." The officers jumped the metal gate and gave chase. For a woman her age, and with only one shoe on, she gave them a run for their money.

"Stanelli, get the owner of this place on the phone so we can get inside."

Detective Spangler turned to us. The look on his face when he saw Nita and me was priceless. It was the first time I'd seen him speechless. Well at least until he started talking.

"Care to explain this?" he asked, pointing to us and, presumably, our dirty faces.

Nita jumped right in. "Anne locked us in her basement and the only way we could get out was climbing up her coal chute."

He did his best to stifle a laugh but didn't quite succeed. "You climbed up a coal chute?"

"It was the only way we could get out. Otherwise, you might have been searching for us for months." Nita looked indignant that he didn't understand.

I tried hard not to sound smug. "I told you there was a link between the deaths of Ian and Damian—and the link could be art. She killed Ian and Damian to cover up her theft of Doris Becker's artwork."

He shrugged. "Things sometimes come to light that'll guide us to the solution of a case. You obviously discovered what it was before we did."

I was surprised he was magnanimous in admitting we were ahead of him in this case. He must be mellowing in his old age.

A driver jumped from his car, walked over to the metal gate, and punched in a code, opening the metal gate. Just about the same time, the uniformed officers came around the corner holding Anne Williamson by her arms. She didn't struggle but looked haughty, assured she was going to be proven innocent of all wrongdoing.

We looked at Anne's fancy Lexus. "I think, Detective, you'll find some paintings in the backseat or trunk signed by Doris Becker." At least I hoped he would.

Chapter 48

A home stager with credentials from a certifying home staging organization can take the pain out of getting your house ready for sale.

The following morning, Aunt Kit and I met Nita at Vocaro's. We needed a quiet morning to recover from our adventures of the previous day, especially after spending hours giving statements to the police. Dealing with Detective Spangler hadn't been quite as difficult as it usually was. Perhaps he was warming up to me—or I was tolerating him better.

Tyrone greeted us as we walked in. "Hey, ladies. Great job solving those murders. Coffee's on the house."

"Thanks, Tyrone. I'm sorry your grandmother won't be joining us." I was exhausted from the previous day's adventures, and I only could imagine how someone Mrs. Webster's age would be feeling.

"You just about wore her out yesterday chasing down Anne Williamson. But she enjoyed every minute of it. She hasn't had that much excitement in years."

Tyrone took off his apron and signaled to one of the other baristas to take over. "Mind if I join you to hear the rest of the story?"

"Join us. It's a hard tale to believe," I warned him as I picked up the tray with our coffees.

We sat down in the comfortable leather club chairs Luigi provided in an adjoining room for customers who wanted to stay for a while. Aunt Kit looked downcast.

"What's wrong Aunt Kit? Are you feeling upset Anne was guilty of those crimes?" I asked her.

"Yes, I am. But I'm more upset I endangered you and Nita, feeding all that information to her about what you'd been discovering. That's why she lured you to that house."

"You couldn't have known. Anne was the last person anyone would have suspected of stealing Doris Becker's art and passing it off as her own. And then murdering two people to cover up her crime. If we had suspected Anne earlier, the message from M. Cassatt to meet at that house might have been a tip-off."

"How so? The message was pretty straight forward," Nita said.

"Anne took great pride in having people treat her like a great artist. When she selected a pseudonym to use in her message to us, she chose the name of a famous woman painter—Mary Cassatt."

"It still makes me shudder to think she could have stabbed you like she did the others," Nita said.

Nita looked pale, but I admired how she'd stood up to finding two bodies, being imprisoned in a basement, and chasing down a murderer.

"Anne probably regrets now she didn't put an end to me." That thought made me shudder. "I believe it was only because of her fondness for Aunt Kit she decided to give me a scare instead of killing me." I gave Aunt Kit, who was sitting next to me on the sofa, a hug. Aunt Kit was a dear, even if she had a dark cloud hanging over her head most of the time. Although it seemed recently she hadn't been filled with as much doom and gloom. Could Nita and I have become a good influence on her?

"Do you think she would have left us to die in that basement?" Nita's eyes were wide, and she still looked shocked at the idea.

"I'd like to think after she got away she'd have called someone anonymously that would've prompted somebody to check out the house. She might not have, but I'd like to think she would." I decided not to say that Anne probably would have left us there without a backward glance. That thought might have given Nita nightmares for months.

"I can't understand how Anne got the paintings to begin with." Aunt Kit shook her head confused.

"I can answer that," Nita said. "I heard the other art group members tried to keep Doris connected to the group when she became too ill to attend meetings. They all took turns visiting her. When Anne got involved with the group, she visited Doris frequently. She told the other members that with Doris's growing dementia it was best she alone visited her, saying too many people confused Doris. The members left it to Anne, who from all appearances was very helpful to Doris. Somehow she must have discovered Doris's hoard of paintings, which no one had ever seen, except perhaps her nephew Ian."

"So that's why she decided to kill Ian—to prevent him from exposing what she had been doing?" Aunt Kit shook her head as though still trying to accept that Anne was a murderer.

I took a sip of my cappuccino, suddenly feeling hungry. "The sad thing is, as a teenager, Ian probably showed little interest, if any, in his aunt's painting and may not have questioned them being missing or noticed that some awful paintings had been brought in to replace them. But Anne couldn't take that chance. Since the police didn't find Ian's wallet, we can only assume she took it, hoping no one would know who he was and never connect his murder to anything other than a mugging gone wrong. And when Damian showed great interest in Anne's painting at the exhibit, she viewed his interest as suspicion. It doomed him."

"Lucky she didn't know Mrs. Webster had seen some of Doris Becker's paintings," Nita said. "She might have gone after her too."

Aunt Kit looked grim. "And when you started showing interest in discovering what happened, she decided to frighten you off. I'm so thankful she didn't...."

Aunt Kit didn't need to say more. I was thankful too. I reached over and placed my hand over hers to comfort her. "It wasn't your fault. Anne knew from the day we had tea at the Orangery that I was inquiring into the deaths."

Nita perked up. "One bright thing out of all this is the size of Doris Becker's estate grew with the retrieval of the paintings, which could prove to be worth something. That should benefit Emily and Brandon Thompson."

Nita put her cup down abruptly. "Would you believe it, there's Monica. They sure were quick to release her from jail."

I looked up surprised to see Monica approaching. She wore a large Nantucket style straw hat covering her hair, probably to cover her darkening roots. She looked good for someone who had been incarcerated, but her eyes showed a seriousness that hadn't been there before.

She walked over to me. "I thought I might find you here. Can we have a word?" She motioned to a table on the other side of the room. Typical of Monica, she didn't say anything to Nita, Aunt Kit, or Tyrone.

I followed her toward the table and took a seat. Monica lowered herself into her chair gracefully, every bit the country club lady.

"You can imagine how difficult this is for me," she said and faltered for a second as though trying hard to find the words, "but thank you. For Damian and me. I couldn't have lived not knowing why someone wanted him dead." She studied her nails, now devoid of polish. "I truly cared for him you know. Following his daughter's death, he was a broken soul—and for once someone needed me."

She took a deep breath and paused, probably to prevent herself from crying in front of me. "Detective Spangler told me all you did to discover what happened to Damian."

"Only because I can't stand an unsolved mystery."

She laughed. "Sister Madeleine also kept me informed about all the ways you were helping my business. I'll be checking to see what kind of job you did."

I laughed too—more a snort than a laugh. "I assure you, Nita and I surpassed your expectations."

Monica became more serious. "I know we'll probably never be close friends, but perhaps we can bury the hatchet?"

"I'd like that."

With that, she stood and walked away. Abruptly she turned. "Just so you know, I never had an affair with Derrick. I wanted to, but he wasn't interested. Not because he was so noble, you knew Derrick, but because he was involved with someone else."

After she left, I sat staring at the wall. Sister Madeleine had been right. I'd been carrying my resentment toward Monica for far too long. Today that weight had been lifted from me.

When I joined the others again, they looked up at me, hopeful looks on their faces that I would share with them what Monica had wanted.

I shrugged. "She wanted to thank me for finding Damian's killer."

Nita looked outraged. "You did more than that. You saved her hide."

"She's aware of that. And she knows I'm aware of that. That's enough." I slid back into my chair and reached for my cold coffee.

"Where do we go from here?" Nita asked.

"I know what I need to do," Aunt Kit said. "Now that I know you two are safe and not chasing killers, I need to go home."

Aunt Kit's sad eyes and pursed lips told me everything I needed to know.

"There never seems to be an end to our adventures, Aunt Kit. Why don't you move back to Louiston? I need you here."

Recipes

Laura Bishop doesn't ply sources with liquor to loosen their lips. Instead, she knows the value of questioning them in a place conducive to sharing secrets—a cozy English-style teashop. Who wouldn't open up while enjoying sandwiches, scones with cream and jam, and fruit tarts, all washed down with fragrant tea? It worked for Laura, and she was able to get good leads that helped her unmask a murderer.

Next time you want to coerce someone into spilling their secrets, serve an English-style tea and include scones like the ones served at the Orangery, the teashop frequented by Laura and her sources.

English Butterscotch Tea Scones

Ingredients:
    4 cups all-purpose flour
    1 teaspoon baking soda
    2 teaspoons baking powder
    ½ teaspoon salt
    ½ cup granulated sugar
    1 stick cold unsalted butter (4 ounces) cut into small pieces
    1 cup butterscotch chips (or substitute 1 cup cinnamon chips, currants, or raisins)
    1 egg
    1 ½ cups buttermilk (or substitute 1 ½ cups milk with 2 tablespoons white vinegar. Allow to sit for ten minutes.)

Preheat oven to 400 degrees. Mix dry ingredients together in a large bowl. Cut in butter until the mixture is the size of small pebbles. Add butterscotch chips (or currants or raisins) to dry mixture and stir to coat well. Set aside.

Beat egg and buttermilk together and add to dry ingredients. Stir to combine all ingredients. Turn out onto a lightly floured surface and knead lightly. Roll dough until it is 1 inch thick or press with floured fingertips.

Cut rounds with a lightly floured cutter or a juice glass and place on a greased baking sheet or one lined with parchment paper. Brush lightly with milk or cream and sprinkle with granulated sugar.

Bake 20-25 minutes or until scones are lightly browned. Allow to cool. Slice in half and spread with butter or whipped cream and jam. Enjoy!

Aunt Kit's Favorite Chicken Dish: Chicken with Mushrooms and Harvey's Bristol Cream Sherry Sauce

Ingredients:
> 2 tablespoons butter
> 4 skinless, boneless chicken breast halves
> 2 cups sliced mushrooms
> 1 can condensed cream of mushroom soup
> 1/2 cup Harvey's Bristol Cream Sherry (or any brand of cream sherry—sweet, not dry) or more to taste
> ¼ cup milk

Heat 1 tablespoon of butter in a 10-inch skillet over medium-high heat. Add the chicken and cook for 10 minutes or until well browned on both sides. Remove the chicken from the skillet.

Reduce the heat to medium. Heat the remaining butter in the skillet. Add the mushrooms and cook until they are tender, stirring occasionally.

Stir the soup, milk, and sherry in the skillet and heat to a boil. Return the chicken to the skillet. Reduce the heat to low. Cover and cook for 5 minutes or until the chicken is cooked through. Season to taste. Serve with rice, cooked noodles, or mashed potatoes.

$\mathscr{Grace}$ TOPPING

Grace Topping is a recovering technical writer and IT project manager, accustomed to writing lean, boring documents. Let loose to write fiction, she is now creating murder mysteries and killing off characters who remind her of some of the people she dealt with during her career. Fictional revenge is sweet. She's using her experience helping friends stage their homes for sale as inspiration for her Laura Bishop mystery series. The series is about a woman starting a new career midlife as a home stager. Grace is the former vice president of the Chesapeake Chapter of Sisters in Crime, and a member of the SINC Guppies and Mystery Writers of America. She lives with her husband in Northern Virginia.

**The Laura Bishop Mystery Series
by Grace Topping**

STAGING IS MURDER (#1)
STAGING WARS (#2)

Henery Press Mystery Books

And finally, before you go...
Here are a few other mysteries
you might enjoy:

PILLOW STALK

Diane Vallere

A Madison Night Mystery (#1)

Interior Decorator Madison Night might look like a throwback to the sixties, but as business owner and landlord, she proves that independent women can have it all. But when a killer targets women dressed in her signature style—estate sale vintage to play up her resemblance to fave actress Doris Day—what makes her unique might make her dead.

The local detective connects the new crime to a twenty-year old cold case, and Madison's long-trusted contractor emerges as the leading suspect. As the body count piles up, Madison uncovers a Soviet spy, a campaign to destroy all Doris Day movies, and six minutes of film that will change her life forever.

Available at booksellers nationwide and online

Visit www.henerypress.com for details

PUMPKINS IN PARADISE

Kathi Daley

A Tj Jensen Mystery (#1)

Between volunteering for the annual pumpkin festival and coaching her girls to the state soccer finals, high school teacher Tj Jensen finds her good friend Zachary Collins dead in his favorite chair.

When the handsome new deputy closes the case without so much as a "why" or "how," Tj turns her attention from chili cook-offs and pumpkin carving to complex puzzles, prophetic riddles, and a decades-old secret she seems destined to unravel.

Available at booksellers nationwide and online

Visit www.henerypress.com for details

Printed in Great Britain
by Amazon

64767202R00145